Salvatore

An In Too Far Novel

Cecy Robson

The Weird Girls Series

Gone Hunting
A Curse Awakened: A Novella
The Weird Girls: A Novella
Sealed with a Curse
A Cursed Embrace
Of Flame and Promise
A Cursed Moon: A Novella
Cursed by Destiny
A Cursed Bloodline
A Curse Unbroken
Of Flame and Light
Of Flame and Fate
Of Flame and Fury (coming soon)

APPS

Find Cecy on *Hooked – Chat stories APP* writing as
Rosalina San Tiago

Coming soon: *Crazy Maple's Chapters: Interactive Stories
APP:* The Shattered Past and Weird Girls Series

New to Cecy Robson? Here's what readers are saying...

"Salvatore is a heartbreaking story of a man forced to sell his soul to the Family in order to save his family. Sal's fight to be worthy of Adrianna's love left me in tears."
–Ebook Obsessed

"You know, I don't think I've ever read a book by Cecy Robson that I haven't just absolutely adored...She gives you characters you can identify with and a story that enthralls you."
 —Two Girls With Books

"Cecy Robson is a phenomenal talent who knows just how to deliver a story filled with suspense, action, humor and romance...leaving you craving for more!"
—Romancing the Dark Side

"Like all of Robson's books, the characters of *Feel Me* are complex and dynamic, the emotions are raw and real, and the ending is sweet and heartwarming."
—The Book Disciple

"Robson proves once again that she can sweep us off our feet with a fun, romantic tale... [*Once Kissed*] is another must-read. I thoroughly enjoyed this novel."
—Rainy Day Ramblings

"Cecy Robson is one of my absolute favorite authors and each book that she writes becomes more gut-wrenching and brilliant than the last."
—Books-n-Kisses

"Cecy Robson has a talent for stepping outside of the classic fantasy and rebuilding the fairy-tale. Realism and connection are mighty weapons and she uses these to the fullest."
 – Hopeless Romantic

"Already [Cecy] Robson was becoming one of my favorite authors but Inseverable sealed the deal. Inseverable shows Robson's different writing style and I couldn't get enough of this new setting and the new characters that were introduced."
—Lush Book Reviews

"Cecy Robson became an instant author to look out for with her great writing, loveable characters, good plot development and a story with just right pace wrapped up in sexy, sweet and swoony delightfulness, and *Crave Me* definitely delivered on all fronts."
—TJ Loves to Read Romance Blog

"Cecy has this fantastic ability to suck you into her stories. She takes difficult topics head on and doesn't cut corners in her portrayals…This is an auto-read author for me and she continues to earn that loyalty with every book she pens."
—Curvy and Nerdy

"Ms. Robson has once again written a tale that I absolutely love. Both characters have captured my heart and the story is so well written and paced that I could not put it down."
—Cat's Reviews

"Cecy Robson is a master when it comes to tugging your heartstrings but leaving you with a satisfied smile on your face."
—Dog Eared Day Dreams

ACKNOWLEDGMENTS

Okay, y'all. I went dark for this novel, real dark . . . and I absolutely love the way it all came out. Salvatore has gasp-worthy moments and enough romance to curl toes. Your heart will break as well as soar. I hope you love every word, just as much as I did.

To Nicole Resciniti, my agent and editor on this project. Thank you for helping to shape Salvatore into the man he became.

To Jamie, who really loved this book. Dark, sexy—it was all the right things, wasn't it, babe? What would I ever do without your love and support?

To Kimberly Costa, my right hand. My left hand. And yeah, feet, too. Thank you for your hard work and friendship.

To Kristin Clifton whose covers are more art than mere images. Thank you for creating such a beautiful cover. Your friendship and patience are everything.

Many thanks to Gaele Hince for (once more) coming to the rescue with formatting. I have the best team this hybrid author could ask for.

DEDICATION

To Jamie:
This was your kind of book, wasn't it, babe?

Chapter One
Salvatore

"What do you think, Salvatore?"

Donnie taps her iPad with her long red nails when she finds yet another pair of shoes she wants. Like I actually give a shit what she's buying with Vincent's money.

"Sure. Get them," I answer, not bothering to really look and fixing my gaze back on the door.

She pouts in that way that annoys me, but probably gets Vin hard. "That's what you said about the other six. I'm serious. Which ones should I get?"

I don't have to tell her that Vincent will buy her whatever she wants so long as she keeps blowing him, but I come close. The muscles along my back are ready to tear away from the bone. Every nerve along my spine fires a warning that shit's about to go down. But I don't show it, my face giving nothing away. "Donnie, I'm paid to watch your back. Not help you pick out shoes," I mutter.

She starts to argue, but a knock on the door shuts her up, so does me motioning her to the corner. She may spend her days worrying about what she looks like and what she'll wear, but she's not stupid enough to ignore me.

I lean against the wall, opposite the door. Donnie might have shrugged off Vin yelling down the hall, but I didn't. He isn't happy. Neither are the other mob bosses in Jersey. It won't be long before hell itself rains down on us. "Yeah?" I ask, keeping my deep voice casual, like my piece isn't already clutched in my hands.

"Vincent wants you in on the meeting," Lucca says.

Lucca's smart. And for someone who hasn't been in the family long, he's tough and good on his feet. But I pick up enough in his voice to know this meeting's not going as planned. So maybe Vin didn't send for me. Maybe Lucca thinks I'm needed. If so, things are a lot worse than I thought.

Donnie looks at me, her preoccupation with shoes nothing more than a memory. "Lock the door behind me," I tell her.

She rushes forward. I snag her elbow and pull her in tight to whisper in her ear. "You hear shots, you leave out the back, through the alley and down the street. Find a diner, a store, any place with lots of people. Got me?"

She nods, but she's trembling already. Shots fired means there are plenty more to come. The other family knows who Donnie is to Vin. But if they don't know she's here, or if they find her with too many witnesses, she'll be okay.

She clutches my arm when I start to leave. "Sal . . ." she says.

Donatella and me are from the old neighborhood. We've known each other since back when we were kids and were too stupid to know shit about organized crime. Now, we're more stupid, because we're willingly a part of it. She wants to say something like "be careful" or "keep him safe" or something else I don't need to hear. So, I don't.

I crack open the door, making sure Lucca's standing there alone, and step out.

His eyes cut toward the hall leading to Vincent's office, where he's meeting with Arturo, the boss in charge of most of South Jersey, including Atlantic City. Yeah. Shit's going down. But I don't move until Donnie clicks the lock behind me.

Lucca starts forward, moving fast. I haul him back. "Easy," I hiss.

That's all he needs to hear. He slows, mimicking my pace and stance, chest out, hand curled near the piece at his waist, face hard and unreadable.

Arturo's men stand in unison when we round the corner. At the sight of me, Vin's men rise, too. They see what I want them to see in Lucca and me. A united front. It solidifies our crew and tenses Arturo's. As Vin's crew fixes their hard stares on the other family, I know they're ready for what the next few minutes will bring.

I reach Vin's office door. It's open, wide open, and it pisses me off. An open door shows weakness and it demonstrates how scared Vin is about being alone with the other boss.

I march in and take point to Vin's right. Lucca starts to head to his opposite side, but he catches the subtle motion of my left hand that tells him to stay by the door. I want to tell him to shut the door and lock it, but I can't without raising the paranoia already thickening the air. Like I said, Lucca's smart. He shuts the door and flicks the deadbolt.

Arturo huffs when he realizes he's closed in. "What the fuck's this?" He doesn't turn around from where he's seated directly in front of Vin, but his second sitting beside him, and his enforcer straighten at my presence. I expected them to react upon seeing me, but I don't expect the same response from Vin's third, Angelo. Their reaction is so subtle that everyone gathered seems to miss it. But me, I don't miss a thing, *ever*. The one time I did, it cost me the only woman I've ever loved.

"Just a little privacy, Mr. Sorenzo." I answer, because Vin waited too long to respond and he's already lost enough face.

Vin eases back in his chair. He knows I'm there and that I have his back, but his fingers digging into the armrest give it away, he's scared shitless. *Christ.* How many times have I told him to keep his hands relaxed and his expression like stone? His ailing father has been grooming him to take over his empire for six fucking years, and Vin's still not ready. The other bosses are honing in on his incompetence. Which is why I'm not sure how much longer I can help keep Vin alive.

"Let's get back to business," Vin says, trying to sound harder than he is.

Arturo smiles in that sleazy way of his and tosses a hand out. "I believe we've reached a standstill," he says.

"You're right, we have," Vin fires back, getting pissed. Good, anger is better than fear and, right now, it's exactly what he needs. He leans forward. "You're not getting the rest of A.C. And you're not getting an eighty percent—"

My 380 auto is out and pointed at Arturo's enforcer before his fingers reach the hilt. "Move and I'll blow your *fucking* head off." Without me telling him, Lucca rams his guns in the back of Arturo's and his second's skulls. Smart guy. I reach for my 9 mil tucked in my leather jacket, not even blinking when I shoot Vin's third in the leg, blowing out his kneecap.

With a scream, Angelo falls to the floor howling. "What the fuck?" Vin growls, leaping to his feet.

I don't explain why I shot one of his made men, someone he trusted. My next bullet goes into the enforcer, the impact and his pain enough to send him flying off his chair. He went for his Sig. I wasn't waiting for him to pull the trigger. Outside, all hell's breaking loose, my heartbeat pounding fast in my chest until I hear the voices of Vin's family taking control.

Less than a minute later, a sharp rap to the door is followed by Benny's deep voice. "Sal?"

"All clear," I tell him, my tone steady. "You?"

It's not my words that he believes, it's the confidence behind them. "All clear," he responds in the same tone, letting me know they have Arturo's men on the ground.

Vin's reaching into the drawer, pulling out his Glock. To his credit, he's not questioning anything anymore, not after Arturo's enforcer went for his piece. He's reining in his shit like he needs to.

Lucca covers me as I strip every one of their weapons. Angelo is wailing like the little bitch he is. The enforcer is swearing, pressing the wound on his shoulder as blood seeps through his fingers. I intentionally missed his heart. But no one needs to know that.

I drop the weapons beside Vin and far out of everyone's reach. Arturo and his second haven't said a damn thing. They weren't scared of Vin before. But they are now.

I'm not sure what Vin's going to say. My fear is, he may say the wrong thing in front of Lucca that makes him look pathetic. Lucca is loyal, so are a few others, but if they keep seeing Vin acting like he's acting, they'll lose whatever respect he's managed outside his title of boss.

"Vin knew you were playing him, you pussy," I tell Angelo, lying through my teeth. "Were you going to kill him in front of Arturo? Was that your way into the family, you lying piece of shit?"

In not answering, he answers enough. At Vin's nod, Lucca puts a bullet in Arturo's second, and finishes off the enforcer.

Vin motions to the door. "Call in a few of my men," he tells me.

I unlock the door and do as he asked, after I make sure everything is still under control. Vin's not ready to be boss, but he isn't stupid, at least not completely. He knows Arturo needs to die by his hands, and that he needs witnesses to see him. I pick three who have started to question Vin's strength, knowing they'll tell the rest of the family what's about to go down, and show them what happens to those who don't stay loyal.

The men pile in, but Vin doesn't let them get too comfortable. He shoots Arturo in the face with his Glock while the last two to enter are still busy taking in Angelo, writhing on the floor. Vin keeps his face neutral, his confidence returning now that he knows his life isn't immediately on the line.

I take a step back when he prowls toward Angelo. Angelo was Vin's trusted third. To be who Vin wants to be, he has to send a message. But I don't tell him that. It's something he needs to realize on his own. "What did he promise you after you killed me, pussy?" he asks Angelo.

Angelo doesn't deny his intention. Doesn't beg for his life. He knows it's over. So, he hits Vin the only way he can. "Your father's the pussy for letting a chicken shit like you take over."

Vin's heel comes down hard on Angelo's face, smashing his nose in. But he doesn't stop there. He snatches the paperweight on his desk and flings himself to the floor, bashing Angelo's face in, not stopping until the side of his temple caves inward.

To anyone eyeing me, it looks like I'm watching everything and immune to it all. Yeah. My face never gives anything away. That doesn't mean my body's not punishing me on the inside. I fight back the nausea working its way through my gut and just how hard my heartbeat thunders out of control. Weakness in the mob and in life gets you killed. I need to live, despite how my sins have all but sliced my throat.

"Fuck," one of the boys says, looking away. He's new and probably has killed with his gun. But shooting someone is easy. Too easy. It's not intimate. Not like killing someone with your bare hands like Vin just did.

Vin stumbles to his feet, out of breath and covered with plenty of Angelo's DNA. His face twists as if angry, which makes him look good, but I know better. "Get rid of them," he says, spitting out blood that hit his mouth.

"What about his men?" someone else asks.

"All of them need to go," Vin says, falling back into the leather seat behind his chair.

"All right, boss," another says.

Vin's focus darts my way. He expects an approving nod from me. But he isn't going to get it. As much as I'm a part of this shit, it doesn't mean I like it.

Or that I don't want out.

I climb into my Range Rover and shut the door tight. Vin's hand is shaking as he takes a drag of his cigarette. I knew he wasn't going to keep it together for long, so I made it like he needed to be away from the cleanup in case someone heard the shots and called it in.

"Is Donnie coming?" he asks, sprawling across the back seat.

"Yeah. She's picking out girls she thinks you might like. Says she'll be right out."

I snagged Donnie at a street festival a few blocks away, after I secured Vin in my ride. She flung her arms around me and started crying when she saw me. I quickly pulled her off me and lead her to Vin. Donnie cares as much as someone like her can, and mostly for all the wrong reasons. I know this and, maybe, she does, too, which is why we're outside a strip club Vin owns waiting on her and whoever she's recruiting to lift Vin's spirits.

"How many girls is she bringing?"

"Two, maybe more," I answer, not because she told me, but more because this has become the norm.

"Yeah, she knows how to take care of me," he says with a laugh, despite how his hand continues to tremble.

This isn't the first time Vin's killed with his hands or the first time I've watched him do it. That doesn't mean it hasn't fucked with my mind or given me more nightmares to stash in my memories. Christ, it took all I had not to puke, seeing all those bodies lying in a mound and the mess Vin made of Angelo's head. But I still have a conscience. Real mob bosses surrender theirs to get what they need. If he's going to be one, he needs to lose what's left of his, fast.

He takes another drag, his forced humor fading. "How long has Angelo been playing two sides?"

"No idea," I mumble.

He straightens. "Then how did you know Angelo was in on it?"

I rub my eyes. I'm only twenty-seven and I already feel too old for this shit. "He tensed at the same time, and in the same way Arturo and his second did."

Vin curses under his breath and reaches for another cigarette. "I didn't see shit and I was looking at them the whole time. How the hell do you pick up on these things?"

"It comes from the years I spent fighting," I answer, looking out through my tinted windows and wondering what the hell is keeping Donnie.

"In the octagon?" Vin asks.

Vin knows I fought in the mixed martial arts circuit for a few years, just like he knows I fought anyone who messed with me on the street. We've known each other since we were kids, long before his father became the most feared man in Jersey. I'm not sure why he's asking, but don't bother to question it. Vin isn't the same guy I once called a friend.

"Yeah," I mumble. "It helped me anticipate my opponent's next move."

"You miss that shit?" he asks.

Considering I was on my way to becoming the next light heavyweight champion? Hell, yeah. Fighting in the MMA put money in my pocket and gave me a way to unleash my rage. But neither were enough when push came to shove. "It was all right," I tell him.

Vin takes a few more drags before he says, "I want you to think about watching my back full-time. I'll pay you a hell of a lot more if you do."

Any other boss would just tell me this is what I'm doing and not give me a choice. But for all Vin's not the same guy I once knew, he was there when my world imploded around me. And in hiring me to watch his mistress, he's able to keep me on the mob payroll without staining my hands with their blood. That doesn't mean I haven't made a lot of people bleed. It only means I haven't killed anyone. Yet.

"I make enough watching your *gumad*," I respond.

Vin doesn't like my answer, but he doesn't push it. After what went down with Angelo, and with his second serving time, I'm the only person he completely trusts. But, despite our friendship, the time's coming when I'll no longer have a choice but to do what he wants.

In killing Arturo, Vin will either gain respect from the other bosses or turn them against him and the family. I don't think any of the higher-ups want war, but they're greedy and looking to expand their domains. My gut tells me that when Vin's father Carmine dies, the cards unfold. But they won't be in Vin's favor, and if he doesn't wise up fast, none of us will make it out alive.

The back door to the strip club opens and Donnie steps out, leading three laughing and almost naked women in clear heels forward.

"I won't forget what you did for me today, Sal," Vin says, right before the women pile in.

He won't. I know that. Just like I know I added a nail to my own damn casket the day I went to him for help.

I'm supposed to take Vin and his dates back to Donnie's. But Vin's not waiting to get there. I crank the engine when I hear his zipper yanked down and the first sound of smacking lips. He groans, likely relieved the day is finally going in the direction he wants.

"*You*, go take care of my buddy, Sal," he says between sharp intakes of breath.

I stiffen and not in a good way, when a blonde with more hairspray than brains falls laughing into the front seat. With a hard stomp, I step on the brake and set my SUV in park. She's already naked by the time I reach into the center console and shove a condom in her hand.

She huffs. "You're kidding, right?"

"No. I'm not."

She looks insulted, but I don't care. She's going to do what Vin's paying her to do, whether I want her to or not. It takes a while for me to get hard enough for her to roll the condom in place. Once she does, she immediately buries her face in my lap.

I lean my head back against the headrest. I should enjoy what's happening. And at one point I did, seeing it as the perks of the job.

Now, all I wonder about is how my life became what it is, and how I'll ever survive it.

Chapter Two
Adrianna

There's a knock on my door. I look up to the wall of glass reinforced with wire to see Tamira Jones. At my smile, she opens the door. "Hey, Miss Aedry. You got a minute?"

I lift the file on Apollo Romero I was reviewing and set it aside. "Of course. Come in, Tamira."

When I started working as a guidance counselor a year and a half ago, the students at James Harris High School took one look at my light skin and blue eyes and heard traces of my southern accent, and quickly sought help elsewhere. Two things worked in my favor: my patience, and the school's limited resources. Aside from me, Miss Jalisa is the only other counselor available for an excess of thirteen hundred students, and the majority are in serious need of counseling.

Jalisa, with over a decade of experience in the Jersey City school system, hung on to her more challenging cases, but began shuffling kids my way. Among them was Tamira.

At first, Tamira was extremely tight-lipped and defensive. Like most of the kids raised in the inner city, she's seen and experienced a dark side of life no one should ever know. She's hard, way harder than she should be at fifteen. But she's still a kid. And while she recognized how different we are, she also recognized I genuinely wanted to help.

She shuts the door behind her and plops down on my brown pleather couch, slipping her heavy bookbag from her shoulders and onto the industrial gray carpet. I sit beside her and cross my legs, causing the hem of my dark blue dress to brush against my shins. In one swoop, she takes me in, from my dark hair down to my tan pumps. My clothes are casual, comfortable, and very different from the tight jeans and shirt that hug and accentuate her generous curves. "You know you're never going to get a man wearing that," she tells me.

I smile. This isn't the first time Tamira has inferred I need a man. I don't bother to tell her that I don't *need* one, even though it's true. But there are moments when I really want one, despite how many have disappointed me in the past.

"Is it the shoes?" I ask, wiggling my foot.

She motions dramatically. "That's part of it. Miss Aedry, you're a hot woman. Hot women wear hot shoes. Get yourself a pair of red stilettos, and you'll get yourself a man."

I grin. "Are you saying there's hope for me yet?"

"Yah. You just need to stop dressing like you're going to church all the time."

She laughs when I do. As my smile softens, so does her humor. "So how are you doing?" I ask.

Her lips tighten to a straight line before she says, "I'm pregnant."

My heart breaks a little, but I try not to let it show. Tamira's grades had started to improve last semester, following tutoring sessions with me after school. Just the other day, we'd met to discuss college, her hope building now that she was doing better in her classes. "Is this something you'd planned?" I ask carefully, knowing how lonely she always seems. She shakes her head slowly. "Would you want to talk about it?"

Her attention travels to the window, even though the shades are partially closed to ease the bright October sunlight. "I was out with Keon around three in the morning the other week. We had sex in his car over at Lincoln Park. The condom broke."

The details she shares come from her trust in me, and because she's scared. My grandma would tell her to go to church and get some morals. My mother would question what a fifteen-year-old was doing out at three in the morning having sex in a public place. And my father would point out that if she'd been taught abstinence in school, instead of being given condoms in health class, she wouldn't be in this mess. But I was raised in the bible belt of North Carolina, and so were they. Yet, unlike me, they never left and saw how harsh the rest of the world can be.

According to her file, Tamira was raped for the first time when she was five by her mother's boyfriend, then again at seven by the next man her mother invited into her bed. So, I don't judge, or reprimand, or turn my back. Instead, I clutch her hand and give it a squeeze. "Aside from the condom breaking, what makes you think you're pregnant?" I ask, keeping my voice soft.

"I was supposed to get my period last week and it didn't come."

"You're still young and your cycle may not always be regular."

She tilts her head in my direction. "You sayin', I'm not pregnant?"

"I don't know, Tamira. It may be too early to tell." I release her hand and reach for the business cards I keep on my end table and pass one to her. "I think the first thing you need to do is see a medical professional. This is Autumn Stone. She's a midwife at the clinic and a friend of mine. Call and make an appointment and ask to see Autumn specifically. If the receptionist gives you a hard time, tell her I sent you."

"Is she nice?" she asks, keeping her attention on the card. "This lady you're sending me to?"

"Yes," I answer quietly.

When her dark brown eyes meet mine, it's all I can do not to tear up. "Like you?" she asks.

"Autumn is really sweet," I assure her, my voice splintering. "We were roommates in college."

She nods and shoves the card in her backpack. When she meets my face again, she laughs. "Miss Aedry, you worry too much. I'm going to be fine. Me and any baby who comes along."

It's what she claims, but I recognize the fear behind that tough outer layer. I'm not supposed to touch my students. Given my line of work and the stories I hear, some days it takes all I have not to reach out and hug them. Today is one of those days. But I do give her hand another squeeze. "I know you're scared, but I'm here if you need me."

Tamira rolls her eyes, laughing, but then her resolve crumbles and the first of her tears release. I let her cry, because, for now, it's the only way I can help her.

Yet, as quickly as those tears come, they abruptly stop. She dabs her eyes with the tissues I pass her. In the silence that follows, that harsh city kid I've come to know and adore returns. She stands, throwing her backpack over her shoulder and pointing at me. "You're too much like a mom," she tells me. "Get yourself some hot clothes and shoes and it won't take you long to have your own kids to worry about."

She's trying to make a joke in order to lock up her vulnerability and keep it safe. It's what's helped her survive everything she's been through. But I don't bother to tell her something she already knows. "I'll work on the shoes," I promise.

"And the church clothes?"

I widen my smile. "That might take a few paychecks."

She shakes her head and walks to the door. As it shuts behind her, my worry for her surges. Keon Monroe, the potential father, already has another child, whom he occasionally supports with the money he makes selling drugs. He's had sex with several young girls who attend the high school. Tamira should know this, since it's no secret. But, like the others, I'm sure she fell victim to his looks and devious charm.

Damn it.

I rise and return to my desk. For the moment, I can't help Tamira. But maybe I can help someone else. My attention returns to the file I was reviewing before she stopped by. Apollo Romero is a freshman who's already missed nine days of school, including today. What's odd is his brother Gianno, a junior, hasn't missed one.

Gianno is a gifted athlete who made the varsity wrestling team his first year. He and Apollo have so-so grades, despite their teachers believing they have tremendous academic potential. They've been in trouble for fighting outside of school, but it's what they were subjected to in their home environment that disturbs me more. According to reports, their estranged father killed their mother in a jealous rage before killing himself. Apollo, only eight at the time, had let their father into the apartment. Gianno, only ten, had suffered multiple injuries trying to protect her.

These poor boys watched their mother and father die. I clutch my chest. Is it no wonder these kids have acted out? I flip through the folder, wondering if a relative took them in or whether they're in the foster system. My brows knit when I see custody was granted to their brother six years ago. "What in the world?"

I pull the file closer. Salvatore Romero, who was only twenty-one at the time, fought for several long months to gain custody. How could a man so young be awarded guardianship? His actions were noble, but, my goodness, he was just a kid himself. I flip through the pages, thinking matters through. A court battle like this must have been costly, especially when represented by what appears to be private counsel. I skim down the page, searching for his occupation, assuming he must work as a plumber or in another trade that pays well. I pause when I see that he works in public relations . . . at night.

"This can't be right," I say out loud. I find a contact number and reach for my office phone to make a call until I catch sight of the long list of messages left by school staff.

My head falls into my hand. According to the email from Apollo's homeroom teacher, if Apollo misses one more day, he'll be automatically suspended.

I call the main office. "Hello, Mrs. Glenn," I say when she answers. "This is Adrianna Daniels. I need to meet with Gianno Romero, a junior—"

"The junior class is on a field trip to the museum today, Miss Romero," she interrupts. "Do you want his homeroom teacher's voicemail?"

"No, thank you."

"All right," she answers and abruptly disconnects, having felt I wasted enough of her time.

Maybe it's her "I could care less" response, or Tamira, or the countless other kids I've lost to the streets in the short time I've worked here. Whatever the reason, I'm not ready to put this case aside.

I pick up my phone and call Jalisa. There's still an hour left in school and I'd blocked off the time to catch up on paperwork, but it will have to wait. "Hey," I say when she answers. "You know how we're allowed to do home visits when a case deeply warrants it?"

She pauses. "Yes?"

I glance back at the file. "Well, I have one that fits the bill . . ."

I drive my trusty white Volkswagen Beetle through one of the rougher sections of the city, but when my navigation system takes me past the area and into one of the more up and coming neighborhoods, I'm more than a little surprised. I find a spot across the street from the building when I realize the underground garage is strictly reserved for its residents.

Perhaps it's better. It might be a nice neighborhood, but I avoid garages at all costs. I make my way quickly across the street, shuddering when the brisk air smacks against my legs and billows my skirt. I stop in front of the main door. Unlike the other mailboxes, the Romero residence isn't marked by a name. But I have the apartment number and that's all I need. That, and access to the lobby, which I quickly gain when an older woman slips out.

The building can't be more than a few years old, something I find confusing. If Mr. Romero can afford something this upscale, I don't understand why he isn't more invested in his brothers' futures.

I tried calling him to warn him that I was stopping by, only to hear a deep male voice on the voicemail say, "You know what to do," followed by a beep. The blatant arrogance in his tone shocked me and left me with an impression that this so-called guardian is nothing more than a thug. But given where he and the boys live, I can only determine he's too caught up in himself to worry about those who clearly need him as a role model.

I slip out of the elevator and hurry to apartment 4B, stopping only to text Jalisa and let her know I arrived. I take a breath before knocking, reminding myself I'm a strong, educated woman despite my young age, and that there's no reason to be intimidated. When only silence greets me, I tell myself I can't just give up. This boy needs me, so I knock again. By my third knock, I'll admit, I'm discouraged. How can I help Apollo if his one parental influence is constantly unavailable? I knock again, this time harder. If this Salvatore guy is truly a PR rep who works evenings, he should be home—

The door swings open. "*What the fuck?*"

My eyes widen at the bulk of muscle standing at the door. This man is at least six-two, shaved head, wearing black boxers that fall slightly below the "V" at his waist, exposing a set of abs hard enough to grind diamonds, and arms and legs that belong on a seasoned wrestler.

Now would be a good time for that confident young woman to make an appearance—the one who came here—the one whose jaw isn't dangling to her toes—the one who no longer has glasses strong enough to see into orbit, or teeth so bucked they end in another zip code.

The man's tight face and stance relax as he leans his shoulder against the door frame. His brown eyes rake the length of my body, the intensity in his stare forceful enough to tug off my clothes. It's not until his attention returns to my face that I catch his approving nod and subtle smile. "Nice," he murmurs.

My face heats, which I absolutely hate. My skin is so fair, there's no masking the blush that follows. I lift my chin. "Shouldn't you put on some clothes?" I ask, well aware my voice is shrill and quivering.

"I would, but then it will block the view of the goods you can't seem to get enough of," he says, adding a wink.

It's the wink that's my undoing. Okay, that and those broad shoulders, and strong jaw, and Channing Tatum-esque face. Who am I kidding? It's the whole package. This man is what some might call more than a little attractive.

"I . . ." It's the only thing I manage to say. By now, it's obvious I'm gawking at him.

"Look, gorgeous," he says. "I've had a long night. Either leave your brochures and get going, or give me a reason to let you inside."

My jaw pops open when I realize he's mistaken me for a Jehovah's Witness—and a slutty one at that! Maybe Tamira had a point about me wearing "church" clothes. "I don't have brochures," I stammer.

"Good, don't read that shit anyway—"

"My name is Adrianna Daniels. I'm the guidance counselor at Apollo and Gianno's school . . ."

Chapter Three
Salvatore

"Fuck me."

"I beg your pardon?" she asks, her voice trembling.

I hold out a hand and shake my head. "Not like that." *Well, at least not now that I know who you are.*

She clears her throat and straightens, gathering courage she doesn't quite seem to have. "Are you Salvatore Romero?"

"That's right."

She clears her throat. Again. "Okay. Well, I'd like to talk to you about Apollo—"

I throw open the door. "Come in."

I stomp inside, turning around when I realize she's not following and catch her eyes glued to my ass. Ordinarily, I'd flash her an easy grin and invite her inside my bedroom for a little fun. I wasn't lying when I called her gorgeous. Those eyes are the bluest I've ever seen, and that red lipstick she's wearing makes her sexy lips that much fuller. And don't get me going on that face. Those supposed girls next door don't stand a chance next to her, especially given the body she's hiding beneath that long dress.

Yeah. Another day, another time, and under other circumstances, I wouldn't be slipping back into bed alone. But considering who she is, *and* following the night I had with Vin and Donnie—and Donnie's freak out when Vin left her and the girls she snagged to go home to his wife—it's not a good idea, no matter how tempting she looks.

"Have a seat, ah . . ."

"Adrianna Daniels," she repeats. "Or Miss Aedry, if you prefer, sir."

Sir? How old does she think I am? "Make yourself comfortable, Aedry," I say, ignoring the "Miss" part. She's already heard me swear and she knows I answer the door in my underwear. It's too late to make like I'm polite. "I'll throw on some clothes and be right out."

I stalk into my room, pulling on a white tank and a pair of black sweats. Damn. Looking at the time, I only slept an hour. I swear when I heard the pounding at the door, I was ready to rip the fist off the arm it belonged to. Now that I've seen that arm, and everything else, I wouldn't mind sliding my tongue along her neck as my hips slam between her spread legs.

I rub my face, reminding myself what she's here for.

Christ. What the hell did Apollo and Gianno do? The last thing I want is some counselor showing up and starting shit I don't need. I march back into the living room, where she's sitting on the white leather couch, clear on the opposite end with her purse placed beside her. She doesn't want me to get too close. *Hmmph. Interesting.*

"Want some water or something?"

"No, thank you." She pushes a strand of her dark brown hair behind her ear as she rummages through her large purse. The waves fall around her face in layers, passing her shoulders, but not by much. The women I know would have added extensions or teased it. Then again, the women I know hang out on poles and wear shoes you can see through. She pulls out a file and, even though she doesn't glance up, I can tell by her nervousness she knows I've been watching her.

"I'd like to talk to you about my concerns about Apollo," she says. "But while I'm here, perhaps we should discuss Gianno, too."

I head to the kitchen, talking as I search through the fridge. "Why did you come here by yourself?"

"I told you. I'm concerned about your brothers."

"That's not what I mean." I snag two bottles of water and walk back, handing her one before I lower myself beside her. I'm close, but not too close, giving her the space I think she needs. "You're a woman, but you show up to some stranger's apartment with nothing but a purse and a smile."

"I don't recall smiling," she says, adding a grin that makes her more beautiful than she already is.

Holy shit. This woman is . . . something.

I twist open the cap of my water bottle and take a swig. "That doesn't answer my question," I say, keeping my face and voice hard.

She angles her chin, analyzing my question and maybe me, too. "I can take care of myself, I assure you," she says.

"You packing?" I ask, motioning to her purse.

Her attention falls to the file. Either she is and doesn't want to tell me, or she isn't and I'm making her uncomfortable. Whatever it is makes her smile fade. Not that I like it.

"According to what I've read, Apollo is really bright and has tremendous potential," she continues. "But his lack of attendance is severely affecting his grades and—"

"Hold up," I say, lifting my hand. "What do you mean his lack of attendance?"

She frowns. "Mr. Romero—"

"Salvatore or Sal. No mister."

"Okay, Salvatore then. Apollo has missed nine days of school. If he misses another without a medical excuse, he'll be suspended."

Now I'm pissed. "I take it the school's called? Sent letters home? Shit like that?"

Her eyes widen slightly. "Yes."

I lean back. "Why are you looking at me like that?" I ask, lowering my rough voice.

She lets out a small breath. "If you must know, your language is rather startling."

"You call it startling," I say carefully, realizing that I'm probably scaring her. "I call it Jersey and honest. It's who I am. I don't mean any disrespect."

"All right," she answers quietly and in a way that tells me she believes me. "As I was saying, Apollo has been frequently absent. Both the administration and staff have made several attempts to contact you." She opens the file and points to a spot on the left. "See for yourself."

I edge close enough to read the communication log. Twenty-two fucking documented calls plus five letters. I hope Apollo's been having fun. I'm going to kill that kid when he gets home. My eyes trail to a copy of the police report, the one filed the night Ma died. "What else does it say about him?"

Her eyes soften and she moves her purse aside to sit closer to me. "Why don't we look through it together, so you can see for yourself?"

"Is that legal? You showing me this?"

"It's not illegal," she responds. "But it's not something I typically do."

Her eyes meet mine with something I'm not used to and can't quite place. "It's too easy to lose sight of Apollo, when all you focus on is what's allegedly wrong with him," she says by way of an answer. "I want you to see the good things others say about him, so you can recognize his potential and we can work out a plan to help him."

"We?" I ask, cocking a brow.

She smiles in a way that holds me in place. "I want to find a way to reach him if I can. Will you help me?"

Given that smile, I, more than anything, want to help her out of that dress. Yet, despite what she's doing to me as a man, I'm not too stupid to see she actually gives a damn about my baby brother. "Fine. Show me what you've got."

She nods and starts on the right side, where the police report is. She hesitates and says, "I'm really sorry about what happened to your mother and father."

She waits for me to say something. But I don't. I earned my G.E.D. at sixteen and left home as soon as I could, using every dime I made bussing tables to train with Lionel Edgar's camp, the UFC's Middleweight Champion at the time. There were days I went hungry and times I slept at the gym 'cause I didn't have enough cash to pay for a motel room. I didn't mind. I was training with the best to be the best, to give my mother and brothers a better life by becoming the next champ. At least that was my intention. The road to hell is paved with good intentions.

When I left, my pathetic excuse for a father spiraled out of control. Ma downplayed the shit he was pulling. I should have trusted my instincts and figured out something was wrong. By the time Gianno reached out to me, it was too late. Instead of helping my family like I wanted, I abandoned my future and returned home to bury my mother and raise my brothers.

That's not the kind of shit you tell a total stranger. It's not the kind of shit I tell anyone, ever. I bury it deep where it belongs.

Her delicate features soften further, if that's even possible, like she latched onto something deep beneath my hard expression. I'm ready for her to ask me to "share" and spill my guts. But instead she flips over the police report and thumbs through the school records.

We go through the file. Every teacher starts with basically the same thing: "Apollo is an intelligent student," but the comments always end with him not applying himself or caring, or mouthing off.

"What about Gianno?" I ask when we're through.

Aedry finishes off her water. For someone who didn't initially want it, she seems thirsty. "He needs help academically. But I think his commitment to wrestling keeps him in school."

"He wants to be in the MMA."

"Mixed Martial Arts?" she asks. At my nod she adds, "He can do a lot more than that."

"MMA is the future in sports, lady."

"It's Aedry," she says casually, even though I'm all but glaring at her. "And I'm not trying to put down a career in fighting. If he can get his grades up, he can probably go to college on a wrestling scholarship."

"College?" I repeat, not sure if she's messing with me. It's something I've wanted for them, and been setting money aside for, but also something I'm not sure either could manage.

She smiles again, but this grin doesn't quite show her teeth. "He has a lot of potential," she says. "Just like Apollo."

Her smile fades when I lock my gaze on her. I've been keeping things easy and professional with her. But the way her eyes shimmer, it's damn hard. The caveman in me wants to have a taste of those lips and a lot more. Except the man who has two brothers to pound into shape doesn't allow me to get close.

Before I can release her from my gaze, she turns away. Maybe she's not interested. Or maybe she knows better than to get close to a man like me.

"Gianno has been on track with regards to attendance and completion of projects," she says, her voice regaining that quiver. "However, he's been in a few fights outside of school grounds that we were made aware of, and there was that incident with him masturbating on the baseball field at Roosevelt Park."

She stops talking when I crack up, her expression stunned. "This isn't a laughing matter, I assure you."

"He wasn't jerking off," I tell her. "He was fucking a girl in the dugout. When the cops showed, he didn't want her to get in trouble. He stepped out to distract them so she could get away, but didn't finish pulling up his pants in time." I shrug. "He saved that girl a lot of embarrassment. You ask me, it was a pretty classy move."

"He was having sex with a girl?"

For a moment I just look at her, unsure why that's the one thing she fixated on. "That's right," I answer.

"He was only fifteen at the time," she says.

I motion to the file with a jerk of my chin. "You know what they've been through and what they saw. They grew up faster than I wanted them to, but it wasn't by choice. Do I like that he was fucking a girl at fifteen? No. He could have waited another two years."

"Seventeen is hardly old enough to start a sexual relationship."

"Men start a lot younger," I remind her. "And I never said anything about a relationship."

Her full lips open slightly. I picked up on a light Southern accent when she introduced herself. But even if I hadn't, it's clear she didn't grow up in the Tri-state area and all its in-your-face brutal honesty. I also pick up on the fact that she thinks seventeen is too young to have sex.

Even though I shouldn't, I can't help wondering how old she was her first time, and whether she enjoyed it. Probably not. The first-time sucks for women, and probably so does their second and third times, which is one of many reasons I only take experienced women to bed.

"They're not men yet," she insists, pulling me back to the moment. "They're boys . . . children really."

"If you think my brothers are the only kids out there having sex at fifteen, you're wrong."

"I'm well aware that teens have sex," she says quietly. "That doesn't mean I approve, or that it should be so easily dismissed as the norm. Rules at this age are important, as are morals that first begin at home."

"Are you saying I don't have morals, and that maybe they don't, either?"

My tone is sharp with each word, but she's not backing down, keeping her voice soft yet absolute. "I'm saying they need guidance to keep them safe in all aspects of their lives."

I cock my head, knowing she means what she says. But, so do I. "My brothers have seen and done things they shouldn't have. And I haven't always been around to protect them." My voice gathers that edge it always gets before I explode. "That doesn't mean I'm not there for them, or that I wouldn't die saving them. No matter who tries to hurt them."

Chapter Four
Adrianna

"Who's trying to hurt them, Salvatore?"

His steel hard expression tightens further. "No one. That's not what I said," he answers, keeping his voice even.

He doesn't blink, yet I don't believe him. "Are you worried someone might?" I ask, trying to press enough to get some answers and maybe attain a better feel for him.

"No," he responds. His gravelly voice grows more of an edge. It's subtle, but my training helps me pick up on it. "I'm only saying I'm there for them no matter what."

No . . . there's more to it than that. I start to tell him when the front door opens and Apollo steps in, leading a young woman into the apartment by her hand. His smile vanishes and so does hers when Salvatore rises and pegs them with a glare that comes down like an axe.

"Oh, *shit*," Apollo says, his eyes rounding when he sees me standing beside his brother.

Sal points to the girl. "You, *out*," he growls, motioning to the hall. The girl takes off in a run. Seeing how Salvatore appears ready to tear someone's spine out, I can't really blame the poor thing. He addresses Apollo, hooking a thumb. "Get your ass in here."

Apollo leaves the foyer. I ease myself between them as he steps into the large open living room. "Hi, Apollo. How are you?"

"Oh, just great, Miss Aedry, real great," he mumbles, keeping his sights on his very immense brother.

I glance at Salvatore. If glares were strong enough to mold and create steel, there would be a tank taking up space in the living room. "Um, your guardian and I have been discussing a plan to help you meet your goals and academic objectives."

Apollo's stare cuts nervously Sal's way. "I can see that," he says, backing away when Sal takes a step forward.

"Watch that smart mouth," Sal snaps, edging closer. "Is this what you've been doing this whole time? Ditching school to bring back girls when you think I'm not around?"

I lift my hand, pressing it against his chest. Ordinarily, I wouldn't touch anyone like this, especially someone so, um, *menacing*. But I have to do something to ease his mounting fury.

My touch is gentle, but it's enough to halt his advancing steps. He looks at me, then my hand, before meeting me square in the eye again.

I offer a gentle smile, or at least I try to. My face is burning and my pulse is racing out of control. I'm not used to being this close to a stranger. "Perhaps a calmer approach would work better?" I offer.

"Calm?" he says, practically growling at me.

"I like calm," Apollo says. "Calm works."

"Don't push me," Sal barks.

This is going to be fun. I turn around and smile at Apollo, who oddly enough seems ready to bolt. "Why don't you sit so we can talk with you?"

"We?" Apollo says, glancing back at his brother. I nod. "*We're* going to talk?" For some reason, the suggestion makes him smile. "Yeah. Let's talk. Wouldn't want to leave Miss Aedry with the wrong impression about us, would we, Sal?"

I don't have to turn around to guess Salvatore's reaction. The tension slamming into my shoulders, coupled with Apollo's large step back assures me his brother's response was neither warm nor cuddly. My nails graze over the ridiculously dense muscles in Salvatore's arm. The motion is light and just enough to draw his attention away from Apollo.

Again, his focus falls to my hand before returning to my thoroughly heated face. "Shall we sit and talk?" I suggest.

He waits for Apollo to lower himself into the loveseat before returning to the couch, a classic demonstration of dominance. Salvatore sits, leaving me space so I'll resume my place beside him. As I take a seat, our legs brush together, sending another wave of heat to flush my skin.

"Okay," I begin, ignoring the feel of him watching me. "You've already missed nine days of school. If you miss one more—"

"He won't," Sal answers for him. "Will you?"

Apollo's stare bounces from him to me. I continue as if uninterrupted. "You can't miss another day without a medical reason and a note from your doctor. But, given your history, excessive absences, and the steps you've taken to hide the school's warnings from your guardian, you'll also have to attend mandatory counseling sessions."

He doesn't appear resistant to counseling. In fact, his entire expression lights up as he steals a glance at Salvatore. "With who?"

"We have a few part-time male counselors starting in a few weeks. I'm sure we'll be able to place you in one of their slots so it doesn't interfere with your classes."

"No," he answers.

"You don't get a choice," Sal fires back. "You had a choice, several, in fact. Go to school. Do the work. Keep your nose clean. You didn't bother with any of them. So now, this is what you have to do, and what you're going to do."

"No," Apollo says, lifting his chin.

"Are you fucking kidding me with this shit?" Sal starts to rise, but somehow my hand on his knee keeps him in place.

Apollo's eyes widen and he swallows hard. "I'll only speak to Miss Aedry."

Salvatore frowns. "What?"

Apollo looks at me when he answers. "No men—and not Miss Jalisa, either. I'll talk to you or I don't talk at all."

"You're under the impression that you make the rules. If so, you're fucking wrong."

Sal's voice is so lethal, I fight the urge to withdraw from him. But knowing that my clasp on his knee is the only thing keeping this massive lion from lunging at the skinny gazelle, I stay perfectly still. "It's okay," I reply, patting him gently. "Apollo," I say, fighting the urge to glance back at Salvatore. "My schedule is full. I can't meet with you during school."

"You hear that?" Sal says. "She's not available."

"I won't talk to anyone else." He bows his head. "Especially a man."

What the . . .

"He's playing you," Sal says, causing Apollo to lift his head.

I steal a glimpse at Salvatore, not missing the way his features darken. Maybe he's right. Or maybe something else happened to Apollo. I can't be sure. What I do know is that I can't abandon this boy. I twist my body around to speak to Salvatore, keeping my voice soft. "I think there may be a way to help Apollo and Gianno. I can meet with them after school in my office and go over their work. On alternate days, I'll take Apollo aside and meet with him privately while Gianno finishes his assignments."

"You're volunteering to stay after school?" Sal asks, sounding doubtful.

"Yes," I respond.

"Without pay?" he clarifies.

"It's not an inconvenience," I assure him. "I'm often there anyway, catching up on reports." I hold onto my smile when his granite expression remains firmly in place. "And this is something I've done in the past that's garnered tremendous success."

"Why?"

"Why have I had success?" I ask, trying to understand why he doesn't appear to believe me. "Because in addition to counseling the students who need it, it's an opportunity to tutor those who are struggling academically."

Sal holds out a hand. "I mean why do it for any of them?"

"I told you. I want to help."

For a long while, Salvatore's brown eyes sear through me, as if trying to catch traces of lies or ulterior motives. It's not until I see him relax his guard that I think he finally trusts what I'm saying. Yet whatever softness he greets me with is lost when his focus returns to Apollo.

"Let's get one thing straight," he tells him. "This is your last chance. You fuck this up, you won't answer to Aedry, the school, or anyone else. You'll answer to me. And you won't like what I have to tell you . . ."

Chapter Five
Salvatore

"Is Vincent fucking someone else? Without me being there, I mean?"

When I don't answer Donnie, she starts swearing and bends forward to snort another line.

"Christ, Donnie," I say. I lift the tray, tossing it, and all the blow, in the trash.

"What the hell, Salvatore?" she screams at me, smacking her palms against my chest. "You know how much that shit costs?"

I snag her elbow and haul her back when she tries rifling through the can. Damn, I'm so sick of this shit.

"A few bills, maybe more?" I offer. "I don' know. What I do know is that you're paying for it with Vin's money, knowing he doesn't want you doing it." She tries to yank herself free, but I hold tight. "Listen to me, you need to get it together. You keep pulling this insecure shit, making demands on him, he's going toss you on your ass—are you listening?" I yell, when she tries to pull away.

She must be, seeing she starts crying. I do a mental groan and ease her back on the bed. Vin was supposed to meet her two hours ago. She's been sitting in here, wearing her silk robe and whatever she has under it, for at least three hours. I told her not to text him, but she did twice, asking where he was and when he was coming.

If she was anyone else, I wouldn't care what was happening. But, like I said, me and Donatella have known each other a long time. Except, where I always dreamed of making something of myself and getting out of Jersey, she always dreamed of landing a rich and powerful man to take care of her. She never wanted to work and, since puberty hit her hard, she never had to, not really.

Donnie is one of those women you can't believe is actually real, she's so beautiful. Blonde hair dyed to perfection, nice rack, tiny waist, and all legs. She's modeled for Playboy and Maxim, but the moment Vin noticed her a few years back, he would only let her model for him, which was fine with Donnie. She played her games, teased and taunted him, made him want her bad. When she finally let him have her, she was sure he'd never let her go. But, instead of making her his wife, Vin married someone else and kept Donnie as his *gumad*.

"Can't marry a whore," I remember him telling me on his wedding day.

It wasn't what Donnie planned on, but she accepted it well enough, too blinded by the money, power, and how well he keeps her. Her mistake was believing what they had would last like a marriage. But she doesn't believe. Not anymore.

Can't say I blame her.

"I fuck those girls for him," she says, sniffing either from her tears, the blow, or maybe both. "I do everything for him."

I kneel in front of her when she takes a seat in front of her vanity. "I'm going tell you something, and I need you to listen and listen good. You push Vincent, he'll cut you loose and not look back. Too much is going down and he can't handle more on his plate, you feel me?"

She wipes her eyes, streaking some of her make-up. But then it's like she suddenly hears me and puckers her lips. "Are the other bosses putting hits on him?"

"Don't know what you're talking about," I tell her. It's not that I think Donnie's wearing a wire. She wouldn't betray Vin, knowing he'd order one in her skull. That doesn't mean I think her place is safe from the Feds.

"Shit," she mumbles.

"Do you have any money saved? Or is it all taking up space in your closet?" Her tight mouth makes it clear she only has what Vin gives her each week. "Maybe you should think about taking a class, going to school, something."

"He is fucking someone else."

I swipe at my face. "Christ, Donnie. I'm trying to give you some advice, so if and when Vin moves on—and he will move on with the way you're acting—you have something to fall back on." Besides another rich man she can dig her nails into.

"I can't," she says, tears sliding down her face. "I have to be available for Vincent when he needs me. How will I do that if I'm sitting in some damn lecture hall?"

For a moment, I don't say anything. Donnie's a little younger than me, but whether it's all the makeup she wears, the blow she's been doing lately, or this life she's carved for herself, it's aging her fast. Is she still hot? Yeah. I see it, always have. But ever since I laid my eyes on Aedry—and given how often I see her now—I don't know, as fucked up as it sounds, I don't look at Donnie the same.

There's no missing Donnie's killer face and body. But Aedry has a rare kind of beauty you don't find in the Tri-State area or, hell, maybe anywhere.

"Fine," I finally say to Donnie. "Your choice. But you have to let him want you on his terms. You fighting with him, trying to tell him when he should be here, it's going to get old fast. Got me?" At her nod, I motion to her bathroom. "Get cleaned up in case he comes. If he doesn't, don't give him a hard time when he does."

She nods and struts toward the bathroom in a pair of crazy stilettos that are probably killing her feet. She pauses before stepping inside. "Thanks, Sal."

I tilt my chin, but that's all I do. When I walk out into the living room, Lucca is already there to take over. Made men don't watch *gumads*, but Vin trusts Lucca, because I trust Lucca. So, for now, Donnie should rest assured Vin doesn't want her fucking anyone else.

"Later, Sal," he says, when he sees me head to the door.

"Later, Lucca," I say, buttoning my suit jacket to shield my piece before stepping out into the hall.

I don't typically watch Donnie during the day, but Vito called me to tell me she was freaking out over Vin and wanted to see me. I came, because despite Donnie's faults, she's a friend. Maybe the blow's making her more paranoid, or maybe it's the shit going down with the other bosses. Whatever it is, she's scared to lose Vin. But her fear is going to drive him away if she keeps it up and where's that going to leave her? On the street for sure, with no one to take care of her.

Shit.

I slam my driver's side door and crank the engine, pulling onto the main road. As I leave the upscale neighborhood, I try not to think about Donnie too much. There's nothing I can do to help her when she's so unwilling to help herself. I'm already putting as much as I can into the trust funds I set up for Apollo and Gianno and investing what remains so, one day, I can open that MMA gym I've been dreaming about. I can't support Donnie, too, especially with how much she's pissing away.

Worrying about what's going to happen to her eats at my gut. But the closer I draw to the high school, the easier it is to let my frustrations with Donnie go and leave her problems behind me.

Gianno and Apollo have spent every weekday afternoon for the last two weeks with Aedry. It doesn't seem like a long time, but already I see a difference in their grades and in their moods. They're not as cranky or as needy. I think the individual attention she gives them has helped. Not that I've spent these last few years ignoring them. I've taken them to the movies, baseball games, vacations, shit like that. But days off away from Vin have been rare since the summer ended.

I haven't been around as much lately. Not as much as I want and, based on how they've been slacking, probably not as much as I need to be.

I pull up to the rear of the building, where all the buses usually idle, to the right of the teacher's lot. The three of them step out as I set my Range Rover in park. Gianno says something I can't quite hear, but it's something that causes Apollo to grin and Aedry to throw back her head and laugh. I've never seen a woman laugh like her. It's like her whole body feels it. She doesn't care how loud she is, or that she's twisting to the side and holding her belly like it hurts. She just puts it all out there. The women I go with, it's like they have to stay in control, always worried about how they'll look if they stray past their well-rehearsed poses.

Aedry's laughter fades, but she keeps her smile when I roll down the window and nod her way. She waves briefly, but then turns to my brothers to hug them goodbye. It's something she does all the time now, and something she asked me for permission to do, so long as it was okay with them and I was present. I agreed, not thinking too much about how she believed it might help them. She spouted some theories, not that I gave them much merit. But seeing the effect it's had . . . I get it now.

The first time she offered, Apollo stiffened and seemed to force himself to accept it. He's not used to affection. The last time he was hugged was at our mother's funeral. He hated all those strangers telling him they were sorry, and touching him because they felt he needed them to. They didn't understand that the only thing he needed was our mother back. We all did.

Except, however awkward and hard it was for him to accept Aedry's show of affection, he did, appearing to relax as she collected him in her slender arms.

Now Gianno was different. Being the ladies' man that he thinks he is, no way was he turning down the opportunity to touch a beautiful woman. But the way Aedry embraces him is very motherly and I think it screwed with his mind the first time. He cocked his head when they separated and looked at her like he was missing something. But then he smiled in a way I hadn't seen in years. He didn't smirk, like he usually does, because he thinks he's too cool to smile, or in that way that tells me he's up to no good. No, this was a real smile, making him look like a kid and reminding me how young they still are.

My brothers like her and that's . . . good. They need a woman like Aedry, not women like I bring to my bed—and definitely not someone like Donnie and what she's become.

Aedry laughs again when she releases Gianno, taking a moment to muss his hair. "See you next week, okay?"

"Bye, Miss Aedry," they both say, before jogging toward my ride and climbing inside.

"Hey," I tell them.

"Hey," they say back. Yeah. We're all about the love.

Apollo drops his backpack on the floor and starts to buckle his seatbelt when a guy about my age hops down the steps and hurries to Aedry. I frown. "Who's that?" I ask.

Apollo pauses. "Some dick trying to get in her pants."

"What?" I ask, keeping the window down.

"Mr. Tavers. He's the basketball coach and our gym teacher," Gianno adds. "But, yeah, he wants to fuck her."

"Watch your mouth," I growl, mostly because I don't like what I'm seeing.

The guy steps closer to Aedry. Aedry steps back, putting some space between them, but keeping her smile. The guy says something and motions in the direction of his car. Aedry loses her smile and shakes her head, saying something else and returning to the steps.

"Asshole," Gianno mutters. "May have to key his car."

I don't hear the last part or maybe I do and don't care. I'm too busy wondering why this idiot can't take a hint and why it's pissing me off to have him so close to her.

Chapter Six
Aedry

It's Saturday night and I have a date.

Okay. Not really. I shift in the backseat of the car, trying to mimic my girlfriends' excitement. I mean, I *am* excited. There's no pretending that I'm not. But I'm also a little nervous and possibly terrified, too.

When I walked Apollo and Gianno out yesterday, I did my best not to gape at Salvatore. Really, I did. Yet a man who looks and moves like him is hard to ignore *and* forget. He was drool-worthy in the tank and sweats he wore, and the way he looked in those tight black boxer briefs rivaled major underwear ads. But in those crisp white-collared shirts he wears beneath those sharp black suit jackets . . . Goodness, it's all I can do to keep my tongue from lolling to the ground each time I see him. The man drips sex instead of sweat.

It's pathetic how I look forward to catching glimpses of him when he picks up his brothers. After all, we've only spoken briefly since I left his apartment. I've tried to keep things professional, especially since he didn't seem interested in me once he knew I wasn't some skanky solicitor. But when I returned to my desk and found a thank you card from him, along with four passes to the exclusive club, Silk, I came close to losing my mind. His note, while simple, tugged at my heart.

Thank you for helping my brothers. Hope to see you Saturday at midnight.

Salvatore

I didn't dare call him to tell him I was usually asleep by midnight. Instead, I rounded up some friends to share my passes with.

My studio apartment is located near the water, on the second floor of a converted warehouse. I have one bathroom and a small eat-in kitchen. A row of sheer curtains separates my cozy living room from my even cozier bedroom. I could probably afford something bigger, but not as nice, and definitely not in one of Jersey City's trendier neighborhoods.

It has its advantages, in spite of the 700 square feet of living space, like access to nearby shops, restaurants, and loads of other twenty-something professionals for neighbors. Case in point, the young single women surrounding me who, based on their delighted chatter, can't wait to make it to Silk.

"Fess up, Aedry," Marilyn says, her eyes skimming to the rearview mirror as she drives. "How did you score these passes?"

"I told you. They were given to me as a thank you." By a hot guy who I probably have no business getting involved with.

"What's his name?"

I try to sound relaxed, but I can't seem to squelch my grin. "Salvatore."

"Oh," they all sing.

"What does *Salvatore* do?" Marilyn asks.

"He's in public relations." *Or so he tells me.*

Christy turns around in the front passenger seat to toss me a wry glance. "You don't get passes to Silk unless you're a celebrity or high-roller. Which one is he?"

"He seems to be successful," I respond, taken slightly aback by what she says. I'm being honest in my response, but I base it on his clothing, residence, and vehicle, and not on anything he's told me directly. "I think he might have connections," I add as an afterthought.

"Is he cute?" Julia asks, twisting in her tiny mini-dress to take me in.

I tug on the edge of the equally small electric purple dress they shoved me into when I showed up to Julia's in black pants and what I thought was a cute blouse and pumps. "Some women may find him attractive," I reply, my face burning under their scrutiny.

"Hmmm," Marilyn says. "I take it you're one of those women?"

I laugh when they do, because it's *that* obvious I'm into him. Salvatore is the sexiest man I've ever had the pleasure of meeting, but that's not something I am willing to tell them.

Our first encounter was strained, given the circumstances, and somewhat scary, given his tough and blunt exterior. Sparks didn't exactly fly, but I couldn't deny the attraction I felt being around him. That attraction intensified when I realized that his brothers mean everything to him, and that he is their world.

I look forward to the simple glimpses of him I catch and, as ridiculous as it sounds, it's the part of my day that always manages to lift my spirits.

I settle back into the seat and try to relax, although it does nothing to wipe the goofy smile off my face. It's been a long time since I've been interested in a man and, aside from Hollywood movie stars, I've never actually *panted* over a man. With Salvatore, I definitely pant and a great deal more.

"Do me a favor," Marilyn says as she pulls into one of the high-rise decks. "If you decide to go home with him, let one of us know."

"I'm not going home with him," I say, wishing my voice wasn't so quaky.

"No pressure," Julia adds, quickly. "We just want to make sure you have a ride back."

"Do you need any condoms?" Christy asks, digging into her purse as Marilyn finds an empty spot.

"No, I'm good," I answer. I do my best to keep my tone light, but fail miserably.

"You sure? I have plenty," Christy says, oblivious to the heat flushing my cheeks.

"Positive."

I try not to react when Julia and Marilyn take Christy up on her offer. My friends are sweet, lovely girls, with alternating shades of blonde hair. They're not promiscuous, but they are sexually experienced.

They don't know that I've never had sex and I don't want to tell them. They like to include me, but it's moments like this I realize how very different we are. They weren't raised in a strict Baptist household like I was, and they've probably always been beautiful.

Growing up, my teeth and jaw were a mess and my vision horrific. When I graduated high school and my parents and grandparents asked what I wanted, I asked for Lasix and braces. Their financial troubles had finally stabilized so they could grant both requests.

My vision repair was easy and successful, helping me toss those awful glasses I used to wear. Repairing my bucked and crooked teeth and the issues with my jaw, however, took a great deal of work. I wore braces all four years in college. During that time, young men finally began to notice me. I dated a few who touched me and who I touched in return, but most were impatient and quickly moved on when I wouldn't have full-on intercourse with them.

"You're a nice girl, Aedry. But I have to get mine while I can," one of them told me. "Understand?"

No, I didn't understand. I wasn't averse to sex, or think it was necessary to be married, or even in love, to engage in sexual activity. The only thing I asked for was a commitment, but even that seemed like too much of a burden for the men I dated.

I graduated from college, enrolled in a Master's program made up mostly of women, and accepted a position at a school where administrators and teachers were mostly women, leaving me with few opportunities to meet many men. So, here I am, likely the only virgin over twenty still left in the area.

As much as I'm starting to, well, *panic*, that the day to lay my "V" card down may never come, I still want to be in a committed relationship when it happens. Is that too much to ask? I groan. Based on the hoots and hollers we hear stepping out of Marilyn's car, it probably is.

"*Oye*, mama, want some of this?" the guy leading his group of friends asks, grabbing his groin.

"I don't touch shit I can't see," Marilyn fires back, hauling Christy away when she grins at the guy in the red hoodie who winks at her.

I think it's fair to say my future baby daddy doesn't hang with this tempting bunch. If there was a doubt, the short guy who drops his pants and smacks his hairy butt confirms my suspicions.

"Ew," we all say, when he can't seem to stop spanking it.

We hit the stairwell and practically run the remaining two blocks to the club. None of us bothered with anything warmer than light sweaters, and the cold October wind is positively brutal.

I can barely keep up in the silver platform pumps Marilyn shoved me into and Julia is all but dragging me behind her. We must look comical to all the cars passing. Here we are, this group of girls trying to run in footwear capable of killing us with no grace to our steps, and our hair flying in all directions. As it is, we're all laughing. But the moment we round the corner, my girlfriends' stumbles morph into struts packed with plenty of attitude.

They sashay past the irate people waiting in line while I do my best not to fall. Oddly enough, the happy-go-lucky clubbers don't appear happy we're skipping ahead of them.

"What the fuck?"

"Skanks," someone else yells.

My, Toto, there really is no place like the northeast.

Christy waves her hands as we pass. "Sorry, bitches," she fires back.

I try to mirror their prancing. But the shoes I'm wearing have already destroyed my toes and all I did was walk from the car. How in the world am I going to dance if Salvatore asks me?

We stop in front of the bouncer. He smiles when he sees us, but then his smile fades when he collects our passes. He motions to the other bouncer who leads us through the velvet ropes. My friends squeal before resuming the flouncing and twitching I'm clearly incapable of. I should have practiced before we left Marilyn's apartment. At best, I resemble someone walking for the first time, following surgery.

Thank God, Julia holds tight to my hand, because the moment we step into the club, I can't hear anything over the blare of loud music or see past the light show smacking against the wall to wall people dancing.

It's as if we've stepped into a world where big hair reigns, short skirts rule, and lots of unprotected sex is sought and expected. My steps slow and I almost freeze.

What am I doing in a place like this? Christy, Marilyn, and Julia frequently club hop, which is why I typically meet them for brunch on weekends or Happy Hour on Friday nights. Silk is a figurative smack-upside-the-head reminder why I prefer to stay home alone rather than join them on their Saturday night adventures.

"Come on, Aedry," Julia yells over her shoulder when she senses my hesitation, yanking me with her.

I clutch my tiny purse against me, gathering my courage and reminding myself that Salvatore invited me. If I can hang in another thirty minutes, I'll see him and perhaps talk him into going someplace quieter. A lot quieter. Good Lord, it's loud.

The techno beat leads into another song with bass heavy enough to vibrate the floor. A group of men nudge each other when they spot Christy and Marilyn. Christy smiles their way, assuring them she's noticed and that she likes what she sees, too.

"Omigod." Julia whips around and shakes my arm, pointing ahead. "We're in the VIP section. Holy *shit*, Aedry, you totally hooked us up!"

We're led up onto a raised platform and to a large table overlooking the dance floor. The moment we're seated, a waitress appears, placing an ice bucket with a bottle of champagne at the center of the table.

"Compliments of the house," she says, hurrying to hand each of us a glass.

"Who is this guy?" Marilyn asks, leaning into me.

The waitress pops the champagne, careful to avoid eye contact, even as we thank her. "He's in public relations," I say again, well aware of the doubt plaguing my voice.

My girlfriends don't seem to notice. What they do notice is all the attention we're attracting sitting in the VIP section. One song morphs into the next as the group of men we saw on our way in make their way to the bar below us.

The one in a silky black dress shirt catches Christy's attention again. She returns his smile, but then turns back to speak to us.

This goes on for another song until the guy holds Christy's attention long enough to mouth, "How about a drink?"

"How about four?" she yells back, holding up her fingers. "Your pick."

The guy grins and holds out a few bills, snagging the bartender's attention. He and his five other friends follow him, their drinks and ours tight in their hands.

"I don't know about this, Christy," I say, taking a nervous sip of my champagne. I'm not much of a drinker and I'm not here to meet a stranger.

"It's okay, Aedry. Nothing has to happen unless you want it to," she says. "Just try to relax and have a little fun."

The men join us, pulling their chairs in close as they introduce themselves. Instead of regular drinks, they brought us shots. Mine hits me hard enough to make me shudder, causing the men closest to me to laugh. "You're cute," one of them tells me.

I don't respond, doing my best to recover and failing miserably. By the time I'm halfway done with my champagne, I'm already drunk.

"Hey, where you going, Avery?" Josh, or something like that, calls to me.

I don't bother correcting him, or tell him where I'm headed.

"I'll be right back," I say. I don't know these men, nor do I want to. Salvatore is who I came to see and the more time that passes, the more anxious I am to have him with me.

I snake my way into the ladies' room, seeking some quiet and peace only to find two women dipping their nails into vials filled with white powder. They glare when they catch me gawking, so I quickly run into the stall.

They're still there when I step out, apparently not in a rush to leave or to hide what they're doing. I don't bother checking my makeup, opting to quickly wash my hands and avoid conflict.

They glare at me with dilated pupils, seemingly ready to lash out. In my haste to leave, I bump into a stunning woman with long legs, a tiny waist, and breasts the size of Miami.

I've never met a supermodel, yet I'm certain this woman has to be one. "I'm so sorry," I say, worried she'll take a swing at me despite her glamourous appearance.

She tosses her long blond hair and grins, giving me a glimpse of her perfect white teeth. "No worries, sweetie," she says, adding a wink.

I hurry out, grinding to a halt when I see Salvatore leaning against the opposite wall with his arms crossed.

Oh, and there's that smile I'd lost.

Beneath the flashing club lights, his crisp white shirt glows against what must be a very expensive suit. I'm not sure what color it is, black, perhaps? All I know is that the dark color does little to shrink his muscular form.

Salvatore is a sculpture of muscle, his body a masterpiece. Meanwhile, I'm in shoes I can't lean forward in without face-planting, and wearing a dress that barely hides my important parts. I'm out of my element, my comfortable clothes, and completely intimidated. Yet I can't help my widening smile as I approach him.

"Hi," I say, beaming that he's finally here.

He turns his head slowly, his eyebrows knitting when he sees me. "Hey," he says.

I run my fingers through my hair and glance down, well aware of his eyes travelling the length of my body. Maybe I should have taken a moment to check my hair and makeup. Regardless, my happiness at finding him is as apparent as his dominating presence.

"I didn't expect this place to be so popular," I say, motioning in the direction of the packed dance floor.

He tilts his chin, his stare cutting away from me. Before I can turn in the direction he's looking, he clasps my elbow, carefully edging me close to the wall.

Two men, who've had way too much to drink or too much of something else, stumble past us. If Sal hadn't moved me, they would have crashed into me, their inebriated state making them careless.

"First time here?" he asks, well aware I'm not used to seeing grown men so wrecked.

"Clubs aren't really my thing," I admit. I hold out a hand. "Not that I don't appreciate it." His frown deepens, as if he doesn't understand. "We're having fun," I add. At least my friends are. "And we're receiving *a lot* of attention."

"I'll bet," he says, taking me in again, but sounding annoyed.

When he says nothing more, I take a moment to build my courage, reminding myself that if he didn't want to see me, he wouldn't have invited me. "Um. Would you like to go someplace quieter?"

He straightens, regarding me as if I asked him an outrageous question. "You want to go someplace quiet. With me?" he repeats.

I'm obviously saying all the wrong things. "We can have a drink first," I offer, even though I've already had enough. "Unless you'd rather dance."

"I don't dance," he says. "And I rarely drink."

I angle my head. "Then what are we doing here?" I ask. I should be relieved he doesn't appear to want to be here anymore than I do, but mostly I'm confused and my tone reflects it.

"What do you mean, *we*?"

"What?" Although I heard him, it's all I can think to say. Salvatore is livid, but I don't understand why.

He closes in, his immense form practically swallowing me whole. "You said 'we.' *We're* not together, Aedry. And I didn't come here for you."

My heart sinks, and I swear it's all I can do not to find the nearest hole to crawl into. "I'm sorry. When you gave me the passes—"

"What are you talking about?" he snaps.

"The VIP passes you gave me with your note," I say, so quietly I'm not sure he hears me over the music and escalating clamor surrounding us.

When his jaw tightens, I realize he heard every word. "I didn't write you a note—and those passes didn't come from me."

The door to the ladies' room opens and the supermodel blonde glides out. Her steps slow when she finds me with Salvatore, but she keeps her smile as she wraps two arms around one of his. "Ready, Sal?" she purrs at him.

The humiliation heating my face spreads to encompass my entire body.

"I didn't invite you," he bites out. "You shouldn't be here, Aedry."

Chapter Seven
Salvatore

I lead Donnie to her usual table in the VIP section. "Are you going to tell me who she is?" she
asks.

"No one," I hiss.

The moment she slides in the booth, I edge to the side and make a call. "Did you give Aedry passes, telling her they were from me?" I bark when Apollo answers the phone.

There's a pause followed by, "It was Gianno's idea."

"You wrote the note and forged his signature, asshole," Gianno hollers from the background.

"And you got the passes from Lucca," Apollo fires back.

"God damn it," I grumble, swiping my face. Gianno and Apollo's stupid idea didn't simply embarrass Aedry, it humiliated her. Even in the dim lighting leading to the bathrooms, I didn't miss the tears forming in her large blue eyes.

Could I have handled it better? Yeah—a thousand times better now that I think back. But I was shocked to hell and back to find her here—that little dress she's in is hugging her curves and giving me an eyeful of the sweet body she tries to hide.

Do I like her wearing what she's wearing? In truth, *no*. Not here and not for anyone else.

I pass my hand along my face again. Christ Almighty, what the fuck is wrong with me? All I can think about is all these assholes here, looking at her the same way I'm looking at her—thinking like me about pulling her close and wanting to make them bleed for it.

Aedry doesn't belong among the scum that crawls in here. I'm pissed my brothers pulled this shit on her—when all she's done is help them! If they were here, I'd knock their thick skulls together. "Why the fuck did you do that to her—and why would you send her to Silk?" I demand. "She doesn't belong in a sleazy place like this."

"Give me the phone," Gianno tells Apollo. For all he seems to want to talk, he takes his time, letting out a breath before finally speaking. "It's like this, Sal. Miss Aedry's a nice lady."

"No shit," I say. "Tell me why you set her up."

"I'm trying," Gianno answers, sounding pissed. "I think . . . I think she likes you."

"You think *what*?" I snap, mostly because I think he's messing with me. "You have to be fucking kidding me. *That's* your excuse?"

"Come on, Sal. I'm not stupid. I've seen the way you look at her every time you pick us up, rolling down the window, even in the rain, trying to play it cool."

"You're really pushing me," I say, even though he has a point.

"Am I? Why you always dressed when you show?" He huffs when I don't answer. "She's not some whore you shoot a look at, then wait for her to come to you. You look at her to *look* at her. And when Mr. Tavers was talking to her yesterday, I thought you were going to fly out of our ride and knock the shit out of him—not that he didn't deserve it."

He must have me on speaker. I hear Apollo's voice. "Her cheeks get all red when she sees you, and every time we say your name. She plays it off and keeps on talking, but it's obvious she's into you."

He laughs then and it pisses me off. "What are you laughing at?" I snap.

"You," Apollo tells me.

"You seriously better watch the next few words that come out of your mouth," I warn.

"I'm not trying to piss you off."

"Too late for that," I say, causing his humor to immediately vanish.

"Sal . . . you didn't see yourself when she came to our place, the way you acted around her. I thought you were going to kill me, but she calmed you down with just her voice. You didn't argue, you didn't fight her, and you let her touch you like you were already fucking her—"

"I'm going to stop you right there, because I'm seconds from driving home and pounding the unholy hell out of you. This bullshit match-up you pulled did nothing but embarrass Aedry and make me look bad."

"Sal, we're sorry," Apollo begins.

"Save it," I hiss through my teeth. As I watch, Aedry returns to the VIP section. Her arms are crossed and she keeps her focus far away from me. I disconnect the call, not bothering to say goodbye and pocket my phone.

"Fuck," I mutter.

She slinks in beside her friend, the one currently not straddling some douche. Her friend stops smiling when she sees her and leans into her. "You okay?" I see her mouth.

Aedry nods carefully, the way women do when they're trying not to cry. I swear, if my brothers were here, I'd wring their necks. Someone like her doesn't belong with someone like me. If anyone should know this, it's them.

Donnie wraps her arms around me and rests her head against my shoulder. "Tell me who she is."

"No one," I repeat.

"Then why are you so pissed?" When I don't answer, she starts pushing like only Donnie can. "She's really pretty. Nice legs, body. Hmmm . . . I wonder which of those men are going to get to taste those perky tits."

"Shut it, Donnie," I grind out.

One of the dickheads trails his hand up and down her spine like he owns her. My blood boils as she stiffens. But what I'm feeling doesn't brew from anger. It's from shit I'm not ready to deal with that Donnie quickly points out.

"You like her, don't you?" she teases, appearing to enjoy the show.

"She's my brothers' teacher. That's all."

"Mmm. I think it's more than that."

Maybe it is, but I don't tell her that.

Donnie's friends show. I'm hoping they'll distract her, and for a long while they do. But she catches me eyeing Aedry and how that fucktard makes his way closer and closer to her, ignoring the fact that she's not even talking to him.

What does Donnie do? She sends a round of shots to Aedry's table telling her they're from me. At first, I don't like it. I don't want these pricks to think I play nice. But then I think it could be a way to make amends.

They all raise their shots and toast me.

Everyone, except Aedry.

She slides her shot across the table to her friend, not bothering to glance my way, even when she stands and edges her way around the table. I think she's headed home alone—at least, that's what I'm hoping. It's not until I see her cut left that I realize she's headed to the restroom. The moron who's been trying to hook up with her all night follows, not that any of her wrecked friends notice. They're too caught up with the men groping them and kissing their necks.

Shit.

I want to go after her, thinking this guy is up to no good. Donnie catches her leave and notices the guy trailing her. "I want to dance, Sal," she says, shoving her friends ahead of her.

Like I said, Donnie's not stupid. She's been at these clubs enough to recognize a predator when she sees one. And she knows me well enough to know I'm plenty pissed, especially when another idiot hurries to catch up to her first.

Donnie moves ahead, stopping near the hall that leads to the bathrooms to grind with one of her girls, allowing me to keep an eye on her while checking on Aedry. This way, when shit goes down, I don't have to tell Vin I left his woman. And judging by the way those two dumb fucks are waiting for Aedry by the bathroom, I know there's going to be trouble.

Just like I know both are going to walk out of here bleeding if they touch her.

Aedry

I don't feel well. Something's . . . wrong. It's more than the shot and the sips of champagne I've had. And it's more than Salvatore's rejection.

My hand sweeps along my brow as I shift through the fog clouding my mind and recall our encounter. God, I feel so stupid for thinking someone like him, so hard, different, and gorgeous would take interest in someone as average and clean cut as me.

I slip out of the stall, taking a moment to run cold water against my wrists after washing my hands. My mouth is strangely dry and I can't seem to snap out of this haze.

I reach to grip the granite counter when I stumble to the side. The women beside me laugh.

"Oh, looks like Snow White got something good," the brunette says.

"Give me some of that," someone else says, giggling in a way that suggests she's more than drunk.

My eyes widen as I realize what they're saying. Those men must have slipped me something. I have to get my friends, we have to get out of here. I force myself forward, stumbling through the door.

I'm not expecting Dean and Mark to be waiting for me. They haven't kept their hands off me all night. If I wasn't so messed up, I would have known they'd follow me, and been more careful. I edge back, my hand sliding along the wall to keep my balance as they slink forward.

"Hey, sexy," Dean says. "How you feeling, baby?"

"Stay away from me," I mumble, inching back. I know I'm headed in the wrong direction and toward the men's room. I know I should scream and charge forward. But the most I can do is remain standing.

Mark clasps my wrist, pulling me to him. "It's okay, Aedry. I just want to kiss you."

I try to stomp on his foot and miss, but somehow manage to break free of his hold. Three other men exit the bathroom, laughing when they see me.

They stop laughing when Salvatore suddenly appears. "Get the *fuck* away from her," he rumbles.

His tone is enough to keep me still, but the menace in his stare and the pure fury etched into his features hitch my breath.

Mark is a big guy and he's not backing down. "Mind your own fucking business."

He lurches forward, only to whirl back when Sal shatters his nose with a sickening crunch. Blood spurts from his face, splattering the wall.

Dean lunges at him. Sal hits him so hard, he flies into one of the men piling out of the bathroom. The man shoves Dean off him, his face tightening when he sees his shirt soaked with Dean's blood. Instead of attacking Dean, the man takes his anger out on Sal.

"What the fuck, bitch?"

They're nose to nose like predators squaring off. I don't see Sal move. I only see the man spin and fall to his knees when Sal locks his wrist. "Try it," Sal rumbles when a man in a suit reaches into his waistband.

My shoulder blades slam against the wall when I see the very large gun in Sal's hand pressed against the man's skull. I don't dare move, terror steeling me in place. Unlike me, Sal remains in complete control, his composure as cool as an ice-covered lake.

"Oh, shit," someone says.

From my periphery, a swarm of bouncers crowd the end of the hall, rushing forward. "He didn't do anything," I stammer, my knees practically knocking with how hard I'm trembling. Salvatore has a *gun,* a mammoth pistol he pulled to defend me. "Those men were trying to hurt me."

The bouncers ignore me as if I never spoke. Two of them haul the man Sal had subdued to his feet, while the others seize more guns from his friends. They were all armed and ready to kill us. It's all I can do to remain upright.

The lead bouncer, the one who cursed, stomps to Sal's side. "How you wanna handle it?" he asks.

Sal whispers something I can't hear, and motions to Dean and Mark. The bouncer nods once, and he and his crew start leading the men out. Sal pulls me to him, shielding me with his body, until every man who threatened us is led away. "Come on," he says, slipping his arm around my waist. "I'm getting you out of here."

I don't argue, succumbing to his magnetic pull with ease, despite how my mind continues to spin from whatever I took and everything that just happened. Still, I'm not so confused that I don't see how those gathered react to Salvatore's presence.

Everyone gives him ample space, despite the densely packed dance floor. It's not simply because of his lethal stride or the stone-cold glare in his eyes. They're scared of him. Everyone here is terrified of the man holding me carefully against him.

What remains of my common sense implores me to run and to put as much distance between us as possible. He's dangerous. Those around us shrinking away and avoiding eye contact as we pass is proof enough. Yet, as he pulls me closer when we round the corner, I don't attempt to lurch free. If anything, my body melds further against his.

His hold is secure, yet oddly gentle, assuring me I'm safe regardless of those cowering in his presence. "I can't leave without my friends," I manage, my voice desperate to compete with the blaring music. "I think those men slipped something in our drinks."

"Your friends have been taken care of."

"What?" His hand slips lower to clutch my hip when I hesitate.

"Don't be afraid," he murmurs, his eyes meeting mine. "The bouncers are rounding them up. An Uber's been called to take them home."

"They're safe? All of them?"

"They are now. Those pricks who were with you are being searched and bounced. Based on how you're acting, they gave you some 'E' hoping for a good time."

"Oh, God." I jerk my head in the direction of the VIP section where my friends are being collected. They appear confused and very wasted, but also annoyed. I don't want them angry, or to worry about me and start to turn in their direction. "I should go with them."

Sal's grip pulls me closer, pressing me against his hip. "No. You're staying with me." His determined brown eyes drill into mine. "I'll be damned if I let you go."

Chapter Eight
Salvatore

Where the hell is Donnie? I catch her in the corner, leaning against the wall and laughing with her stupid friends. Shit, I leave her alone for fifteen seconds and she's already high. As I near her, Aedry stiffens and tries to ease away.

"Your girlfriend will get mad if she sees you touching me," she says.

"She's not my girlfriend." I hold tight. No way am I letting her go, not after she's been doped, and especially not after what those pricks tried to do to her. God *damn*. It's taking me all I have not to order Stefano to bring them out back so I can beat the unholy fuck out of them.

I spent years ripping my father off my mother. Nothing sets me off more than a man trying to hurt a defenseless woman. Ma *never* fought back unless she was protecting us. She'd shield us with her body, taking the blows for us. She even went after Pop with a pan the time he was wailing on me, just because he could. She was a good woman, sweet and kind like Aedry, which is why I saw red when those bastards tried to herd her into the men's room.

Donnie laughs when she sees us. "Just your brothers' teacher, huh, Sal?" She flicks her tongue over her teeth playfully. "Did you feel her up yet? Or are you waiting for the next parent-teacher conference to make your move?"

I don't have to look at Aedry to know her face is red. She tries to be strong, but there's an innocence to her I've never quite seen.

Donnie wraps her arms around my neck, giving me an excuse to focus on her. "What the hell did you take?" I ask her.

"Does it matter?" She doesn't wait for me to answer, lust creeping into her glazed stare. "Vincent called. He wants me back at my place."

"Fine. Let's go," I tell her. I snag her wrist, but keep Aedry against me.

I don't have to tell the bouncers shit. By the time we hit the street, my ride is already hugging the curve. "Later, Sal," Stefano says to me.

I nod, my way of letting him know I owe him. Another bouncer, one I don't know, opens the rear door for Donnie and helps her inside. I cut in front of him when he tries to do the same for Aedry, the lingering anger in my expression forcing him back.

He edges away, hands up. "Didn't mean any disrespect," he tells me.

He thinks Aedry is my woman. I don't bother telling him otherwise, mostly because that crazy instinct to protect her is searing a hole straight through my gut.

"Here, get in," I say, helping her up.

The second I pull away from the curb, Donnie lights up a joint. "Christ, Donnie," I mutter when the smoke drifts to the front.

Aedry's eyes widen. First "E," now some potent ganja by the smell of it. This little thing is going to take the first train back to Georgia, or wherever she's from, and never look back.

Donnie takes another drag, blowing it out slowly before leaning forward. "What's your name, sweetie?" she asks.

"Leave her alone, Donnie," I growl.

Aedry frowns, angling her chin like she's trying to figure me out. "It's Aedry," she answers. "Adrianna Daniels to be exact."

"I'm Donnie. Donatella to be exact," she adds, laughing. "Do you want a drag?"

Aedry shakes her head slowly. "No, I'm getting more than enough from you, thanks."

And then she giggles.

I cover my mouth, trying to hide my smirk. This woman is seriously cute.

Donnie laughs. "Is this your first time getting high, Aedry?"

Aedry nods in that slow way of hers, like she's worried her head will fall off her shoulders if she moves it too fast.

"Do you get drunk?" Donnie presses, having her fun interrogating Aedry.

"Not really," Aedry answers her. Her words are simple, but it takes her a long time to say them. "But I did tonight. It didn't take muck."

"Muck?" Donnie asks.

"Ah-hah," Aedry answers.

Donnie turns to me. "She's adorable. I can see why you like her."

"You don't know shit, Donnie."

"Yeah, I do." She takes another long drag, releasing it slowly and leaning in to whisper in my ear. "A whore will never get to you. But someone like her, hmmm, I can see why you went all alpha tonight."

I stop at a light, cupping her chin so I can get a good look at her face. Her eyes are so glassy, I'm surprised she's as coherent as she is. "What did you take?"

"Just a little blow and a few drags."

My hand slips from her face. "You have to stop doing this shit," I tell her.

She holds onto her smile, despite the misery dulling her stare. "I will if Vincent keeps wanting me."

"And if he doesn't?"

She doesn't have an answer, at least not for that. She motions to where Aedry is slinking into her seat, her eyes closing. "Take it easy on her, Salvatore. Someone that good doesn't belong around people like us."

"This the place?" I pull into an open spot along the curb.

"Hmm?" Aedry mumbles. Since dropping off Donnie with Vincent, Aedry's fallen asleep half a dozen times, impressive, seeing she only lives fifteen minutes away from Donnie's.

I kept her awake long enough to ask for her address and punch it into my GPS. I reach out, intent on clasping her shoulder and shaking her gently. Instead I lift my hand to her face and carefully stroke my knuckles against her cheek. "Hey, Sleeping Beauty. Wake up. You're home."

"I'm Snow White."

"What?"

"That girl called me Snow White," she slurs.

"Nah. Snow White's too pasty."

She laughs, causing her head to slide against the side window where she's leaning. She stretches slowly, blinking her heavy lids open.

"Thank you," she says. "I appreciate you looking out for me."

I clutch her arm. "Hold up. I'll walk you in."

"You don't have to," she mumbles.

Her lids start to close again. "Texas, you're as high as a Learjet. No way are you walking in alone."

She tilts her head. "Why did you call me that?"

"What? Texas?" She barely manages a nod, so doped up I'm sure she'll fall asleep. "Isn't that where you're from, cowgirl? I heard the accent."

She laughs again. "I'm from North Carolina, just outside of Raleigh. Huge difference. *Huge*."

"Sure it is," I tell her, smirking. I slip out of my ride. She doesn't wait for me to come around and all but slides out of the passenger seat.

Her dress rides up to her waist. I barely catch her before she falls.

"Oh, God," she says. She pulls down the skirt, but not before I get a nice view of the perfect round globe that peeks through her tiny panties. "I'm so sorry."

I'm not. *Damn*.

"Don't worry about it," I respond, lurching my attention ahead and away from her body. "Do you have your key?"

"Yes. Just give me a second." She rummages through her purse and pulls out a set of keys as she reaches the top of the concrete steps.

She opens a heavy metal door, revealing a brightly lit foyer with white tile. On the left, wide plank stairs lead up to the next level. To the right, a long hall with several doors on either side extend to the rear of the building.

"Thank you, again," she offers.

"You on this floor?" She shakes her head. "Then I'm not done with you yet," I tell her.

Her eyes widen. "I'll be okay."

"Yeah. You will. Because I'm going to make sure you make it up to your place."

She seems ready to argue, but doesn't, hooking her arm through mine. Maybe it's the drugs or maybe she knows I'm not ready to leave her.

I keep her steady, allowing her to lead me through the foyer and up the large staircase. There are four floors, but she stops on the second. Good. The only way she was getting up the next few levels in her condition was if I carried her.

Vincent is expecting me back to watch Donnie after he's done with her. I should head back, but I'm not in a rush. I'm so done with their drama, and tired of the life that I lead. It feels good to be here with someone who's not a part of any of it.

It's a dangerous game I'm playing, being connected to the mob like I am, but I need to keep moving my pieces. I'm only hoping I can stay alive long enough to see Apollo and Gianno grown and on their own.

Aedry takes a breath, turning away from the staircase and leading me back to the front of the building. "I'm really thirsty," she says as we reach her apartment.

"It's the drugs and the alcohol," I tell her, watching the careful way she slips the key into the lock and opens the door.

"I suppose." She waits by the threshold. "Do you want to come in? Maybe have something to drink with me?"

"Yeah. I do," I respond, my voice dropping an octave.

She doesn't notice the shift in my tone, offering me a small smile before stepping inside.

The first thing I notice is a framed picture of her on the wall, hugging what appears to be a yellow Labrador with fur that's almost white. Shit. Aedry can't be more than fifteen in the picture. Despite the thick glasses and crooked teeth, she looks the same—younger, yeah, but pretty like she is now, smiling wide as she hugs the animal against her.

"Was this your dog?"

"Yes," she answers quietly, placing her keys and purse on the table beneath the photo. "Moonlight."

"What?"

"That was my puppy's name, Moonlight." Her voice fades like she's remembering. "She was my best friend for fifteen years, but we had to put her down the summer before I left for college. Worst day of my life."

I don't tell her if that's her worst day, she's had a good life. Especially since it's obvious the memory still causes her pain. "Did you get another dog?" I ask.

"No. But I've wanted to for the last few years. I'd love another lab, because I adore the breed, but I wouldn't want a yellow one since I don't want to feel like I'm replacing Moonlight." She shrugs. "It's just never been the right time."

She walks ahead. Her place is small, but modern and clean. There's a kitchen to my right and a bathroom with a claw foot tub directly across from it. The tiny living room extends past the kitchen, yet nothing keeps my focus like her bedroom further back.

A large shelving unit that makes up her closet is perched against the wall just behind her headboard. Shoes neatly stacked in vertical shelves make up each side while a rack filled with clothes runs along the center. A sheer curtain separates her room from the living area. Without it, the entire apartment would basically be one large room.

I wonder briefly how many men she's invited to her bed. I stop wondering when I realize how much the thought pisses me off.

"Would you like some water?" she asks. She's bent over, searching through her refrigerator, her tiny dress riding up her smooth legs and barely keeping her ass covered. "If not, I have some wine or root beer, if you prefer."

Her voice cuts off as she turns around, my slowly lifting gaze demonstrating that my mind hadn't been on anything but her.

"Water's fine," I tell her, sensing her sudden unease.

Maybe another guy would be put off or possibly turned on by her fear. I'm not. I've seen the terror in a woman's eyes inflicted by the cruelty of a man. As much as I'm coming to grips with how bad I want her, I'd never intentionally scare her.

I edge away. "Water is good," I repeat. "Where would you like me to sit?"

Fear seemed to sober her up. She blinks back at me alert, her voice quivering slightly. "In the living room?"

She phrases her comment more like a question, like she's not sure what to do to with me. I tilt my chin and head to the couch, sitting on the opposite end to give her as much space as possible. She joins me moments later, passing me a glass filled with ice water and surprising me by lowering herself directly beside me.

I'm not sure what she's thinking, whether she's trying to be brave, polite, or something else. I don't know Aedry and, while I can usually read people and anticipate their moves, in many ways this woman's a mystery. Maybe it's 'cause I've never met anyone like her.

Aedry doesn't play or manipulate. She's not out to get everything and anything she can. She simply *is*, a genuine entity among a sea of cut-throats.

I wish I could do that, go through life like I'm actually living it, instead of just trying to survive it. But I don't have that luxury.

"Are you sure you don't want something else?" she asks, motioning to my glass with a subtle tilt of her chin.

I do, but not because I'm thirsty. My gaze hones in on her full lips. No, right now thirst is the last thing on my mind. "I'm good," I tell her, lying through my teeth.

She crosses her legs. She's close, within my reach, but not close enough to touch me. I'm wondering if it's intentional or if she's waiting for me to make a move. Like I said, she's hard to read.

Her hand passes along her skirt to cup her knee. She's not trying to flirt, at least that's not how I take it. But the motion draws my attention to her bare legs. She notices, her focus returning to her glass as she takes large but careful sips.

I wait for her to empty her glass before asking her something that's been bugging me all night. "Can I ask you something?" She dabs the corner of her mouth with her fingertips and nods. "What were you expecting tonight, coming into Silk to see me? As you saw, it's not a place for someone like you."

"No. It's not." Those bright blue eyes scan my face as she considers her words. "I thought . . ." She glances down. "I thought you'd invited me to spend time with you."

"Like a date?" Her blush answers me enough. *Shit*.

"Apollo and Gianno set you up," I tell her when she says nothing more.

"I figured as much." She rolls the glass between her hands. "I'll admit, I'm disappointed in them. I thought we were connecting, and that they liked me."

"They do."

She lifts her chin. "Then why would they do that to me? I feel like such a fool."

"You're not a fool," I say, my steeling features showing her I mean what I say. "And my brothers never meant to embarrass you. They don't know what goes on in Silk. All they know is what they've heard: that it's hot, exclusive, and that people line up every night to get in. If they knew it like I do, they would never have sent you there."

She leans in. "And how do you know it as well as you do?"

"I take Donnie there all the time."

"Why?"

"It's one of her favorite clubs. You can see why. She likes the atmosphere, the exclusiveness of it all, and the drugs that are easily offered."

"But she's not your girlfriend."

"No," I answer.

She gives what I say some thought. "The way she touches you, it seems like she is or at least wants to be."

"She's like that with people she trusts and we've known each other a long time. But I've never fucked her."

Her eyes round. "Wow. You don't mince words do you?"

I shake my head slowly. "No."

Her hands clutch the glass. "You're not in public relations, are you?"

I was waiting for her to ask that. "I work security for Donnie's lover. With what she does, and the places she frequents, it's my job to keep her safe."

Her brows knit. "You're a . . . bodyguard?"

"No. I'm in public relations," I answer, even though we now know it's a lie. Aedry's been good to my family, but she's still an employee at my brothers' school. By law, she's obligated to report any concerns about their welfare.

"Why can't you just say you work security detail?" she asks. "It's an honest living."

"Public relations sounds more impressive. When people hear security detail, they think mall cop. A twenty-one-year-old mall cop didn't stand a chance at gaining custody of two kids in grade school."

I'm not sure she's buying what I'm telling her, but when she speaks, she latches on to my reasons for doing what I did in a way that cements me in place. "I can't imagine how stressful your life must have been back then, losing your mother and fighting to hang on to the family you had left. It must have been a nightmare."

Yeah. It was.

My jaw seals tight. The last thing I want to do is remember that time or even talk about it. I'd toss and turn all night, wondering if my brothers were safe, if anyone was messing with them in that group home they were dumped in, and whether my efforts were in vain.

The judge, he didn't like me and neither did the social worker assigned to the case.

"Too young to provide appropriate care," she'd told the judge.

"Nothing more than a thug," she'd whispered to the other caseworker.

If it weren't for Vin stepping in, dropping the bills to support me, and replacing my shit-bag attorney with one of his, I would have lost my brothers to the system.

You might say I owe Vin everything.

"I'm sure everything you did was for them," Aedry says, bringing me back from that dark time.

Her smile is soft, sympathetic without showing pity. "What?" I ask, even though I heard her.

"I'm trying to tell you that I know that you love them, and that everything you did was to help them."

Her smile loses its luster in the quiet that follows. "What are you thinking?" I ask her when her attention drifts toward her bedroom.

"That they're great kids with good hearts," she answers quietly. "Just like their brother."

She thinks I'm good man. But she's wrong.

"But I'll be honest," she continues. "I'm confused by their actions tonight, and why they would pick me of all people to target for prank."

I mull over what to say to maybe spare her or to make her feel better. In the end, instead of more lies, the truth comes out, even though maybe it shouldn't. "Near as I can figure, you remind them of our mother."

"I don't know what you mean by that," she says. "Are you saying I resemble her?"

"Not even a little bit," I admit.

"Then where are you going with this?"

"She was everything to us," I say without thinking how much I'm telling her. "You're nurturing like her, affectionate like she used to be. I think they miss it and maybe need it." I set my glass down on the coffee table and look up at her. "You might have noticed I'm not the warm and cuddly type."

She laughs, placing her glass beside mine. "I might have noticed."

"I'm pissed at what they did," I confess. "Don't get me wrong. But I know they meant well."

"How?" she asks, grimacing. "It was so embarrassing. I can't imagine what they'd hoped to accomplish."

"They were trying to get us together."

It's like I'm watching a movie at home and I hit pause. For a long few seconds, Aedry doesn't move.

But I do.

I lose the space between us, my hand cupping her face as her full lips part. "They think I'm attracted to you," I murmur, trailing my thumb over her cheek. "And they're right."

I lower my head, passing my lips gently along hers until she invites my tongue to penetrate her deeply. I'm not sure how she'll respond. I half-expect her to break away from me.

But she doesn't, flicking her tongue over mine as I strengthen our kiss and my arm hooks her waist.

The kiss is slow, not as fast as I want, or as hard as I'm used to. But then something switches, turning us more aggressive. Her nails trace over my chest to dig into my shoulders, tightening our embrace and inviting me to curl around her.

I don't want to pull away. I don't want to stop. What I want is to peel away her dress and spread her legs wide.

The only thing that stops me is knowing she's not sober, despite how she's acting. Ecstasy can do a real number on your head. I won't take her now, not like this.

I break the kiss, even though I'm as hard as a metal railing. "I have to go."

Surprise sweeps along her delicate features, but when she bites down on her bottom lip, I come close to tossing my sense of right and wrong aside and carrying her to bed.

"Are you sure?" she asks, barely above a whisper.

No. I'm not. But that's not what I tell her. "I have to get back to Donnie."

Donnie's is the last place I want to be, especially with Vin there. I don't need their dysfunctional shit messing with my head. I'd rather be here, with Aedry.

I almost tell her that, but I shut my trap and force myself to my feet.

Images of taking her behind that sheer white curtain pound against my skull like a wild storm as I walk toward the door. She follows me, tugging down her skirt as she reaches my side. Christ, does she know what she's doing to me and how bad I want to rip that thing off her?

As small as her place is, it seems to take forever to reach the door. I won't lie, I change my mind about leaving more than once.

I grasp the knob, but then let it go, speaking before I think things through. "Do you want to have dinner with me tomorrow night?"

"Dinner?" She smiles. "I'd love to."

I frown when her grin fades, and she seems to want to say more. "What's wrong?" I ask.

She watches my hand when it drifts to play with her dark hair. "I just wanted to thank you, for being such a gentleman."

My hand stills. "I'm no gentleman," I growl, pegging her with look that halts her in place. "Have dinner with me and you'll find out what kind of man I really am."

Chapter Nine
Aedry

Salvatore's comment is meant as a warning and that's how I take it. He's not like the beta men I've always dated. Oh, no. He's *very* alpha, his mere presence commanding respect, or else.

I'm not blind or naïve. The way he held the gun with ease demonstrated his readiness to pull the trigger. He's a man used to violence and seizing control. It makes sense, given his family history and the rough streets he grew up in, but I'll confess, it was hard seeing that side of him.

I don't want to believe that he'd tread on the wrong side of the law, so instead of focusing on what he might be capable of, I remind myself that almost everyone in the south, including my immediate family, owns a gun. "You have to be ready to protect yourself and those you love," my granddad told me every time I'd find him cleaning his rifle.

He's right and Salvatore did use his gun to protect me.

Despite witnessing his aggression, I don't cancel our dinner plans.

I pause in the middle of sweeping my lashes with mascara. There's something about him that invites me closer, luring me into his dark embrace and stirring my primal need like a cyclone.

A knock on my door has me hurrying to finish. *Oh, no. He's early.*

The second knock has me racing. "Aedry?"

My steps slow as I reach the door, the familiar voice of my former roommate and loving bestie making me grin. I open the door. "Hey, Autumn."

She yanks me against her, hugging me against her tall, slender frame. "Hey, stranger," she says. "One of your slutty friends was nice enough to let me in." She glances back to where Christy is standing outside her apartment, scowling and clutching her bag of groceries under her arm.

Autumn whips her head back, her eyes wide. "Do you think she heard me?" she whispers frantically.

Given how hard Christy slams the door, I'm certain she did. I try not to let it bother me. When I checked on her and the rest of the girls earlier, they were pissed their good time ended, and annoyed they were escorted out. Unlike me, they'd taken the ecstasy willingly and it hadn't been their first time.

I haul Autumn inside. I love her dearly, but smooth and unassuming are the last two words I'd use to describe her. She steps back enough so I can close the door. "You look nice. Are you going out?"

"I am," I say beaming. "If you can believe it, I'm going to dinner with a hot guy I have no business dating."

"You're kidding?" She shoves her quirky green glasses back on the bridge of her nose. Despite the silly frames and the pile of messy red hair held on top of her head by a well-placed number two pencil, she looks beautiful, even though she wouldn't believe anyone who told her. "Who is this stud and how did you meet him?"

I scrunch my nose. "His name is Salvatore. He's the guardian of two students I council."

"Whoa, Nellie."

"I know."

"*Aedry*."

"I know!"

She tilts her chin. "I'm guessing our Dr. Who marathon is off for tonight."

"Oh, God. I'm so sorry. I forgot all about it."

She holds onto her grin, but I don't miss the disappointment in her features. Like me, Autumn spends too much time working and most of her free time alone. In a way, she's worse off, hindered by her awkwardness and her disastrous track record with men. Two of her serious boyfriends became priests, choosing God over her. The other two chose men. Autumn blames her performance in bed for permanently turning them off to women. I can't really blame her. It's safe to say her experiences haven't exactly been confidence boosters.

"Aedry, don't look so sad. It's okay. If I had to choose between a make-believe man on TV and a real one, I'd choose the real one for sure."

"I'm really sorry."

"Don't be," she says, gripping my shoulders. "One of us has to get a view of something other than vagina."

I laugh. As a midwife dedicated to serving the public sector, she always seems to have an array of genital jokes. I suppose it helps her cope with all the difficult aspects of serving those from underprivileged environments. She loosens the buttons to her white coat. Poor thing must have spent her day at the homeless shelter, and here I am ditching her.

I take her hand in mine. "Would you like to come with us?" I offer.

"On the really hot date with the really hot guy, so I can bask in all the hotness? Hmm, I think I'm better off with Dr. Who, a bowl of popcorn, and the box of wine taking up space in my fridge. But don't worry, I also have Pop Tarts."

I wish she was joking, but back in college, Autumn and I frequently drowned our lonely Saturday nights with the cherry-flavored ones.

"I really am sorry," I tell her.

"It's okay, Aedry. But I miss you. Call me soon, okay? Oh, and take a picture for me."

"Take a picture of what?"

"The hot guy."

I gasp. "What? I can't do that!"

"Why not? If he's that good-looking, you need to prove it. Living vicariously through you is almost as good as placing fourth in the Hermione Granger lookalike contest at Harry Potter World last year." She makes a face. "Granted there were five of us and third place went to a dude, but it's still cool, anyway."

"Of course, it is," I tell her.

"So, you'll do it?"

"Do what?"

"Take a picture of your yummy date?" she clarifies.

"No!"

"Why? If you're dumping me and the Doctor, I want proof, damn it!"

I'm about to tell her she's out of her mind when a hard knock rattles my door. My face warms and we both still. "I think that's your proof at the door," I whisper.

"Do you want me to leave through the window?" she offers.

"And die? No."

"He better be hot," she says, not so quietly, as I walk to the door.

I bat my hand to silence her. My navy sleeveless dress is casual, yet fits me in a way that boosts what remains of my confidence. I'm a nervous wreck, and more than a little scared.

"Who is it?" I ask, just to be certain.

"Salvatore," he rumbles.

I open the door, smiling. A black leather jacket hangs over his black silk shirt and dark slacks cover his muscular legs.

I try to be subtle and not drool, or gawk, or straddle. I think I'm doing well until his stare drags the length of my form, heating my body to nuclear meltdown digits.

"Hey," he says, leaning forward. I'm sure he's going to kiss me until his attention cuts behind me.

"Oh, I'm sorry, I'm being rude. This is my best friend, Autumn. We were roommates in undergrad together."

Autumn remains standing where I left her, barely moving and not really breathing. Unlike me, she's not going for subtle. Not even a little bit. In fact, if "subtle" was a college major, she'd be kicked out of the program and asked never to return.

Her jaw unhinges to the floor as Salvatore follows me in.

A blush creeps up my neck. "Autumn, I'd like to introduce you to Salvatore."

"Good to meet you," he says. Based on her response, I don't think he means it.

"Pleasure," she spits out, smacking my upper arm awkwardly. "Well, have fun."

She bolts toward the door, whipping around to point frantically at Sal's back. *Holy shit*, she mouths.

Something in my expression causes him to glance over his shoulder, in time for poor Autumn to crash into the raised breakfast bar separating the kitchen from the living room.

I lurch forward. "I'm okay," she says, clutching her side as she limps out the door.

Sal meets me with a frown when the door slams shut behind her. "What the fuck's wrong with her?"

"She's just nervous," I say. *You see, she's not used to seeing hot guys She stares at vaginas all day.* "She's actually a well-respected midwife."

"You serious?"

"Um. Yes." I reach for my coat, draped over the armchair of the couch. "Shall we?"

"Here. Let me." He takes the coat from my grasp and helps me into it. My heart flutters. Despite what he claims and what I've experienced, I'm convinced he's a true and honest gentleman.

It doesn't take long to discover how wrong I really am.

Sal takes us to an elegant restaurant in the city, originally founded in Little Italy. "This is lovely," I say as we step inside.

"The atmosphere is great, but the food is even better," he murmurs against my ear, stroking my back gently.

The maitre d' straightens when he notices us. Sal's caress remains gentle against my spine, but his expression isn't as endearing. It's that one he most frequently demonstrates, a quiet lethality few could pull off.

"Good evening, Mr. Romero," the maître d tells him as he draws closer.

Sal holds out his hand. "Just a table for two tonight, Suvio."

The man releases a breath, appearing relieved. I'm not sure what's happening, but I know this isn't the right time to ask.

"This way, please," he says. He leads us to a quiet booth at the rear of the dimly lit restaurant. It's large with dark leather seats, its mere size enough to swallow us whole.

I smile at him and at the other man who appears with two leather-bound menus. Neither seem to notice me, their full focus on Sal.

"Do you want wine?" Sal asks me.

I smile. "I thought you said you didn't drink."

He smirks. "I said I *rarely* drink. But I always take my pasta with a glass of red." He looks to the waiter, who materialized from nowhere. "A blend of your best."

Sal tosses his menu to the side and slides across the leather booth, dissolving the small distance between us. His arm seeks my waist. I quiver at his touch. "Are you cold?" he asks.

"No. Just a little nervous," I admit.

The corners of his mouth lift. "You have nothing to worry about. Not with me next to you."

"I know," I answer.

I want to keep looking at him and that smile he offers. But shyness has me averting my gaze. I catch sight of the maître d as he hurries to speak to the staff, appearing anxious. "Is he all right?" I ask, when he dabs his forehead with a handkerchief.

"Business isn't what it used to be here. The restaurant might be shutting down," he tells me.

I scan the room, and with the exception of another booth similar to ours, the place is packed and there are several people waiting at the entrance. "It looks like a popular place," I say.

"It's because it's a weekend." He takes a sip of his water. "You need more than two good nights to keep a restaurant this size running in New York."

"I suppose," I reply, although I admit I remain very much confused. As I skim through the menu, the array of dishes along with the exorbitant prices overwhelm me. I place it aside and motion to his abandoned menu. "Are you going to look through the selections?"

"Don't need to." His brown eyes spark with heat. "I already know what I want."

My eyes open wide. Is this really happening? His knuckles drift over my side in a slow and lazy caress, sending another course of shudders along my spine. Oh my God . . .

"Do you know what you want?" he asks.

"No," I reply, wishing I didn't sound so breathless. "Will you help me decide?"

His free hand reaches for my hair, allowing the pieces to glide through his fingers. "What do you like?"

"Everything," I whisper, unable to rip my stare from his. "You pick," I add, hoping we're still talking about food.

"All right, then," he murmurs.

The waiter returns with a bottle of red wine. He shows it to Salvatore, who nods in approval. I expect him to give me space, now that we're not alone. Yet he keeps his hold on me and resumes his gentle strokes to my hair. He's sweet, endearing, and not afraid to demonstrate affection, despite who's near.

He passes me the glass of wine the waiter places in front of me, clinking my glass with his as he lifts it. "*Salud*," he says.

"*Salud*," I repeat, taking a careful sip. A bold blend of grapes reaches my tongue, its richness enveloping every taste bud. "Mmm. Good choice," I say.

I'm hoping I don't sound as unsophisticated as I feel, especially with how suave he is.

"Tell me something about yourself," he says.

I grin. "What would you like to know?"

"I don't know. Anything. Tell me what it was like growing up in Kansas."

I laugh, almost spilling my wine. "You mean North Carolina?"

"Same thing," he says, smirking.

I laugh again. "To begin with, I grew up on a farm."

He frowns. "People still do that shit?"

"Believe it or not, yes. My parents had a working farm of almost six-hundred acres passed down to them by my grandparents, and my great-grandparents before them. We didn't have a lot money growing up, but with the population in the area growing like it is, they sold the land to a lucrative builder. In doing so, they were able to put me through school and set aside a nice retirement for themselves."

"They got rid of the farm," he acknowledges.

"The original farm, yes. But they're farmers at heart, so they bought another twenty acres outside of town and are now raising dairy cows."

I laugh when he regards me like I'm crazy. "That sounds like a messed-up way to retire." He pauses as the waiter approaches.

"Are you ready to order, *signore*?"

He lifts his brows at me. "You trust me, right?" At my nod he places our order. "We'll start with the sautéed calamari. The beef and gorgonzola pasta for me and the *quattro formaggi* for the lady. Also, the pesto olive cheese bread with our meal."

"*Si, signore.*"

"Sounds perfect," I say, smiling back at him.

And it was.

Hours later, Sal pulls into my neighborhood. I'm tired, well fed, and happy, but I also can't help feeling confused. The dinner was among the best I ever had and the service exceptional. The staff fell all over themselves to please not only us, but everyone present. I don't understand why their business is failing.

What I also found odd was how the maître d seemed to fear displeasing Salvatore, and how skittish he appeared. Sal was quiet and polite and never once did he criticize or complain. He even left an exorbitant amount of cash for a tip.

I dismiss it as the stress of a failing business, and while I feel terrible on their behalf, Salvatore's kindness and continued affections lure me away from our meal and into the present.

He rolls to a stop in front of my building and places his SUV in park. "Thank you for such a wonderful evening. I had a really nice time."

"You're welcome," he murmurs, lifting my hand and sweeping a kiss over my knuckles.

I'm not sure who moves first. Maybe I do, succumbing to the desire to feel closer to him and surrender to the privacy behind his tinted windows. His seatbelt buckle smacks against the arm rest when he hits the release seconds before mine and moments before his arms encircle my waist, hauling me to him.

Like the night before, his lips stamp against mine. I don't hesitate to open my mouth, immediately inviting his tongue to explore and tease. With each pass of his hand along my back our kiss deepens, causing me to involuntarily moan. Sal leaves my mouth, trailing his teeth down the curve of my neck, his gentle bites causing my neck to arch and my eyelids to flutter.

I don't expect his aggression, but that's exactly what I receive. My breath increases as he smooths his palm across my breasts, popping open the buttons of my dress faster than I can process what's happening.

As his hand kneads and massages, my mind insists that I should stop him and tell him he's moving faster than I'm used to. But when he yanks my bra up and tugs at my nipple, all I can do is gasp.

No man's touch has ever felt so sweet.

I part my lips to speak, but my words fail to form. My focus is solely on him and his hard body pressing into mine. The scent of his cologne, and the way his mouth and hands roam, cause lust to scorch a path through my veins. I grunt, falling back against the window when his head dips down and he starts to suck.

My shoulder blades smack the rim of the door. But it's when he shoves his hand beneath my skirt, and his fingers circle over the crotch of my panties that my moans dissolve into whimpers.

"*Shit*," he groans, my heat building along his hands.

"Salvatore," I stammer. I need to say something, but I'm so turned on I don't want him to stop.

With motions of a skilled lover, his circles increase. I'm no longer breathing, I'm panting, my shoulders trembling as an unfamiliar ache overtakes me. It hurts a little, but the pleasure it stirs is so worth the bite, ensnaring me with delicious lust.

My orgasm (*that's* what *this is*!) builds, crashing hard enough to make me jolt. Before I can recover, he slips in a finger, followed by one more. My head lolls back. I'm not sure what to do, but my body does, responding and surrendering to his strokes.

My hips swivel against his touch, the turns as forceful as my cries.

He lifts his head, his irises clouded with need. "You're so wet, so *tight*," he whispers, delving deeper, his palm smacking against my folds. "How long has it been?"

His words are slow, lascivious murmurs against my ear, sending me into a dark sensual world I've never experienced. I can't think, my head spinning with the start of another orgasm. I manage to bite out the truth. "I haven't . . . I'm a virgin."

He freezes, grinding everything I'm feeling to a startling halt. Abruptly he pulls away, the warmth he'd given me withdrawing in one painful strike.

I wish I was exaggerating and that this isn't really his response. Yet it is. What's worse is he doesn't just lift off me, he slumps into the driver's seat, putting as much space as he can between us.

My breath releases in ragged spurts, mimicking the rise and fall of his chest. But while I'm looking directly at him, he keeps his focus ahead.

His hands grip the steering wheel tight. Only inches separate us, but never have I felt so alone, a sudden chill claiming my soul like a winter storm and isolating me within its shadows.

My body shudders as I struggle to sit back in my seat, my legs rubbery and useless. With trembling hands, I pull down my skirt and button the front of my dress. My buttons are off-center. I don't care. I'm too distracted by the dwindling bulge in Sal's pants and stunned stupid by his reaction.

He isn't speaking. He won't even look at me.

I wait for our breath to slow, trying to give him time to say something. When it's clear that he won't, I pass a hand through my disheveled hair and work up my courage. "What's wrong?"

He doesn't answer.

I lick my lips and try again, hating how hard my voice is trembling. "Please tell me what's wrong."

The expression he pegs me with as he slowly turns is laced with what I can only interpret as betrayal. "I don't fuck virgins," he grinds out.

My breath lodges in my throat, his tone and words like stabs to my already deflated confidence. Humiliation fills me, stinging my eyes with tears, until anger replaces my shame with brutal vengeance.

"I wasn't asking you to," I fire back. This time, my voice doesn't shake and it's his turn to stare back stunned.

Everything in his deepening scowl tells me he's ready to talk. I don't stick around to hear what he has to say. I snag my purse from the floor and fling the passenger door open.

"Aedry—*wait*," he says, reaching for me.

I smack his hand away. "Don't touch me!"

I lurch out of his SUV, hurling the door behind me.

"Son of *bitch*—Aedry! God damn it, wait!"

I don't wait, moving fast when I hear the driver's side door swing open. His footsteps echo a mere breadth away as I unlock the main door to my building and slip inside, slamming the reinforced door hard in his face.

Despite the layers of metal, Salvatore's deep voice booms through it, calling my name. I don't care. Not about him, or us.

I only care about the tears he causes and how fast they're dripping from my eyes.

Chapter Ten
Salvatore

I've screwed up before. I'll be the first to admit it. But this shit with Aedry is messing with my head two ways from Tuesday. A virgin. Of all things she can be, why does she have to be that?

With any other woman, I'd shrug the whole thing off. But this woman, God *damn*, I can't stop thinking about her no matter how hard I try.

Four women. That's how many have offered to fuck me since Aedry slammed her door in my face. Unlike with Aedry, I didn't bother chasing after them when I told them to walk and they stormed away from me pissed.

Before Aedry, I would have taken each up on her offer. Hard and more than once. My hips would have pounded, their mouths would have sucked, and they would have begged me to stay. That's how it's always been and what's always been enough for me.

They should have been exactly what I needed to forget everything that happened Saturday. But they weren't. None of them held my attention.

Every thought I have wanders back to Aedry—her laugh, her smile, and that body.

Shit. When the hell did I become such a pussy? It's like every time I close my eyes—and sometimes even when I don't—that night in my ride plays over again. She liked what I was doing to her. I could tell by the way she arched her neck, letting me slide my tongue along her skin while my hands played with her nipples and slipped beneath her dress.

She could have told me to stop. I would have. So why the hell didn't she? Why did she seem so willing to let me fuck her there on that damn street?

"Sal? You there?"

I'm not even listening to Lucca. "Bad connection. Say it again," I lie.

"The boss wants you with him for a sit down. Thursday night at eight," he says, but I can tell he knows I haven't been paying attention.

A sit down. Aw, hell. "Where?"

"Tomasso's."

No wonder the maître d was so nervous when I took Aedry there. He must have known a meeting at his place was imminent. I played it off like his business was in trouble, which was a total lie. But then, it's not the first time I've lied to this woman.

"You going?" Lucca asks.

What choice do I have? "I'll be there. You?"

"Yeah, I'll be there."

The edge in his voice tells me Lucca's already set to kill. That doesn't mean I'm stupid enough to think I won't have to. Each meeting Vin agrees to, and each step his father takes toward death, put him at risk. I've managed to dig myself into this shit so deep, it won't be long before I fire a round into some bastard's skull.

Or take one myself.

"Who's covering Donnie?" I ask.

"He didn't say anything about Donnie. Guess she's on her own."

He disconnects. I wait for the three consecutive beats that signal the line is clear before swearing. If Vincent is calling me in for a sit down, he's either scared of who he's meeting, what's coming, or setting me up to guard his back full time.

If I watch Vin, no way in fuck can I end up not filling some asshole full of lead. I'd have to kill. I'd have to torture. I'd have to finish becoming one of them.

I do a mental check of the enemies Vin's made and curse again. Yet my next few swears are all about Donnie. I walked in on Vin getting head the other night in his office. The girl going down on him on the couch couldn't have been more than twenty. But he liked what she was doing to him and she didn't care that I was there. He called me for some stupid shit that could have waited. I didn't need to see what I saw. Except I think he wanted me to. Maybe even needed me to. He's not a big guy. Someone like him needs to feel important any way he can.

My fingers flick the button to crack open the window, needing to get some air despite how frigid the fall day has become. This wasn't the first time I'd seen this girl with Vin—her name's Tina, I think. But every time I see her around, she has another piece of jewelry, newer clothes, and more attitude. Donnie's on her way out and there's nothing she or I can do about it.

Just like there's nothing I can do about getting the hell out of Vin's hold. I sold my soul to him to save what remained of my family. And now he wants some serious payback.

I roll to a stop a few cars down from Aedry's little white Volkswagen. I'm fifteen minutes early until her time with my brothers end. But that's how I planned it. For the last two weeks she's either stayed just inside the confines of the school, or sent my brothers out on their own. Being who they are, they knew right away something had happened.

The first day I had to deal with them was the previous Monday, less than twenty-four hours after our date. Gianno had glanced back at the closing door, and so had Apollo. Gianno met me with a frown. "What's going on?"

"Nothing." I rolled up the window when it was clear she wasn't coming out, and didn't want to see me.

Apollo was more nervous, scared even. "Sal, what did you do to Miss Aedry?"

"I said, '*nothing*'," I bit out.

I shot out of the school lot, feeling them watching me. I didn't bother with an explanation. I didn't think I owed them one. But when Gianno started swearing, and Apollo wouldn't say shit, I assured them I hadn't hurt her. Even though I guess I did. "I'm not the right man for her."

"What the hell is that supposed to mean?" Gianno snapped.

"It means we didn't get along and we didn't have a good night."

That was only partly true. The night was good up until I took her home. I enjoyed learning about where she came from and getting to know her. I also liked how she felt against my body and how hot she made me when she came. But I didn't tell them that.

"Stay out of my business and keep your head in school where it belongs," I added when they wouldn't stop drilling me.

My brothers weren't happy. They didn't like what I had to say, but eventually backed off.

I figured after a few days, a week tops, I'd catch a glimpse of her and eventually she'd start waving again. Now here we are, two weeks later and she still won't return my calls.

I hop out of my car and slam the door shut. Well, this shit ends today.

"Hey," someone calls to me. "That's the teacher's lot."

"So?" I mutter without another glance back. The school is locked up tight, but I catch a break when a kid walks out. He moves back when he sees me, *way* back like he should. I jog up the steps to the next level. Her office is on the second floor, that much I know, so I follow the blue signs glued to the wall directing me to the guidance offices.

I'm a few steps from reaching the end of the hall when I catch sight of Gianno in what must be Aedry's office. His long body is sprawled across a couch and he's reading something he actually seems to be paying attention to. Last time I saw him reading this intently, he'd slipped a porn mag between the pages of a history text and was reading tips on how to go down on a girl. I ripped that shit in half. The last thing he needs at his age is an STI.

I glance through the window lined with wire. Her office is small, nothing more than a box with a glass front. Even still, it's clean like her apartment, with bits of her personality poking through, a painting here, a vase there, and a flowery window treatment running above the industrial-looking blinds.

Aedry leans toward Apollo where they're sitting at a desk, pointing to whatever he's scribbling and speaking quietly. She nods, her smile widening the more he writes. When he pauses and shows her his work, her entire face lights up like the sun.

"You got it!" she says, giving his hand a squeeze.

I can't see Apollo or make out everything he says, but based on his excitement, I know he's smiling. Gianno glances up, shaking his head as he takes them in. His profile is only slightly visible, but I see enough of his grin to know he's happy, too.

I don't watch them long. Aedry straightens when she sees me, her smile dissolving.

"What's wrong?" Apollo asks. He and Gianno turn around at the same time, neither thrilled to see me.

Nice.

I rap on the door out of courtesy and open it slowly. "Hey," I say.

Aedry is the first to avert her gaze, flipping through Apollo's notebook. "Don't worry. You're going to do well on your test," she tells him like I'm not even there. "Just take your time and don't rush."

"Got a minute?" I ask, refusing to be ignored.

She stiffens, but it's Gianno who answers. "We still have another ten with Miss Aedry."

"This won't take long," I say.

Aedry meets me square in the eye. "If you want to discuss your brothers' progress, you need to make an appointment. Otherwise, I'm not available."

"Looks to me like you are." I lean against the doorframe. "Like Gianno said, you have time."

Maybe it's me, but I'm pretty sure she's about two seconds from flinging her hole- punch at me. My stare fixes on each of my brothers, long enough so they know I mean business. "Wait outside."

Neither one of them moves and it pisses me off. Whose damn side are they on, anyway? After what seems like too long, and right when I'm ready to snatch them by their throats, Gianno lowers his feet to the floor and reaches for his backpack.

Apollo stays where he is. "Get going," I tell him.

He stands, his gaze locking on mine. "No," he says without flinching.

I push off the door frame and prowl forward. "I'm not asking," I growl.

This time he does flinch, as he should. Aedry tries to step in front of him to shield him from me, but Gianno beats her to it. We face off, his nose just below mine. Hell, when did this little bastard get so tall? Doesn't matter. I can still beat his ass, and he knows it.

Unlike Apollo though, Gianno isn't looking for trouble. "Let's go, Apollo," he says.

No one moves, pissing me off more than I already am. Apollo opens his mouth, but Aedry cuts him off. "It's okay," she tells him, assuring him in that soft voice of hers.

He swallows a swear, but he bends to shove his crap into his backpack. He doesn't look at me when he storms out, but my eyes stay trained on him. I don't expect Gianno to shove his face into mine. But that's exactly what he does. "Don't fuck this up," he says.

I tighten my jaw, not happy with how my brothers are pushing me today. "I'm serious, Sal," Gianno says. "Don't be an asshole."

I don't like the way he's talking to me and if we were at home, I'd smack him upside the head. He knows I'm plenty mad and that this shit going down between us won't be over when he walks out. Except he doesn't care, keeping his attention on me when he calls to Aedry. "Bye, Miss Aedry," he tells her.

"Bye, sweetie," she responds.

Sweetie? *Da hell?*

I wait for him to shut the door behind him before turning back to Aedry. She's sitting in her chair with her legs crossed, the skirt of her denim dress brushing against her shins.

"Hey," I say like a dumbass.

She raises her brows. "Let's get one thing straight. We're going to talk about your brothers and nothing more. Am I clear?"

Most women who meet me want to shove me into bed. Aedry's glare suggests she'd like to shove me through a window, without opening it first. I didn't come here to argue so I take a seat at the sofa, putting some distance between us.

"How are they doing?" I ask.

The strain in her shoulders eases enough for me to notice, but not much more. She swivels in her seat and opens her file. "Gianno has shown tremendous improvement. His biggest challenges remain in history. I've started counseling him—"

"Why? He's fine."

She lifts her chin. "He asked to meet with me. It's nothing formal, not like it is with Apollo. Just questions here and there, and brief talks during his tutoring."

"Talks about what?"

"His past and some of the stress he's going through."

"Stress?" She nods. "All he has to do is go to school. How much stress can he have?"

She taps her finger against the desk. I don't ever remember her being this, I don't know, *impatient* with me. But as I keep looking at her, "impatient" isn't quite the right word. Fit to be tied is more like it. Except, when she talks, her voice stays even and relaxed. "I think you're forgetting what it's like to be sixteen. There's a lot of pressure to act a certain way, be accepted, and feel like you have a place in the world. It helps that Gianno is a natural leader—"

"He gets it from me."

I mean it as a joke to loosen her up. Aedry doesn't take it that way and is irate that I cut her off. "Do you want to discuss your brothers, or would you prefer to use this time to inflate your already immense ego and take control, like always?"

Damn. I start to tell her that I don't have a big ego—and that I don't always have to be in control, but that's a lie and we both know it. A certain satisfaction sparks her eyes. It should piss me off, and it would with anyone else. But it's not like that with her. Like I said, this woman is . . . yeah, I'm in deep shit.

I try to keep my face hard, but I don't pull it off in time. Another spark lights her irises when she catches my smirk. I lean back. "If Gianno's a leader, like I've taught him to be, he should be better off, right?

"He should be. And in a lot of ways he is. But he's also very alpha," she says, looking right at me. "Which gets him into trouble."

"How?" I frown. "You mean the fights?"

"He doesn't back down when he feels he's been disrespected."

"And he shouldn't."

"Sometimes he needs to." She holds her hand up when I start to interrupt. "Disrespect at this age is different than it is in adulthood. The things we would let go could lead to an altercation between teens. Yesterday, in the cafeteria, another boy subbed out his chair for one Gianno was going to sit in. There was nothing wrong with the chair and Gianno hadn't yet sat. But it set Gianno off. He had it in his head that the chair already belonged to him. I was on lunch duty and I managed to deescalate the situation. But if I hadn't, those boys would have gone to blows over an old plastic chair."

"Okay. I get it. I'll talk to him." I wait a breath. "Does he talk about the past—about what happened between our parents?"

"I let him talk about anything that upsets him."

"But you won't tell me what."

She doesn't blink, even though the sharpness to my tone suggests she needs to spill the details. "I won't betray Gianno's trust, or Apollo's," she says. "We agreed that I could discuss general concerns if you asked, but never anything specific unless their safety or someone else's was at risk."

I want to argue, but I can't. I know trust doesn't come easy for my brothers. Hell, for any of us. If they're talking to Aedry, it's because they need to, and I won't take that away from them.

"What about Apollo?"

She shifts through the files on her desk. "He's improving in all his classes, but his progress is slower. As his confidence in his academics continues to blossom, I'm certain that will change."

"But how is he doing in counseling? Is he talking to you, opening up?"

"He is," she answers, carefully.

I lean back, watching her brow crease with concern. "Something wrong?"

This time when she faces me there's no attitude, her perfect blue eyes warm enough to melt even a guy as cold as me. "He's deeply affected by his past and struggles more with his decisions."

"He seems fine to me," I say, more because I want to believe it's true.

"He's not," she adds, quietly. "Apollo carries a tremendous amount of guilt, and while Gianno is traumatized by what he saw the night of your parents' death, his guilt is slightly alleviated because, like you, he tried to save your mother."

Anger clenches my gut, but it's not directed at Aedry or my brothers. It's all due to that shit for brains man I used to call my father. "They've talked about me?"

She considers her words, her posture relaxing so maybe I will, too. "They talk about everyone who's impacted them."

I tilt my chin and try to relax my clenching fists as I remember how Gianno took over our mother's protection when I left. It wasn't fair of me to leave them behind—to put all that hell and responsibility on them. But I had to make something of myself for her and for them.

"What are you thinking?" Aedry asks, keeping her tone easy.

"That I want them to be okay," I admit. "Despite what they've been through."

"I have faith they will be."

"Yeah?"

"Yes." A small smile arcs her full lips as she glances at the wall clock perched above my head. "Time's up."

I furrow my brows when I realize what happened. "Did you just pull that counseling shit on me?" She purses her lips as if trying not to laugh. "Son of bitch," I groan, causing her to lose it.

I didn't realize how much I missed that pretty face until then, but there it is. Her humor vanishes the longer I take her in, but that infamous blush returns. She swivels in her seat, giving me her back.

"Have a good weekend," she says, busying herself at her desk.

She's trying to dismiss me, but I came here for a reason and I'm not ready to leave. "I'm sorry for how I treated you," I say, causing her to still. "I didn't mean it."

She doesn't say anything for a long while. I'm working through what else to say when she finally speaks. "You didn't mean what? To treat me like a monstrous douche or all those asinine things you said?"

Well, shit. This went downhill fast. "I meant what I said about not fucking virgins. That doesn't mean I meant any disrespect." She's not saying anything. I force out more. "The last thing I'd ever do is intentionally hurt a woman." Dead silence. "There's nothing wrong with being how you are," I finally add.

All I said sounded right in my head. That's sure as hell not how she takes it.

"You didn't mean any *disrespect*?" she repeats. If I didn't think she could stiffen anymore, I was wrong. "And there's nothing wrong with how I am?" she asks, spinning her chair slowly to face me. "Really?"

"That's right."

She glares at me with enough hate to kill. "And, how am I?" she asks.

She's *pissed.* I'm not used to anyone—especially a woman calling me out. I should walk on outta here before I bury myself deeper than I am.

But I don't.

"Sweet," I tell her, my deep voice dropping. "It's why I like you."

Her jaw pops open, but she recovers fast. "That's not how you made me feel," she says. "You made me feel—" She steals a glance at the window and sighs before turning back to me. "You made me feel dirty."

"*What?*"

She waits, as if debating whether to continue. For as mad as she is, it's the hurt I pick up on when she finally speaks. "The way you pulled away from me was so abrupt, it was as if I was something loathsome to touch."

"That's not how I meant it," I grind out. Shit. I messed up and my actions crushed her.

"Whether you meant it or not, that's how I felt." She brushes her hair away, even though it's not in her face. "You believe in a promiscuous lifestyle, which is why you barely blink knowing your brothers are sexually active. I don't share your perspective. I never have. But I don't judge you or think less of you for your beliefs. Because of it, I expect the same respect back."

I lean forward, placing my forearms on my knees. "I respect you. I respect you more than anyone I know. But I'm not going to lie. When you told me what you were, you knocked me on my ass—given what we were doing and how hard you were making me—it's the last thing I expected you to say."

Her eyes widen in time with her flushing face. "My, you just put it all out there, don't you?"

I hold her gaze. "Yeah. I do." I give her a moment to collect herself before I ask what I've wanted to know. "Why didn't you tell me to stop or to slow down?"

She lowers her chin and rubs her hands, surprising me by returning her gaze to mine when she answers. "I liked what we were doing and I became carried away."

My focus drifts to the floor, the lust in her tone and the heat in her deep blue irises making me instantly hard.

"I didn't mean to tease you," she adds, luring my attention back to her face. "And I apologize if that's what it seemed like. It wasn't my intention." Again, she strokes her hair, giving away her nervousness, showing me how bad it's killing her to say what she says. "But like I said, I was carried away with how you were touching me."

"Have dinner with me," I say before I can stop myself.

She stills. "What?"

I rise slowly and stalk toward her. "I said have dinner with me. Tomorrow at six or later if you want."

She stands and starts to gather her things, giving me her back. "I don't think that's a good idea. It didn't work out well last time."

I edge closer, curling my body so that it hovers above hers. "Last time I screwed up," I whisper. "It won't happen again."

Her shoulders rise and fall with her deep intakes of air. I don't notice I'm doing the same until she pivots to face me. "I don't think it's a good idea," she repeats, her voice shaking.

She's right. It's not. But that doesn't stop me from cupping her face and meeting her lips with mine.

My hold on her is gentle despite the aggression of my tongue. It moves deep into her mouth, seeking her out, claiming her as mine.

My lips are fastened to hers, but my fingers barely brush her skin. If she wants to step away, she can. But she doesn't, giving me everything I give her, her moans inciting a deep growl in my throat.

She breaks our kiss, backing away and slamming her ass against her desk. "I think you should go," she says.

"Why?" I ask, unable to keep the heavy rumble from my voice.

"I'm not going to sleep with you."

"I wasn't asking you to."

It's like a repeat of what went down in my ride, only now the roles are reversed. She realizes and laughs, covering her mouth. I wish I could laugh with her, but I'm so hot for her right now, all I can do is stare at her gorgeous face.

She lowers her hand. "I'll see you later, okay?" she tells me quietly.

"You won't have dinner with me?"

Although she keeps her smile, there's a hint of sadness I'm not used to seeing. "No."

"Why?"

"Salvatore . . ." she says, shaking her head. "You couldn't handle someone like me."

"What's that supposed to mean?"

My frustration and need for her leaks into my voice, making me sound angry, instead of what I really am: ready for more than just a taste of her tongue.

She steels her expression. "It means that I hope you enjoyed that kiss. It's the last time I'll ever let you touch me."

Chapter Eleven
Aedry

"You told him *what*?" Autumn squeaks into the phone.

I finish munching on my salad and take a sip of water before answering. "That I didn't want him touching me."

"But that's a lie, right? I mean this guy gave you your first *and* second orgasm for heaven's sake—Oh, hey, Dr. Marvin, how are you?"

I pause in the middle of placing my water bottle back on my desk. I don't have to be with Autumn to know she's blushing.

"Oh, shit," she whispers, when she finishes her small-talk with Dr. Marvin.

"Who's Dr. Marvin?" I ask.

"Oh, no one, just the Chief of Staff for the organization."

"Autumn!"

She groans. "I know. Do you think she heard me?"

"*Yes*. You totally screamed my orgasms into the phone," I laugh through my teeth.

Although I'm embarrassed for me and for her, we both start laughing. Ordinarily, I don't make personal calls at work, but I've been dying to speak to Autumn since my talk with Salvatore last week. With her schedule, it would have been easier to meet with the president. But this is technically my lunch break and I finally got a hold of her.

"You're not going to go out with him, again?"

"It's not a good idea," I say for the millionth time.

"Even though you like him."

I start to argue, but I won't pretend with Autumn. "He's too alpha."

"And that's a bad thing?" she asks. "I don't know, it sounds kind of hot."

"Autumn . . ."

"In fact, he *is* hot. Aedry, this isn't some idiot with a Napoleon complex trying to act like a bigger man than he is. Yeah, yeah, he might have a little bit of an attitude and sort of an over-inflated ego."

"Little? Sort of?" I fork a piece of cucumber. "He's all attitude and all ego."

"But he also has the goods to back it up." She sighs. "Princes Leia on Alderaan, did you *see* his ass?"

I did. I stared at it every chance I had . . . even as I watched him walk out the door. My heart sank when he shut it behind him and didn't look back. To his credit, he didn't slam it.

Yesterday was the first time I walked the boys out, and the first time I saw him since Friday. We fell back into that same routine consisting of him rolling down his window and nodding my way and me waving like his mouth hadn't sucked on my nipples and his fingers hadn't slipped beneath my panties. I lean my forehead against my hand as my typically neglected body parts begin to throb to the beat of Cardi B's latest rap song. This man doesn't make me quiver. No, not at all.

"He's too controlling," I say, attempting to resume my conversation.

"Did you ever ask yourself why?"

"Hmm?" I'm only half-listening, my feminine areas aching as I recall what he did, how he did it, and what he said. He used words like "tight" and "*wet*." Comments so graphic and straight to the point and so, so, *arousing*. My last boyfriend had used words like "nips." It's safe to assume it didn't generate the same response.

"Aedry," Autumn says. Her voice remains patient. She knows my crash and burn with Sal devastated me.

"Yes?"

"I asked you if you realize why he is how he is? A man who always has to be in control is that way for a reason. My guess is he's not only witnessed severe abuse, but suffered it as well."

I flop back into my chair. "I know," I say. "I've given a lot of thought to it. But his potential history of abuse reinforces why I should stay away."

"But you like him," she points out.

"Yes, I do. He's very generous and he can be extremely kind."

"Then don't you think he deserves a shot?" she asks. "He wasn't the one who hurt his mother, Aedry. And he couldn't help the childhood he was given."

"I realize that. But I'm a counselor. It's what I do and love. I don't want a lover I need to play therapist to. I'm not sure it's healthy."

"I get it. But how can I say this? Okay. Here goes. Your relationships have all *sucked* and the men you were with were total vaginas."

"Vaginas?" I ask, chuckling.

"You know I don't like saying pussy! —Oh, hey, Dr. Marvin. . . . Yes, ma'am, I'm all over that . . . stuff."

"Shit. Shit. *Shit*," she mumbles again. "That woman is either going to fire me or promote me. Did I tell you she looks like Jane Goodall?"

"No." But the visual makes me laugh harder.

"Well, she does. But like I was saying, your past boyfriends were ball-less little bitches . . . granted you didn't turn them gay like I did, but all they cared about were themselves, getting laid, and what *you* could do for them. Salvatore can get into any woman's pants."

"Clearly," I say, trying not to think about it.

"So why waste his time with you? Believe me, I'm not saying I like how he treated you when you were in his ride—in fact, I'm mortified on your behalf. But look at it from his perspective. He practically pulled your thong off with his teeth only to realize you were wearing a chastity belt with no freaking key!"

"Thanks," I mumble.

Her voice softens. "My point is, if this dominant alpha male with hard as cinderblock ass cheeks and a face that could melt panties can have anyone he wants, why waste his time on you? He swallowed his pride and went out of his way to apologize, because he felt bad for being an asshole. I think that's what you should hang onto, Aedry. It's what makes me think he really likes you."

"Maybe. But he comes with a lot of baggage," I remind her.

"We all do, sweets. And it sounds to me like he'd benefit from therapy. From what you tell me, this guy doesn't necessarily need a lover. But what he may need is a friend . . ."

Autumn's words stay with me after she disconnects and long after my cup of soup gets cold. I'm picking up my trash when someone raps on my door. I lurch to my feet as Tamira hurries in and slams the door shut behind her. She's not pregnant and she's doing better. But you wouldn't know it by how frightened she appears.

"What is it?" Her gaze shifts from side to side, as if unsure whether she should speak. "Tamira, tell me what's wrong."

Her expression is that of the tough city kid I know, but her quickening breaths reveal the extent of her fear. "Keon hit me."

"What?" I move closer, my eyes sweeping over her frame to look for injuries.

"I'm all right, it didn't hurt that much."

"That's not the point, he shouldn't be touching you—"

"It's because he saw me talking to Gianno Romero. You know him, right?"

My belly churns. I already know where this conversation is headed. "Did Gianno see him hit you?" Her lips seal shut, but she nods. "You need to give me more information than that," I press.

"Gianno is nice," she says. "He's always been nice to me. He said something that made me laugh. Keon saw and grabbed my arm and pulled me into the boys' bathroom. Gianno followed us in and saw him hit me. They're going to the Block to fight."

A sense of nausea fills me as I feel the blood drain from my face. "The Block" is an old basketball court on the worst side of the town. It's where the local kids buy their drugs and settle disputes. Most fights end with someone in the hospital. But a fight over the summer resulted in a kid shot in the face and another left paralyzed.

"When?"

"They already left," she says.

I snag my purse and coat. "Miss Aedry, don't go!" she calls.

I'm already racing down the hall, fumbling with my phone as I shove myself into my wool coat.

"9-1-1. What's your emergency?"

"My name is Adrianna Daniels. I'm a guidance counselor at James Harris High School. I just learned two students are about to fight at the Block."

"Where?"

"The Block." I curse when I slip on the first step and twist my ankle.

"What did you say?" the irate operator snaps back.

"It's a basketball court. I think it's near Halladay and Communipaw."

"Holliday and what?"

"Halladay and Communipaw," I say louder.

"What city?" she asks, getting testy.

I curse again, this time with frustration as I limp out the door. This is the problem with calling from a cell phone. "Jersey City."

"Please hold while I connect you."

I'm cramming myself into my car with my purse smacking against my side and my dangling coat only half on when the call disconnects. "Hello? . . . Hello? *Damn it.*"

I stare at my phone, debating whether I should call again. But instead of dialing 9-1-1 again, I scroll through my contact list. Beneath Autumn's phone number is Salvatore's. I close my eyes briefly, take a breath, and punch the number.

"Hello?" his sleepy voice answers.

"H-Hi. It's Aedry."

Suddenly he's awake. "What's wrong?"

"Gianno went to the Block. It's an old basketball court near Halladay—"

"I know where it is. What the hell's he doing there?"

"He's meeting a kid he's supposed to fight."

He swears and I can hear him rustling in his sheets.

"Sal, what's wrong?" a woman asks in the background.

I pause in the middle of yanking my coat free from my closed car door. There's a woman in his bed . . . just four days after he kissed me.

I shove aside my petty jealousy and focus. "Salvatore, I'm scared," I tell him truthfully. "This boy Gianno is meeting is violent and a known drug dealer—"

"I'm on my way."

"I've tried calling the police—"

"No, no cops," he snaps. "I'll take care of it. Just stay where you are and I'll call you when I have him."

He disconnects, leaving me to stare numbly at the screen.

My mind races with what to do. It shouldn't take Salvatore long to get there, but it won't take long for Keon to hurt Gianno . . . or possibly shoot him.

I'm closer to the Block than Salvatore is. I know I can arrive sooner. But I realize that in going, I'm rushing into danger.

Yet, when I think of Gianno's sweet, smiling face, and consider how far he's come in just a few short weeks, I can't in good conscience sit back and wait.

I crank the engine and shift my car into drive, peeling out of the school lot and onto the main road.

The ten minutes it takes me to reach the Block are the longest of my life. I called 9-1-1 again and was able to get through. Yet despite my frantic and detailed call, there are no blaring sirens upon my arrival, no scrambling men and women in uniform, no approaching vehicles. There's no one besides me.

The old buildings and trees surrounding the basketball court cocoon the area, separating it into a dark urban world of its own. I'm not sure where to park, or if I should even be here. But I can't abandon Gianno with the hopes that help will eventually arrive. I settle near a busted hydrant and pray that at least a meter maid will arrive to the rescue.

I'm not scared. I'm terrified. I gather my coat around me, buttoning it to the collar to offer me an extra layer of protection. It's an absurd gesture. I know I'm being insanely stupid and I'm ready to high-tail it back to my car when the escalating voices of kids swearing and fists crunching bone resonate ahead of me.

"Fuck him up. Fuck that bitch up!"

"Yeah. *Yeah!*"

I was ready to skitter away and hide. Now my boots clomp against the hard sidewalk as I race toward the sounds. My heart almost stops as I skid to stop. Keon is the first one I see in a crowd of swinging fists, lying on the ground holding his side as blood pours down his face.

Gianno busted his face, except now he's in trouble. He and—oh, my God! —he *and* Apollo are being attacked by Keon's friends.

I lurch forward only to be hauled back. "Hey, baby. Whatcha doing here?" a man sneers against my cheek.

"Get the *fuck* away from her!" Gianno growls when I scream.

He lunges forward as I struggle to break free, punching an older teen so hard in the nose, I feel the impact from where I stand. Another boy grabs him, and another, until he's swallowed up by the crowd.

"Aedry!" Apollo yells. His eyes fling open when he sees me being dragged toward the driveway of an old house, his fists swinging wildly as he tries to fight his way to me. But neither he nor Gianno are a match for the number of young teens gathered.

Their anger fires my will. The man holding me swears as the heel of my boot crashes firmly against his shin. I smack him hard across the face.

"How dare you touch me?" I shriek at him.

I dig my hand in my coat and withdraw my stun gun as another hand reaches for me and hauls me back by the crook of my arm.

I don't hesitate. In one motion I ram my stun gun against his chest and squeeze the trigger.

"Mother *fucker*." Salvatore grunts, crashing to the asphalt on his knees.

His T-shirt smokes. "Oh, no. No, no, no," I stammer. "No, no, no, no." I crouch next to him. "Are you all right?"

He lifts his glaring face, his jaw tightening as he staggers to his feet. "*I told you I would handle this*," he growls.

The man who first grabbed me takes off in a sprint as everything around us grounds to a halt. Slowly, the gang who attacked Apollo and Gianno circle out and away from them, their hardened expressions wary and splitting between fight or flight.

Swelling contusions litter Apollo's and Gianno's faces, their shirts dangling in pieces from their frames. As hard as they fought, they weren't immune to the vicious blows and violence that street kids are ingrained to inflict.

Blood trickles from Gianno's busted lip and from some scratches to his face, likely wreaked when he was on the ground fighting. Apollo is worse off with a swollen nose and eye, and a longer laceration along his crown line.

At least I think he's worse off. The stiff and careful way Salvatore stalks toward the large group informs me I may or may not have blasted the hell out of him.

I cover my mouth. Anyone else would be crawling away if moving at all. But, again, Salvatore is very alpha. He won't show weakness before this pack of wild dogs.

I follow behind him, trying to remain alert.

Keon's friends rallied against Apollo and Gianno. They do nothing when Sal hauls back and kicks Keon hard in the stomach.

"You know who I am?" Sal snarls, his lethal stare trained on Keon.

Keon squares his swollen jaw, but doesn't respond, clutching his side harder. I try not to react when Sal kicks him again, yet I can't help but gasp.

Sal flips him over and presses his large foot against his chest. "I asked you a question, you little bitch."

"Yeah," Keon says, no longer appearing so tough. "I know who you are."

"Then you know who I work for," Sal adds, causing Keon to tighten his already rigid muscles. "These are my brothers you fucked with."

"I didn't know they were your brothers," Keon says at the same moment a few from the surrounding group mumble a round of "oh, shits."

"Now you do." He motions to me. "Just like you know she's also with me. This won't happen again. Understand?" Sal's tone is laced with so much venom, I involuntarily step back.

He lifts off Keon, dismissing him. Keon staggers to his feet only to crash to his knees, swearing in agony.

I almost go to him, but Sal's voice keeps me in place. "Let's go," he tells his brothers.

All three back away and toward me, keeping Keon and his friends in their sights. They stand as a united front, waiting in silence until everyone disperses.

"Sal," Apollo begins.

Salvatore holds his hand up, quieting him instantly. "Just get in the damn car."

I follow them to where Sal parked across from me. "What were you thinking?"

Gianno squares his shoulders. "He challenged me when I stopped him from beating on a girl. I—"

"Not you," Sal quips. "You, me, and Apollo are going to have a nice talk on the way back home." His stare cuts my way. "I was talking to Aedry," he says, stopping in front of my car.

I frown as he hits the key fob to his Range Rover and the boys edge away. "I couldn't simply sit there and wait," I snap, ramming my hands on my hips.

"Yeah, you could have. It's what I told you to do. But you didn't listen," he says, shoving his face in mine. "You're a woman *and* you were outnumbered. Do you have any idea what could have happened to you? What the hell were you thinking, charging in all defenseless?"

"I wasn't defenseless. I had my stun gun," I fire back, motioning to the holes seared into his shirt.

It's as if the world stops spinning. Sal glowers at me as if I punched him in the nose. Today he's in dark jeans, a white muscle T-shirt, and a dark suit jacket, likely clothes he yanked on in his rush to reach his brothers. On anyone else, these clothes would look ridiculous and comical. Yet the T-shirt grips the muscles of his chest like it refuses to let go and the rest resembles something a stylist at GQ would hand-pick for a photo shoot. But he doesn't look hot. Absolutely not hot. Not even remotely sexy.

I'm such a terrible liar. Throw in his current brooding persona and I'm ready to peel my clothes off on the street.

"Get in your car," he says, through his grinding teeth. "You're following me back to my place."

My emotions get the best of me and without thinking, I shove my face into his. "Don't you think it will be a little crowded back at your place?"

His brows furrow deeper until understanding lights his stare. "You really gonna go there with me?"

I clamp my mouth shut, hating the way my blush lifts his full lips into a smirk. He steps closer, his broad chest brushing over mine. "It was Donnie and she's already gone," he says.

Donatella, his stunning friend, had spent the night. I shouldn't be hurt. After all, I'm the one who rejected him and told him I didn't want him touching me. Yet, here I am, devastated to learn how quickly he moved on without another glance back, and with whom he moved on.

I haven't been able to rid him from my mind, but, apparently, he didn't have that difficulty.

Sal leans in closer, his breath tickling my ear. I try to inch away, not wanting to smell another woman's passion against his skin. But his clasp to my elbows holds me in place, forcing me to inhale his aroma.

I sigh as I exhale, then re-breathe his scent. There's no hint of another woman. There's only him, his deep male musk, traces of his fading cologne, and an underlying fragrance that screams of dominance.

"She doesn't mean anything to me. Not like that," he whispers, his lips trailing against my ear.

My heavy lids close as an army of goose bumps swarm my arms. This isn't appropriate. We shouldn't stand this close. I'm a guidance counselor, miles from my assigned post during school hours, with a man capable of extreme violence. I shouldn't speak to him. I should keep quiet, climb in my car, and speed away. It's what most intelligent women would do. Yet, I don't, turning my head to face this man who's ensnared me in his seductive web. "Did you tell her that before or after you bought her dinner?"

If I didn't think his smirk would infuriate me more or grow any cockier, I'm dead wrong. "I didn't buy her dinner," he says, returning to speak low against my ear. "She's a friend who needed a place to crash."

I almost ask him if I was just a friend when he was pulling up my skirt in his car. But I'm not so brave and I'm too afraid to hear his response.

"Come back with us," he says. "I want to try and make things right."

My heart wants to believe and trust him, despite how my instincts warn me against either. But around Salvatore, I'm never really sure of anything except that he's dangerous . . . and that I can no longer resist his touch.

Chapter Twelve
Salvatore

Aedry shocks the hell out of me by following us back. As I stretch out against my white leather couch, the same couch I slept on after giving Donnie my bed, I watch her zip around my apartment, tending to my brothers.

Donnie was a hot mess last night, worse than I've ever seen her, and crying over Vin cancelling their plans to go see a play with his wife. Whatever she'd taken before she arrived hit her hard. I spent an hour talking to her in my room and away from my brothers until she passed out. They know her and like her, but this isn't a side of Donnie I want them to see. I'd rather they know her for the good person hidden beneath all that pain than the one who stumbled in at three in the morning.

Except I don't want to focus on Donnie now. Not with Aedry here taking care of my family.

Gianno and Apollo . . . damn. They barely flinched on the ride back, acting hard like nothing could hurt them. Now that we're home, they're acting like a bunch of wounded vets. Can't say I blame them. Every grimace, every groan, earns them more attention from Aedry.

"I don't like peas," Apollo says when he sees Aedry smashing the stuffed frozen bag against the counter.

She wraps a dishtowel around them as she nears. "They're not to eat. They're for your face." She places the bag on his head, stroking his hair when he holds the bag in place. "I'm glad you're okay," she says quietly. "But you shouldn't have been there."

"I had to have my brother's back," he says.

"You should have told me, instead," she insists, stepping away. "I would have handled it. Now, you're risking suspension." She shoots her reprimanding look at Gianno. "And so are you."

"Sorry, Miss Aedry," they mumble.

"Does the school have to know what went down?" I ask.

Hell, and doesn't that earn me the glare of death. "I'm not lying to my employer."

"I'm not asking you to. I'm just saying you don't have to come clean about everything."

"Actually, I do," she answers with smile that's none too friendly. "Gianno," she says, hurrying back to him. "Don't scratch your face." She lifts the bottle of Witch Hazel, or whatever that shit she found is called, and dabs another cotton ball.

"Is that going to sting? —*Ouch.*"

"A little," she tells him quietly. "But for a tough guy like you who took on an entire gang, this should be nothing."

Gianno grins at her. "Yeah, I did kick some ass, didn't I? That bitch Keon went down like a pussy."

"Language," she reprimands, dabbing his skin a little harder.

He and Apollo start going off on how hard they fought. I won't tell them I'm proud of them. At least not in front of Aedry. But I am. Gianno stood up for a girl getting beaten, and he and Apollo watched out for each other.

They even watched out for Aedry. Christ. When I saw that guy dragging her off, it took all I had not to pull my piece out. Somehow, I kept my head.

Not an easy task around this woman.

"When are you making us dinner?" Apollo asks her.

Aedry straightens, her cheeks turning pink when she's realizes I'm watching her. "You're making us dinner?" I ask.

"No. I'm making *them* dinner. You're welcome to have some if there's any left over." Her voice is shaky like it always gets when she's nervous. She fumbles with the bottle of Witch Hazel, as if she can't close the tiny plastic lid tight enough.

A smile eases across my face. "Why are you making us dinner?" I ask, ignoring the fact that she said it was for my brothers, and that I was only welcome to their scraps.

Apollo speaks up when Aedry takes too long to answer. "I aced my algebra midterm and Gianno aced history." His grin locks on Aedry. "Ms. Aedry promised us homemade fried chicken and biscuits if we both got A's."

"No, shit," I say. "When are you coming over to cook?"

"I never said I'd come and cook here," she says, her voice continuing to tremble. She hurries to clean up the cotton balls and Band-Aid supplies she used on my brothers. "I'll go home first and bring it by later, if it's okay with you."

"If I didn't want you here, I wouldn't have asked you to come," I tell her. Something in my gravelly voice slows her movements. Out of the corner of my eye, I catch Gianno levelling his gaze on Apollo.

He motions to their rooms down the hall. They rise as one, Gianno pulling Aedry into a hug, something that bothers me way more than it should, considering how motherly Aedry returns his affection.

"I'm glad you're safe," she tells him. She releases him and strokes the side of his face. "But nothing like this can happen again. Do you hear me? I don't want anything to happen to you."

Had it been me talking to Gianno like that, he would have reacted with anger, annoyance, or maybe both. With Aedry, his reaction is thick with guilt. He knows he disappointed her, and he probably senses her fear. "Okay," he tells her.

She keeps her hand on his face and lifts up on her toes to kiss his cheek. When she releases him, he skulks away. I rise from the couch and move toward her when she gathers Apollo in her arms. My youngest brother isn't a big guy. He's getting taller, but he has a good twenty pounds of muscle to put on. Even still, Aedry seems so fragile against him. It's not her height or her small frame that makes her appear so delicate. It's her gentle nature. How could someone so soft have survived a world this hard . . .

I don't ask her directly. I simply watch how this delicate woman attempts to shield my brother from harm within her embrace, and how easily he welcomes her. She whispers in his ear. I don't hear everything, catching only bits and pieces. "You really scared me" and "Don't ever be afraid to come to me." But it's the last thing she says that's like a sledgehammer to my chest. "I love you."

I don't think I could feel anything harder than the blow that comes with those words until Apollo says, "I love you, too," and I have to turn away.

Aedry has a major effect on my brothers, except I didn't understand how much until that moment. She loves them, for real. And they love her right back. She's a good woman. I should leave her alone and let her find her peace. But I can't.

The moment she releases Apollo, I close in. I don't wait for him to disappear down the hall and into his room before I touch her.

My hand trails down the length of her back as she tries to gather her things. "Hey," I say, working to keep my voice tender.

Her grip tightens around her purse strap and she clutches her coat against her. "What are you doing?" she asks. Her voice is shaking, but in a different way than before.

I angle my hips and bow my head so my lips skim over her ear. "You said I couldn't kiss you, again. You never said I had to keep my hands to myself."

Her body shudders, causing her hip to lightly brush against my groin. I'm getting to her like I was when we were talking in front of her car. The way she reacts when I stroke her is like power firing through my veins, pumping liquid sex through me. I like having this effect on her. It gets me hard—no, *she* gets me hard.

Whether she knows it or not, she's the one in control, the one calling the shots. If she tells me to stop, I will, no matter how much the rejection will rip me in half. For now, she hasn't said anything, so I keep going, my caress of her body slow and thick with lust.

"So, when are you bringing me dinner?" I ask.

Whether she wants to smile or not, she does. She knows I'm messing with her and she wants to mess with me back. "I never said I'd cook for you."

"Even though I want you to?"

"You'd like that wouldn't you? Having some half-naked female in your kitchen slaving over the stove to make your manly self a hot meal."

"Never said you had to be naked." My lips skim over her ear, hitching her breath. "If you want to, though, I'll let you. Just don't plan on my brothers being here for the show." I circle her waist. "My manly self wants you all to himself."

I pull her back against my front, trailing my tongue over the curve of her ear. "I'm not sleeping with you," she whispers, her voice tight.

"I'm not asking you to," I say. "We'll take things as slow as you want or not at all." I step back enough to grip her waist and turn her.

Her face is pink with enough sizzle in her eyes to deepen my voice. "I don't date women," I tell her truthfully. "I sleep with them once or twice and don't look back."

She smiles then, but it's not all that friendly. "That's sounds like an awesome proposition. Where do I sign up?"

I chuckle, because she is that fucking cute. "Ask me when was the last time I took a woman to dinner."

She stiffens, but that's her only response. "I'm not sure if I ever had," I confess. "It's not my thing."

"But sleeping with women is?" She's not being bitchy. If anything, she sounds disappointed, and maybe sad, too.

My first instinct is to lie and protect her, exactly how I've been doing. But lying isn't something I like doing, especially with her. So today, I spare her and tell her the truth. "Yeah."

"Then what are you doing with me? Touching me like you are . . ." She shakes her head. "Salvatore, this isn't a game. I won't pretend that I don't like you, because it's clear that I do. But just because I'm attracted to you doesn't mean I'll allow myself to be used or mistreated."

My thumbs skim over her hips. I'm trying to behave and not be so bold. But when she's near me, I like her close and it's where I want to keep her. "I'm not trying to do either," I respond.

"Maybe not. But your actions warn me to keep my distance."

"My mother was a virgin," I say, cutting her off before I realize where I'm headed. "Until she married my father. She saved herself for someone good, except he was never good enough for her."

I sometimes forget what Aedry does for a living, and this is one of those moments. Her stare softens so I know she's listening and picking up on more than I'm telling her. "Why?"

Both my brothers have talked to her about our past. She knows a lot. But right then, she wants to hear it from me. Maybe I should keep my yap shut. It's something I'm good at. But I don't. Not this time.

"He ran around on her, made her cry, and then beat us to get back at her for rejecting him. But in his own sick way, he was committed to her and promised to love her forever."

What I'm saying should have her running out of here. Instead, she moves her hands from where they're clasped between her breasts and skims them over my chest. "How could he claim to love her when he'd leave her to be with other women?"

She's not judging me. Her careful tone tells me she's trying to understand the old man. I do my best to explain, although I've never understood him myself. At least not in a way that made sense or excused what he put us through. "In his mind, he remained faithful by loving only her. Those other women meant nothing, or so he'd tell her."

"I see," she says quietly.

"When she filed for divorce and left with me and my brothers, it made him do a one-eighty, or so we thought. He started courting her, or whatever that shit is called, and for a while we thought maybe he was changing. He'd take us out as a family and started acting like a real father. But he kept cheating. Ma found out and went through with the divorce."

I quiet, remembering that time, but mostly realizing I've just spilled more about my father than I've ever told anyone. The old man and I weren't close. We couldn't be with the way he treated my mother. Except some things he taught me, I've hung onto, and keeping quiet about shit that goes on in your house is one of them. Family secrets. That's what he called them. Is it a wonder I'm so tight-lipped and a good liar?

Aedry, being who she is, doesn't let me stay quiet for long. She lures me back to those demons in a way no else would dare to. "What was he like, following the divorce?"

It surprises me how easily I answer. "Pathetic," I tell her truthfully. "He'd show up, crying and begging her to come back to him. But it wasn't until Ma started dating years later that something in him switched. My father, he couldn't handle it. He . . ."

I can't tell her he said he'd kill anyone he saw her with, or how no one else could have her. That shit's too fucked up. What I do is allow her embrace, folding forward so she can link her arms around my neck.

"I'm sorry," she whispers.

She told me not to kiss her, but when I turn to take in her face, that's exactly what I do. My tongue sweeps over hers, going deep. She moans, but then quickly pulls away. I don't let her get far, holding tightly to her hips.

"I don't want to stop kiss kissing you," I rasp.

She turns away, glancing toward the door. "I don't want to stop either."

I tilt her chin so she'll look at me. "Then let's not stop."

I attack her mouth. She doesn't fight me, pressing her body tight against mine.

"Oh, shit," Apollo says, causing Aedry to jump and break our kiss.

"What the hell?" I say, keeping my hold on her.

"My peas melted," he says tossing the bag into the sink. "I didn't know I was going to walk in on this shit," he adds, laughing.

Aedry waits until she hears his door shut before lifting her bright pink face. When I try to kiss her, she presses a hand against my chest, keeping me in place. "I'm sorry, but it's hard to kiss you—"

"Didn't seem that way just now."

Her mouth twists. "I mean, knowing you already kissed another woman today."

"I didn't kiss her. She only spent the night—"

She holds her hand up. "I'm going to stop you right there, big guy."

"She stayed in my bed, but I didn't stay with her. I slept on the couch."

It's the truth, but she still seems hurt.

My lips brush over her forehead as I speak softly. "Look, Aedry. I don't know what's up with you and me. Like I said, dating women isn't something I do. But I want to do it with you or at least try."

"I want to try, too," she admits.

I don't say anything more. I've already said too much. But maybe it's enough.

"I like you," she tells me. "I think despite everything you've been through, you're a good man. But I'll be honest, sometimes you really scare me."

I frown. "I wouldn't hurt you—or force you to do anything you don't want or like. You have my word."

"Okay," she says, like she's been waiting to hear it.

"You want to date me?" she says after a moment. I answer with a stiff nod, even though I'm still asking myself when I became such a pussy. "All right," she says. "But even though we're not sleeping together, I won't keep dating you if I know you're with other women."

I raise a brow. "You're asking for commitment? Already?"

No sooner do I spit the words out than her finger glides along my lips, silencing me. "Not a commitment, only honesty. If you're with someone, tell me."

"But you'll walk away." I'm not trying to tell her I'll lie to keep her. I'm only pointing out what I know she'll do.

"I will," she admits. "But only because I don't want to get hurt." She sighs. "I don't know what it is about you, but I already know you have the power to hurt me like no one else . . ."

Chapter Thirteen
Salvatore

The sit-down Vin has with Raphael goes as well as I thought, which means everything goes to shit. Raph didn't mince words and told Vin flat out he wants his domain. Vin, being who he is, answers with an immediate nod that gives Lucca the okay to shoot Raph point blank in the face.

We had a plan, me and Vin. Hear Raph out, give him the terms. "Stay loyal or pay the price." Vin jumps straight into pay the price, so now me and Raph's enforcer are fucking each other up.

Monster—no shit, that's what he goes by—takes a swing. I duck out of reach, but he still catches me in the skull, sending me flying into the wall. My foot nails him in the gut when he hurtles towards me. He stumbles back just far enough for Benny to empty his clip into him and not shoot me.

Vin is still hiding beneath the desk where I shoved him. I stagger to him, holding tight to my upper arm where the Monster stabbed me. Inches. He missed my heart by inches. If I hadn't turned when everyone started swinging—

The barrel of a gun comes flying out over the desk. I dive out of reach when Vin sets off three rounds. Benny isn't so lucky.

"Mother fucker," Benny howls, falling to the floor.

"Vin—*Vin!*" I shout. I'm ready to kill him my damn self. I keep it together enough to control him. "It's over, boss," I say.

Vin stands, blood pouring from his mouth from his brief interaction with Raph's second. What the hell would this little bitch have done without me? He can't do shit right. Problem is, he knows it, which is why he demanded I show. I mutter a swear, nailing him with a glare as I address his men.

Everyone is breathing hard from the fight and from the rush. Eight dead. Two of them ours, and now Benny's lying on the floor bleeding. I kneel next to Benny, ripping what's left of my jacket off and pressing it to his thigh. "What do you want us to do, boss?" I ask.

It's my way of giving control back to Vin. His men are looking at me, waiting for *me* to make a decision. He needs to answer and call the shots, and he needs to do it fast before he loses any more face. "Boss?" I question, louder. Like his men, I can't wait to get the hell out of here.

Vin hurries out from behind the desk, but it's not to talk. He kicks Raph's already mutilated face. "Mother fucker!" he yells.

Christ.

The men gathered look from Vin to me, their expressions hard, annoyed, but mainly pissed. This is the man they took an oath to. The one they're risking everything to stay loyal to. Almost in unison, they meet my eyes. I swipe my face, knowing there's nothing left to do but lead. "Sam, Dino, Mattie, you're in charge of clean-up. Lucca, call the doc, tell him you're bringing Benny over and to be ready. Tony, you help."

They nod and move. By now, Vin's stopped kicking. He's breathing hard from the breakdown, but also because he's pissed, probably at himself. I want to fly out of here. I want to rage. I want fucking out!

I glance away from the bodies, from the splatters of blood painting the walls like I'm forming a plan. I'm not planning shit. My head is pounding brutally from the stress, and from how hard I had to fight to stay alive.

I can barely see straight. Each heartbeat is like a stab through my lungs. I'm ready to lose it, but I know I can't if I'm going to survive.

Without trying, my mind fills with images of Aedry. We had dinner at that converted church where they make brick oven pizza a few nights back. The pressure in my skull lifts the more I focus on the details, how she looked in that dark dress. How she laughed when I dripped sauce on my chin and how she smiled when I kissed her goodnight. It's the only thing that keeps me from falling to my knees and heaving.

I don't speak again, not until the bodies are taken away and the rest of the crew files out. "You can't pull this hysterical shit again," I tell Vin. "We'll both end up dead if you do."

He lights a cigarette and takes a long drag. "I wanted to go big, make a statement. It would have worked if . . ." He drifts off and, for a second, it's like he's no longer there.

He's crumbling, falling apart. I bring him back with the truth, fast. "You looked weak," I tell him, meeting his narrowed eyes with my own. "You want to play big, then play big, go strong. Don't pull this half-assed shit."

"I have to do something, don't I?" he asks, understanding where I'm going with this.

I nod, but I don't offer anything, even though I know that's what he wants.

He lifts his cell phone from his pocket and makes a call. "Dino, it's Vin. Cut out Raph's heart. Send half of it to Leo, the other half to Marlo . . . yeah, that's right. The other two bosses in New York . . ."

Aedry

"How's it going with tall, dark, cranky, and hot?"

I grin as I place the roast in the oven. Autumn always has a fun way with words. "Good. It sounds silly, but I feel like a teenager."

"Because you're horny?"

I laugh. After two weeks of only kissing, she's not far off. I'm ready for more. "He's taking things slow."

"It's what you wanted, right?"

"Not this slow. Even annoying Marlon had whipped off my bra at this point. Sal . . ."

"Makes you hot?"

"Yes."

"Sharpens your girl parts to Number 2 pencils?"

I think about how he kissed my neck and left me those hickeys and how I've had to wear scarves all week at school. "Yes, that, too. But what I mean is —"

"Makes you want to ride him into the sunset like a bronco with no saddle while wearing a prairie maiden dress—sorry, that was my fantasy about him."

"Autumn!"

"Aedry, can you blame me? I have no one. I look at vaginas all day and treat for syphilis. The least I can do is live vicariously through you. Seriously, think about getting a prairie maiden dress. It's a little-known fact, men like hot prairie maidens."

"I'll keep it mind," I tell her.

"Are you going to tell me what's bugging you?"

"I will if you let me."

"What do you mean?" she asks, laughing. "I'm all ears."

"Sure, you are," I say. I shut the oven door and set the timer on my cell phone. "Autumn, it's as if now that he knows I'm a virgin, he's afraid to touch me or hurt me, or something."

"You're kidding? He doesn't, like, *touch you*, touch you?"

"Not as much as I'd like. I think it's because I remind him of his mother."

"Oh, um. How can I say this? Oh, yes, *ew*."

I burst out laughing. "Not like that."

"Okay, then please explain. You're seriously killing my hot cowboy fantasy."

"You have more than one fantasy about my almost boyfriend?"

"Aedry, I have needs, girl."

"Clearly." I carry the plates and silverware from the kitchen to where I made up a small dining area in my living room. As I set my borrowed table, I do my best to explain my situation. "His mother was a virgin before Sal's father came along. His father wasn't good to his mother and I think it hurt Salvatore to see her in pain. From what his brothers tell me, she's the only woman he's ever loved."

"Mm. He has daddy issues."

I place the fork down over the carefully folded napkin. "Yes."

"And mommy issues."

"Apparently."

"And now, because of it, he won't touch you."

I sigh. "I think so."

"Well, that sucks."

"I know," I agree, trying not to grumble at the thought. "It explains why he reacted the way he did when he found out I was a virgin."

"Yeah. It does. I think you should put it all out there. Let him know you have experience, even though you haven't played the 'V' card. Otherwise, he may never touch you—you do want him to touch you, right?"

My body heats at the thought. "You might say that."

"Then, go for it. In the meantime, I'll look online for naughty prairie maiden outfits. I may be able to find something cheap now that Halloween's over."

"You're a real friend, Autumn."

We disconnect at almost the same time Salvatore rings the front door. I buzz him in, but I'm not expecting the condition I find him in when I open the door.

His right eye is horrifically swollen and an array of bruises line his jaw. "Holy—what the—*shit*!"

I haul him inside. "I'm fine, Kansas," he says.

I place him on the couch. "No. You're not. You need ice." My gaze sweeps over his face again. "Lots and lots of ice." I hurry into the kitchen and sort through my bags of frozen vegetables. "What happened?"

"Donnie wanted to go into the city for lunch at this restaurant she heard about. It wasn't in the best part of town and some guys gave us trouble on the way out."

I reach for a towel to wrap the frozen bag of corn in, my movements slowing as his words sink in. "I thought you weren't seeing Donnie today."

"What?"

I walk slowly back into the living area, my hands squeezing the bag with how nervous I suddenly feel. "When you called me this morning, you said someone else was watching her today."

He straightens slightly. I stop with my knees just in front of his. "You weren't with Donnie, were you?"

He tightens his jaw, a motion that must kill him considering how swollen it is. "No," he says.

Silence settles between us, neither of us moving or speaking. It's as if he's waiting for me to ask him to leave and not come back. But I don't.

Salvatore is a hard man whose life is probably harder. But that glimpse of vulnerability he shared with me gave me a view of his tortured soul, and a better understanding of this man I've completely fallen for. Instead, of pushing him away like he probably expects, I sit on his lap and place the bag of frozen corn on his face.

His arms find my waist as my free hand lifts to stroke his temple. Small soft bristles of thick hair tickle against my fingertips. He hasn't shaved his head in a while and I'll admit I like the way it feels beneath my touch. What I don't like are the lies.

"What really happened today?" I ask.

He waits, as if debating whether to speak. "You know how I work security for Donnie's lover, Vincent?"

"Yes."

"I mostly watch Donnie, but sometimes I have to watch Vin, too."

"He's successful, but not the way corporate men are in the city. Most of his businesses are small, delis, bars, some mom and pop shops. They're scattered throughout the Tri-State and not in the best areas."

"Why doesn't he just move them to better locations?" I ask, once more taking in his injuries. "Or invest in other means."

His voice lowers. "You take businesses out of struggling areas, it destroys what's left of the economy. The area turns to shit and never comes back. Look at all the places that have ever had riots. Businesses leave, but it's the residents who suffer."

He considers me a moment, as if debating whether to continue. "Early today, he was rounding on some bars he owns in Newark. I went with him, but word got around to the local gangs that he was in the area. We got jumped on the way out."

"My God," I say. "A gang tried to rob you?"

"They tried," he says. "Since I was with him, they didn't succeed."

I cover my mouth. "Did you call the police?"

"We did, but the police can't do shit until after the fact. That's why I'm late. We had to fill out a bullshit report."

"Salvatore, I don't like this," I say. "Anything could have happened to you. Those people could have had guns—"

He takes the bag in my hand and tosses it on the table, then clasps the back of my neck and pulls me in for a deep kiss. "I don't want to think about them anymore," he says between kisses. "Not when I'm here with you."

He slips off the scarf I'm wearing and dips his mouth to claim my neck. I'll admit, his switch from tough guy to lover catches me off guard. That doesn't mean I don't welcome his tongue or the brush of his hard chest against my breasts.

As my muscles tense further, he breaks away. "What's wrong?" he asks. I don't answer. He frowns. "Do you want me to stop?"

Heat crawls its way along my face. "No," I admit.

He glides his hand between my breasts. "Why does it feel like something's wrong?"

"It's not that anything's wrong," I say, my skin warming further.

"What is it?" He cocks his head. "If you have something to say, just say it. I don't want things to come between us."

Neither do I. I owe him the truth, not that it's an easy truth to share. "I'm not ready for sex," I tell him. "But I am ready for more than kissing."

He leans back a little, watching me closely. "Yeah?"

I force the word out. Salvatore is simply that intimidating. "Yes."

His already gravelly voice grows gruff. "Have you messed around in the past?"

Without meaning to, I laugh, causing him to smirk. I should be embarrassed and I am, but laughing seems to lift the tension I'm feeling. "Just because I'm a virgin, doesn't mean I'm completely inexperienced. I've done plenty of things with other men . . ." My voice fades in time with his deepening frown. "Why are you looking at me like that?" I ask, realizing he's majorly pissed.

"I don't want to think about you with other men."

What remains of my humor dissolves. I know exactly what he means. Envisioning him with other women in any capacity absolutely crushes me. But neither of us can change our pasts, or the fact we've experienced intimacy with other people.

"I'm not with those men now," I assure him. "Nor do I want to be."

He keeps his expression tight, but his strokes along my spine remain tender. "I still don't like it," he murmurs.

The intensity behind his gaze drills straight through me, stimulating every part of me that for too long has been ignored, including my heart.

Yet, it's what he says next that fires a need only he can invoke. "You've had your breasts touched, your nipples sucked?" he asks, his voice lowering with every word.

My breath quickens as I struggle to speak. "Yes," I manage.

His hand leaves my back to slide around my hip. "Have you had fingers slip beneath your panties?"

Now he's the one breathing hard. "Yes," I stammer, trying to keep from trembling.

"Did you like it?" His fingers dig into the fabric of my dress as he reaches my inner thigh.

"It's been . . . okay," I gasp.

He leans forward, whispering close against my ear. "Just okay?" he asks, his hand lowering.

"Um." Oh, my God, I have nothing better.

His fingertips swirl, grazing just above my folds. "And has anyone kissed you here?" he teases, two fingers skimming down. "Licked you until you were begging for it—"

My cell phone timer goes off, making me jump.

"*Damn* it." I reach for it on the coffee table and tap the screen to silence it. He withdraws his hand and chuckles. "Sorry—sorry," I add.

I point at him as I scramble to stand. "Hold that thought. Just . . ." I shake my hands out, realizing how desperate I sound. "I'll be right back."

I hurry into the kitchen and reach for a towel, practically throwing the roast on top of the stove. I barely finish shutting the oven door when Sal snags me, gripping my hips and slamming my butt against him. I gasp with surprise . . . and from the length and thickness of his erection pressing against my back.

"What if I don't want to hold that thought?" he murmurs against my ear, sliding my side zipper down. "What if I tell you all my thoughts are about making you come?"

He yanks the straps off my shoulders and pulls them down, removing the arm anchored around my waist only long enough to finish stripping me out of the dress. "Will you let me make you feel good?" he asks. "Or do you want me to walk away?"

My need for him is so feral and strong, it hurts to speak. I crane my neck to face him, my voice shaking. "No," I plead.

He freezes and begins to withdraw. I snag his arm around my waist, keeping him with me. "I mean don't walk away," I whisper, melding my lips with his.

His hand slides beneath my panties and his body curls around behind mine. I can't hang onto our kiss. Not now.

A deep groan releases from my throat as I fall forward, slapping my hands against the counter.

I whimper as he pushes his fingers inside me, clenching my jaw. My ass rubs against his erection, keeping pace with the movements of his hand.

"Aw, *hell*," he rumbles, increasing our friction.

My breasts bounce as he unsnaps my bra in one motion. He pushes his fingers deeper into me, stretching me, teasing me, making me cry out from the pain mixed with pleasure.

I jolt when his palm passes over the sensitive bud. Passion clenches my stomach, my pelvis rocking fast with my building orgasm. I'm trying to keep quiet and not thrash or lose control.

Sal won't let me. "Don't hold back from me," he growls against my ear, pinching my nipple. "I need to hear how loud you can come."

He increases his efforts, talking dirty, his voice leaden with sex. Perspiration builds along my breasts with how aroused I am and how perfect he's working me. I fight to keep quiet. Yet, as my orgasm releases in one hard jerk, he gets his wish.

A lust-charged scream rips through my throat, enticing him to slide his finger out and circle my swollen folds.

He has me swearing, my quivering thighs batting his hands. Another orgasm peaks, hitting me hard enough to fall forward. Sal holds tight, nipping my shoulder. "I want you, Adrianna," he moans.

My heavy lids blink open. He called me Adrianna, every syllable laced with a mix of devotion and desire. No one has ever said my name like this. No one.

He makes me feel good . . . and naughty . . . and sexy. I need to do the same. "Have you been with anyone else?" I ask him.

His breath is hot and ragged against my skin. "No."

"And you're clean?"

"Yes."

I nod, my head feeling heavy. "Good to know." I turn and fall to my knees, watching him as I unbuckle his pants and reach inside.

He collapses forward as I move fast and take him deep into my mouth. This time, he's the one clenching his muscles and using the counter to keep him standing. The fingers of his left hand thread through my hair, pressing gently against my head and encouraging me to go deeper.

"That's it," he says, his breath hitching. "Just like that—*fuck*—yeah, like that, baby."

This isn't my first time doing this, but it's the first time I'm enjoying it. I like taking control, but it's how he moans as I'm driving him crazy that I absolutely love, craving his pleasure more than my own.

My lips press tighter, increasing the suction and encouraging him to pump faster. The speed in which we're both working, combined with his sounds and mine, are such a turn on, I almost slip my hand between my legs. But I want this moment to be solely about him and that's what it becomes. He roars with his release, his body spasming as he watches me finish him in my mouth.

The moment he's done, he takes a breath and hauls me to my feet. "I don't want to be with anyone else."

I nod, agreeing. It's all I can do.

"And I won't be," he says, continuing. "But that means you don't get to be with anyone else, either."

"Okay," I say, my body unbearably aroused.

His grip on my elbows tighten, not enough to hurt, but enough to demonstrate he means what he says. "I'm serious, Adrianna. As long as you say you're mine, I will fuck up any man who touches you."

I know where this is coming from, but the heat and possessiveness shimmering his irises make it clear that now isn't the time to play psychoanalyst. "I don't want anyone, but you," I tell him honestly.

His chest rises and falls as he continues to watch me, the angles along his face appearing to sharpen, as if he's expecting me to reject him or somehow turn on him. But then he does something that catches me off guard. He relieves me of the bra dangling on my arms and kneels to rip off my panties, leaving me only in the black stilettos I recently bought.

His steel eyes drag the length of my body as he rises. "Jesus," he groans.

I release a shuddering breath. I don't remember ever feeling this naked, this exposed, this, this . . . *vulnerable*. As much is it unnerves me, I have to allow Salvatore to see me this way. He doesn't seem to trust anyone. I need him to trust me.

He kicks out of his heavy boots, socks, jeans, underwear. I clench my fists, forcing myself not to withdraw or cover my body. The way his ravenous features seem to take every inch of me in tightens the tips of my breasts hard enough to sting. No one has ever looked at me so sinfully.

God help me, I like it.

His muscles strain as he edges back, his voice dropping another octave. "God damn, you're beautiful."

I lick my lips nervously when he strips out of his T-shirt, my need to touch him driving me insane. But it's the bandage covering his arm that has me rushing forward. He catches me in an embrace as my fingers trace the edges of the dressing.

"What happened?" I ask, my fear for him distracting me from the warmth of his bare skin.

"We were jumped," he reminds me. "It was bad, but I'm fine."

"Salvatore," I say, trying to keep myself from flat-out telling him to quit his job. "I don't like what you do."

He answers me in a way that completely shuts me up. "I've had a rough day," he says. His erection is so stiff and full against my thigh it strains his voice. "This was a good start." His hand pushes between us. "Let's keep it going."

He doesn't want to talk about what happened and, considering how close my body is pressed against his, I can't blame him.

"How?" I ask, knowing he wants me to.

Once more, his dark gaze clamps on mine like a vice. "I want to go down on you, all night. Will you let me . . ."

Chapter Fourteen
Salvatore

I pull Aedry against me, her bare skin hot and moist with sweat. "Are you scared?" I ask.

"No," she says. Her pretty eyes skim along my face as I stroke her jaw.

"You're shaking pretty damn hard."

"I think it might be due to the multiple orgasms you gave me." She smiles. "But, what do I know, I'm new to this whole being pleasured by a hot guy thing."

I laugh when she does, relieved she's all right. I try not to be rough with her when we mess around. She gets me so worked up, it's hard not to be more aggressive. Sometimes I think I've gone too far. More than once, I've wrenched away from her, worried I'm hurting her. Each time, she's pulled me back, begging me not to stop.

Except, I do. The thought of causing Aedry pain rips me apart. She's not like other women I know. Hell, she's not like anyone I've ever met. She's good, too good, especially for a man like me.

"I'm glad you spent the night," I whisper against her neck between flicks of my tongue.

"Me . . . too," she says, her head lolling to the side. She shudders when I start to bite, groaning slightly. "Sal . . . I have to go, love."

"Not yet," I say, rolling on top of her.

"Love." That's what she's been calling me lately. The first time she said it was like a punch I hadn't been ready for. I wasn't sure what she meant by it or if she expected me to say something back.

My reaction caused her to laugh, despite the blush that filled her cheeks. "What's wrong, big guy? Do I scare you?" she teased, batting her thick lashes at me.

It wasn't easy to hear something like that. The physical connection between me and Aedry alone is a big change. I usually walk away from women after one or two nights. Here we are, weeks later and the thought of leaving her hasn't crossed my mind.

The bat-shit crazy thing is, for all we've done in bed and around her apartment, we still haven't had sex, the kind that involves me pumping inside her and filling her. Do I want to? Hell, yeah, and wake up hard because of it. Every waking thought revolves around Aedry and how bad I need her.

Call me a pussy, but I'm the one holding us back. The last few times especially, she's begged me for it. Every time I've turned her down, rubbing one off while I go down on her to sate us. I don't want to ruin her by taking what remains of her innocence. Dragging her into my world is bad enough. So are the lies I keep feeding her.

My brothers learned from a young age when to keep quiet and to not ask questions. But Aedry asks all the time. Maybe it's because I'm such a good liar that she believes each one, or maybe it's because she's a good person, and believes in the good left inside me.

It's the latter that stabs at my conscience. I don't want to keep lying to her. And I want out, so I don't have to. I'm stashing money away like a greedy bitch and I almost have enough to start a new life. But, for that to happen, I have to survive this nightmare I'm stuck in. The other night, Vin gave one of his men the go ahead to kill Soto, just because he thought Soto was trying to leave him. There's was no proof, just Vin's paranoia getting to him. But it was enough to leave Soto dead.

"What are you thinking?" Aedry asks.

I'm lying on top of her, shoving away everything Vin's putting his family through, so I can focus on her and everything she's doing to me as a man. "That you should spend the night here more often," I tell her, my lips attacking her nipple and my fingers slipping between her thighs.

That much I mean. This is her first time staying over. Even though my brothers know we're together, she doesn't think it's appropriate we "shove our intimacy in their faces." Those are her words, not mine.

"Sal," she moans when my sucks grow stronger and my fingers circle deeper.

Last night, she finally stayed. All this shit with Vin and Donnie, too, had kept me away from her all week. Her texts to me became fewer and fewer over the days. I think she was worried I was running around on her, especially after hearing how sad she sounded those few times I managed to call her. It was a stupid thought if she was thinking it. By now, she should know I'm hers and that she has me right where she wants me.

My fingers slide in and out, her dark lashes fluttering and her back arching as she peaks. She seems to fight her release. But I don't let her, working her until her head wrenches to the side and she screams through her teeth. She's trying to be quiet, but it turns me on when she's loud.

"You going to scream for me, baby?" I ask, clamping my teeth on her soft flesh.

She breaks away from me with force I don't expect, shoving her face in my lap. I bite back a growl, the sound vibrating against my throat. But when I shove up on my arms to watch I see something that sends jolts of pleasure from my lower back, straight into my groin.

Aedry grips me with her tight lips and one hand while her free hand disappears between her legs. *Damn.* She's never done that, but it's hot and I want a better view. I shove up into a sitting position and grab her ankles, adjusting her kneeling position, and spreading her open so I can watch and tell her what to do.

"Faster," I gasp. "That's it." It's not like she doesn't know what she's doing, but me coaching her fires that scorching heat between us. The movements of her fingers on her and her mouth on me, gets us both ready. She finishes me off, but her hand falls away from her body too soon and she loses her orgasm.

I haul her hips toward my face, pulling her down on top of me. No way in hell is she not getting off with me lying next to her. I want her screaming, and that's exactly what happens no matter how hard she clasps her mouth and tries to be quiet.

My hands grip her tightly, holding her in place as my tongue swirls and my lips suck. Her entire body jolts with the force of her release. I keep going, gradually slowing until she collapses on her side next to me. I leave her there, my palm stroking her ass and thighs, expecting her to adjust her position so that she's lying beside me.

When she still won't move, I lift her and tuck her against me.

She lifts her head, her breathing still fast as she brushes her wild hair away from her face. "That was . . ." She seems confused, her eyes glazed until she smiles. "I'm sorry, what's my name again?"

I laugh before stamping my lips against hers, my tongue diving deep to play. No matter what, I can't get enough of her.

Unless Aedry tells me to, I'm not going anywhere. Problem is, even if she tries to walk away, I'm not sure I can let her go. She takes care of me and my brothers, cooks for us, fusses over them, and makes sure they do their work. She hasn't missed a single one of Gianno and Apollo's wrestling matches, losing her mind right there beside me when they win, and covering her face when she thinks they might lose. She also listens—even though I never realized how badly I needed to be heard.

There are a lot of things I didn't think I needed, until Aedry came into my life and proved how wrong I was.

I called her late last night and all but begged her to stop by. I didn't feel right leaving my brothers. With the exception of the past few weeks, I've always made it home to my boys. No matter how late, I'm always there when they wake up. It's my way of giving them stability. But with Vin's screw-ups, I haven't even been able to give them that.

Like with Aedry, I've barely seen my brothers all week. Aedry knew they were alone and stopped in to make them dinner. She also made sure they picked up and did their laundry. Each morning or afternoon, whenever the hell I was done cleaning up after Vin and Donnie, I'd stagger in, expecting to find the place wrecked to shit. Each time, I was wrong.

Except, as much as Aedry watched out for them, and as much as I appreciate it, they're my responsibility. I couldn't leave them to be with her. But I could have her here. She snuck in, but I didn't let her sneak back out, and given how the past few hours have gone and how content she seems, I doubt she regrets it.

"I have to go," she says again, her small nails skimming the surface of my chest.

"What if I don't want you to?" I ask, pushing up on my side.

"I have to work," she insists.

Pounding on the door interrupts what she has to say next. "*What?*" I ask, craning my neck.

Aedry scrambles beneath the sheets when Gianno throws open the door and sweeps in, followed closely Apollo.

"What the fuck?" I yell, clutching Aedry against me.

Gianno stops at the foot of my bed, more pissed than I've ever seen him, pointing at me. "You're an asshole," he snaps.

At first, I think he and Apollo are pissed, since I haven't been around, until Apollo lets loose.

"How the fuck could you do this to Miss Aedry?" he demands.

"Wait," I say. "*What?*"

Gianno lays into me. "You dragged in this whore, knowing Aedry's been waiting on you all week," he says, motioning to the lump in my arms. "That makes you an *asshole.*"

"Watch your mouth," I warn, not because of what he's calling me, but how he's referring to Aedry. He doesn't know it's her burying her face against my chest. That doesn't mean anyone gets to put her down.

"Fuck you," Apollo says.

"And your whore," Gianno adds.

I drag my hand down my face, torn between laughing my ass off and reaming my brothers out for how they're talking. They're protective of Aedry. I know that. The more they're with her, the more they want her to stay. It's good and bad. Good, because I know they love her, and bad, because . . . yeah, because they love her.

"You finally meet a good woman and this is the shit you pull?" Gianno demands.

I hold out a hand, trying to silence them as Aedry continues to squirm against me. "You don't know what you're talking about," I start to say.

"Like hell," Apollo snaps. "We heard you—last night and this morning!"

"Oh, *God*," Aedry squeaks against me.

Apollo's and Gianno's scowls dissolve. They exchange confused glances. It's not until Aedry pokes her bright red face from the mound of covers she tried to cocoon herself in that their jaws collectively drop. "Sorry," she offers.

I crack the hell up. Apollo backs away, smacking into the wall before taking off in a sprint—like any kid would after finding his parents in bed. Gianno just stands there, watching Aedry cover her flaming face as I laugh my ass off.

"Ah, sorry I called you a whore," he says. He starts toward my bathroom before realizing where he's headed. He quickly turns around and heads out to the living room, slamming the door behind him.

"Oh, God," Aedry says again.

She breaks through the tangled sheets and leaps out of bed. I try to snag her waist, but she's too fast, racing around the floor and snatching up her clothes.

"Babe, come back to bed."

She pauses in the middle of pulling up her panties. "Really? That's all you have to say?"

I smirk. It's either that or crack up again.

"Salvatore," she whispers. "They *heard* us."

If I didn't think her face could get more red, she proved me wrong then. I throw my legs over the edge and march toward her. "They were bound to hear something sooner or later."

She hooks on her bra, her thin brows drawing tight. Even when she's pissed, she's still damn cute. "If you're trying to make me feel better, it's not working," she fires back.

She slips her sweater dress over her head, but when she reaches for her leggings, I clasp her arms and kiss her. "They like you," I say between kisses. "Take their anger for what it is. They don't want me with anyone else." My tongue slips into her ear. "Not that I blame them."

She jerks away from me. "I have to go."

I shake my head, following her toward the bathroom. "Call in sick. Stay with me. Let's make up for our time apart. We'll go to brunch or order in. Your choice. I just want you with me."

She smiles in that way I love that tells me she doesn't want to leave. But that's not what she says. "I can't," she tells me. She lifts up to kiss my chin before disappearing into my bathroom.

For a long few seconds, all I do is stare at the door. She's my woman now. It's the old school man in me that wants to take care and provide for her—so she doesn't have to work and so she's stays with me permanently. But she's not my wife. And, unlike Donnie, she doesn't want to live as a kept woman.

I tug on a pair of sweats, wrestling with what to do. If I offer to pay for her to take the day off, I'm only treating her like a whore. I can't make her stay, even though I want her with me. Again, I remind myself that she's not my wife. But the fact that I'm even thinking the word "wife" is messed up.

She slips out of the bathroom, her face freshly washed and her hair brushed. No make-up, and her eyes swollen from lack of sleep.

And she's beautiful.

"There was an extra toothbrush that hadn't been opened, so I used it. I'll pick up a new one for you when I go to the store later." She tilts her head. "What's wrong?"

I sit on the edge of the bed, scowling. What am I supposed to say? Don't go. I've missed you and need you with me? No, I'm already enough of a pussy around her. "You don't owe me a thing. Take whatever you want," I offer.

I lean back on my hands as she reaches me, trying to put some distance between us so I can let her go home. Aedry doesn't make it easy. She bends forward to tug on my bottom lip with her teeth. She says she has to leave, but that bite to my lip is practically begging me to pull off her panties.

"Don't be cranky," she says. "It's nothing personal. I have a job and responsibilities, just like you do."

"I'm not cranky," I mumble like a dumbass.

"It shows," she says, laughing.

Anyone else would run for their lives at my glare, but Aedry isn't anyone. "Has anyone ever told you that you do dark and brooding well?" she teases.

I smack her ass as she walks away, making her jump. "Behave," she says.

I don't bother listening, stalking after her when she tries to escape.

She sees me coming and keeps her hand out as she snatches her purse off the floor. "Salvatore," she says laughing, as I loom closer. "I'm serious."

She ducks out of my reach and races out the door. I storm after her, watching her pace slow when she finds my brothers in the kitchen. Apollo is bent over a cereal bowl, spooning in the contents for all he's worth.

Gianno is pretending to read the paper. "Um, see you at school," Aedry stammers as she swoops past them. Her back is to me, but I don't have to see her face to know she's blushing again. This whole scene and how embarrassed the three of them appear should make me laugh. But I can't, not now.

I follow her out, the coolness in the hallway sweeping against my skin as she stops in front of the elevator and she pushes the button leading down. "Bye, love," she begins as she turns to face me.

My lips smash against hers, my arms encircling her waist to pull her tight against my body. "Say you'll stay with me again tonight," I say, when I break our kiss.

She glances around. "I don't know. The boys—"

"The boys will deal. You and me are together and what we're doing is normal. They're just not used to it being with you."

She averts her gaze. She didn't like what I said, probably because it was a stupid comment on my part, reminding her of all the women my brothers have heard me go at it with. But that's not how I meant it. "I'm sorry," I say quietly. "I'm only trying to tell you I want you with me."

She nods as the elevator chimes open and the doors part. "All right. I'll stop by tonight."

She slips from my hold and into the elevator, taking a part of me with her.

Chapter Fifteen
Aedry

"Come shopping with me tomorrow," Donnie chimes on the other end of the line. "We'll hit a few shops uptown and maybe catch a late lunch."

When I first met Donnie, I never expected someone like her to be friends with me. She's a fabulous city girl, and I'm very much a small-town girl at heart. I was taken aback when she stopped by Sal's the other week unannounced. I was making them dinner and I wondered how often she dropped in in my absence.

Sal and the boys weren't particularly excited to see her. They assured me it wasn't something Donnie often did. Sal especially appeared tense and he kept encouraging her to leave. I convinced him to let her stay for dinner. I'd made a lot of food and she seemed lonely and sad, despite the smile she repeatedly flashed.

Donnie chatted up a storm during our meal, insisting I give her my number. She left abruptly when it was time to clear the table. I didn't expect her to call, but she had every day since, reinforcing my belief that she lives a lonely life.

"I can't tomorrow," I tell her. I race around my office with the receiver tucked between my chin and shoulder as I tidy up.

"Why not? We had so much fun Monday. And, you said yourself, Sal liked the dress I picked out."

I don't mention to Donnie that Sal also loved the shoes and the lingerie, but she can probably guess as much. "We're taking the boys to a winter festival in Pennsylvania," I explain. "Food, sleigh rides, that sort of thing."

The first few times Donnie reached out to me, I made excuses to avoid meeting her. I had trouble believing that she and Sal were always "just friends." She'd spent our entire dinner clinging to him and the boys. It was hard to watch and almost too much to handle.

Donnie is . . . *gorgeous*. I'm not typically insecure and I'm comfortable with the way I look. But Donnie has a face and body that belongs in *Maxim*. The only way I'll ever grace *Maxim* is if I tape a picture of my face to the cover.

It's when I realized how desperate Donnie seemed for a friend that I finally gave in. I'm glad I did. Like I suspected, she doesn't have anyone in her life to lean on. Those women I saw her with at the club were more devoted to what she could do for them than what they could do for her. And regardless of how confident she is in her beauty, those uncertainties she hides beneath trendy clothes and expensive cosmetics poke through when she thinks I'm not paying attention.

"Would you like to come with us?" I ask, realizing how quiet she becomes.

She laughs. It seems forced. "Can you seriously see me on a back of a sleigh?"

I see her point. Our most outdoorsy excursion included a walk through Central Park, following lunch at Tavern on the Green. "No. Not really."

"Vincent doesn't like that kind of thing," she adds quickly, trying to add merit to her argument. "He won't even take me on a carriage ride through the city."

Donnie does that a lot, bounces from talking about herself as if she's single, to reminding me that she's not. She doesn't discuss their relationship, aside from comments like, "Vincent says this" or "Vincent bought me that." From the tidbits I've gathered, their relationship is volatile at best. She's told me she wants more of a commitment, but that Vincent isn't ready to settle down. She also talks as if Vincent and Salvatore are the best of friends.

When I've asked Salvatore about Vincent, Sal shuts down, telling me he doesn't like to talk about work or his boss when he's with me.

I sit at my chair and file the folders I've been working on all day. I feel bad for Donnie. Everything about her behavior demonstrates that she loves Vincent and that he's everything to her. I can't be certain he shares those feelings. His needs always come first and his availability is severely lacking. There are days that I don't think he calls her at all.

Salvatore and I have been together almost six weeks. We spent Thanksgiving apart when I flew home to North Carolina. Despite how much I've missed my family and friends, I was crawling out of my skin with how badly I missed being in Salvatore's arms.

And I wasn't alone.

Sal texted me constantly and so did the boys. He picked me up from the airport, greeting me with one hell of a kiss and a few more on the drive back to my apartment. When we arrived and I found almost every square inch covered with vases spilling roses, I teared up.

"Just wanted to show you I missed you," he said when I turned to kiss him.

Yes. . . Vincent and Donnie have been together longer, but Sal is far more committed. What's challenging is he still won't make love to me, even though I'm begging him every time he touches me.

"Aedry?" Donnie says.

I ram the last folder into my drawer. "Sorry," I offer. "I'm trying to do too many things at once."

"Oh," she says, clearly upset that she didn't have my complete attention.

"I'm sorry," I say again. I shove my heavy filing cabinet closed. "It's hard for me to talk at work." It's something I've often told her, but it doesn't stop her from calling. It's only because it's the end of the day that I was able to take her call this time.

I don't think most people would be offended. But Donnie is sensitive. I feel terrible about not offering more to the conversation. When she stays silent and all I can think about is her spending her weekend pining over Vincent, I add, "Give some thought to coming with us to the festival. It won't be an intrusion. My girlfriend, Autumn, is going to join us, if she doesn't have to cover a shift."

"Family isn't my thing," she says, her tone stiff. "You know that."

I pause in the middle of shutting down my laptop. As much as she's repeatedly made this claim, I believe it's the opposite and something she desires. "Okay. But if you change your mind, send me a text. We're leaving after breakfast, but by nine at the latest so we can enjoy the day."

"Nine?" she repeats. "You're leaving at nine *at the latest*?" She sighs. "Honey, you know I'm never awake before ten. Besides, I don't do the mommy thing. Making sure everyone eats and wiping noses is your department, not mine."

"All right," I say, slowly. I don't miss the backhanded compliment, or the insult behind it.

Donnie isn't mean. Really, she's not. But she often teases me about becoming the mother Apollo and Gianno need and the one Salvatore needs for them. At first, I took it as good-natured needling. However, she brings up my role this way so often, I'm starting to think she envies the closeness I share with Salvatore and his brothers. I hope that's not the case. I want her to be happy for the good things Sal and I have, including my relationship with his brothers.

"I have to go," she says when I remain silent. "I have a nail appointment and I can't be late if I want to look good for Vin."

Her constant need to look perfect for Vincent is another thing that worries me about Donnie. I always want to look good for Sal. But considering he's seen me without makeup and woken beside me after minimal sleep, it's safe to assume he hasn't always seen me look my best. But he still greets me with a kiss and longs for my affection. I can't be sure Vincent would be as forgiving or as kind.

"All right, sweetie," I say. "I'll see you next weekend for lunch."

My term of endearment and my promise to get together brings her back to the Donnie I adore. "Hey, Aedry," she says, struggling to gather her words. "Have a blast tomorrow, okay?"

"I will, thank you," I reply, smiling.

"Later, then," she says and disconnects.

Donnie always has to end the conversation first. What's the old term, "cut 'em loose, before they cut you first?" It's something I've come to know about her and it adds to my worry. She's not perfect, but she's someone I consider a friend.

My thoughts are on Donnie as I button my black wool coat. Although it's cost me money, I've invested in more clothes, and thanks to Donnie's tutelage, definitely more style. The knee-high boots and black leather pencil skirt I'm wearing are prime examples, as is the red scarf wrapped around my neck.

A knock to the door has me glancing up. "Hi, Aedry. Are you walking out?"

I return Max's smile. He's one of the new part-time counselors, who is connecting well with the students. He leans against the door, the buttons of his coat opening to reveal his cashmere sweater and khakis. "Yes, just give me a minute," I tell him.

I shut off the desktop lamp and snag my purse. He steps out into the hall, watching me as I lock my office door. It's not too long ago that I think I would have been attracted to Max. But since meeting Sal, no man can compare.

We walk down the hall. "I was asked to help out with the basketball tournament this weekend," he says. "Are you going?"

"No, I have plans. When I help out, it's usually with wrestling." I don't add that Gianno and Apollo are on the team and that I attend the meets with Salvatore.

Max grins. "You're leaving me to fend off the single moms on my own?"

I laugh as we step out of the building and toward the staff parking lot. Max is a pretty boy, one who draws ladies (including some on the staff) like a magnet despite his best efforts to keep a professional distance. "Perhaps Coach Stevenson will let you borrow a bat to beat them off."

"What I need is a pretty lady by my side. But, if you're not available . . ." His smile vanishes as a car door slams shut ahead of us.

Salvatore stomps forward. His long black leather coat flying open like a cape and exposing the stone hard muscles pressing against his expensive suit. Menace drips from his pores. I do a double-take, unsure what he's so upset about. "Hi—"

Sal yanks me to him, crushing his lips against mine and ramming his tongue deep enough to flick my tonsils.

The kiss is brief, but his claim on my waist and the sizzle behind those lips are more suggestive of our time in bed than a simple hello. My face burns as he keeps me anchored to his side and offers Max a hand.

"Hey," he says, his gravelly voice laced with an extra dose of kick-ass. "I'm Salvatore."

Poor Max. His eyes widen as he clasps Sal's hand. I nudge Sal hard when he doesn't release him.

Max shakes out his hand. "Hi," he stutters.

I speak through my teeth. "This is my friend, Max. He's one of the counselors we recently hired."

Sal fixes Max with a hard stare. "Is he?"

I cover my face, mortified. With a sigh, I drop my hand away and smile, doing my best not to kill my behemoth and insanely jealous boyfriend. "Have a wonderful weekend, Max. I'll see you Monday at lunch."

Sal glares daggers at Max. "Why are you meeting him for lunch?"

I meet Sal with a frown of my own. "We have lunch duty together," I explain. When nothing changes in his features, I jab him in the chest with each word that follows. "You be nice."

I turn to apologize to Max, but he's already gone. Seriously. The last thing I see is the back of his foot and the door to the building slamming shut behind him.

"You scared him," I accuse.

Oh, and look at that, he's smiling.

"Good," he responds.

From the inside of his SUV, Apollo and Gianno are in hysterics. I narrow my eyes at Sal. "What?" he asks.

"What do you mean 'what?' You were horrible to him. Max is a nice man."

"Who can't wait to take your panties off," Salvatore finishes for me.

He huffs when I blink back at him. "Come on, Aedry. I saw the way he acted around you, hanging on your every word, checking you out. I'm not blind and I sure as shit ain't blind to what a man wants when he sees you—and the way *you* were, laughing at whatever lines he was feeding you. He's lucky he's not laying on the ground bleeding."

I peer behind his back and along the ground, taking a step back as I make of show of passing my gaze along the cracked sidewalk. "What are you doing?" he asks.

I shrug. "Oh, nothing. Just looking for your club, caveman."

"I'm not acting like a caveman," he snaps. "I'm just looking out for my woman."

"Is that what that was? Here I thought you were just being a jealous lunatic. Silly me."

His scowl turns into a smirk. A sexy smirk, but a smirk, nonetheless. "You saying he wasn't hitting on you, wasn't asking you out?"

I start to argue until I realize Max was pretty flirty. But the last thing I want is to justify Salvatore's outrageous behavior. My problem is, I wait too long to respond. "No."

He quirks a brow. "He wasn't inappropriate," I insist. "He just didn't realize I'm in a relationship."

He closes the distance between us. "He knows now."

I duck out from under his arm when he tries to kiss me. "You can't do that," I insist, pressing my hands into his chest when he closes in. "I'm serious. Some women may like this possessiveness, but I don't. It worries me."

"I would never hurt you," he answers, as if offended.

"If I believed you would, I wouldn't be standing here. But the way you acted isn't okay, nor does it set a good example for Gianno and Apollo."

His stance solidifies, assuring me he's listening and that he understands what goes unsaid. "I'm not my father," he tells me.

"I know you're not," I answer quietly. "Jealousy is an unintentional emotion. But when you feel it, you need to pause before your actions lead to something you'll regret."

He bows his head, thinking through the situation and maybe a lot more. But when he meets my face, only one thought comes through. "I would *never* hurt you," he promises.

His lips meet mine. The way he kisses me isn't like a man trying to insert his alpha-ness or stake his claim over his woman. It's sweet, and loving, and so very sexy.

"I'm sorry," he whispers against my lips.

"Thank you," I reply.

I turn when I realize we have company. At the top of the steps, there's my sweet girl, Tamira, and a group of her friends, eyeing Salvatore with their mouths dangling open.

I point to my feet. "It's the shoes," I mouth.

Salvatore slides his hand against my lower back and leads me to the lot. "Come on. I'll follow you home."

"You don't have to, love."

He frowns. "Yeah. I do."

Maybe he does. Sal is a rough and "I'll break you in half" kind of man, but this side, the one that wants to ensure I stay safe, is the one I most cherish.

"What time do you think you'll be ready for dinner?" he asks me.

I pull the keys out of my coat pocket when we reach my car. "By seven at the latest. Why? Are you hungry?"

"No, I just—pack a bag, okay? After dinner I want us to head back to my place."

"All right," I say, even though that's what we'd planned.

"What's wrong?" I ask, when he grows abruptly silent.

For a moment all he does is stare blankly at the row of houses across the street. "What do you think about moving in together?" He does a one shoulder shrug when I grow quiet. "We can get a bigger place. Maybe even a brownstone."

I should be losing my mind based on the level of commitment he's offering. Yet, I don't, realizing this isn't something I can give him. How do I explain that it has nothing to do with him or us, and everything to do with my upbringing and beliefs without scaring him?

"It's not something I can do," I answer truthfully.

"Why?" he asks.

"I'm old-fashioned in that respect," I carefully explain. "I don't believe in living with someone until I'm married."

He leans back on his heels, squaring his jaw. "Marriage" evidently affects him the same way moving in with him affects me. "I'm not asking for that," I clarify. "I know it's something you're not ready for. But, Sal, neither is me living with you."

"We practically are now," he reminds me.

"That's different."

"All right." He bends to kiss me, although he doesn't seem happy. "I'll see you in a few."

He waits for me to slip into my car and start it before stalking away. He wants me to live with him and feel close to me. But why does it seem like sometimes he wants to keep me so far away?

Chapter Sixteen
Salvatore

More snow drifts up and into my face. Sleigh rides aren't my thing and this is why. Aedry giggles beside me in that cute way she does and lifts her chin to kiss my cheek.

"This is *fun*, isn't it?" she teases.

"Yeah. Fun," I respond, working to keep my face hard.

She laughs and snuggles closer. She knows me well enough to guess I'm having a good time. It bothers me, to some extent, that she can see past my steel exterior. What bothers me more is how much I've lied to her.

The shit I've been dealing with has made me more of a liar than the man I'm trying to be for her and my brothers. It's one of the reasons I agreed to this trip. Out here, far from the city, it's like the life I'm leading doesn't exist and like the danger I breathe in and out is nothing more than pollution skimming along the New York skyline. I want this time for us. It connects me to that human side I all but lost before she came along.

Christ. How is it possible for a woman to make me feel this way in such a short period of time? As if reading my thoughts, she curls against my body like she belongs there, reminding me of the little things she does to make me feel like I'm the most important thing in this fucking world. I kiss the top of her head, she draws my affection as easy as that.

Gianno and Apollo turn from where they're seated in front of us, both smirking. "Pussy," Gianno mouths to me.

I lean forward and shove his head. "Behave," Aedry insists.

"I am," I say, the corners of my mouth lifting when Apollo cracks up. "He's still breathing, isn't he?"

The sleigh slows to a stop in front of the barn where our excursion through the snow-covered hills first began. I hop out and help Aedry out. Two teenaged girls edge closer to the sleigh, lured by the sight of my brothers. Gianno and Apollo are growing up fast, their faces and developing muscles earning them second glances from young women everywhere we go. Aedry doesn't like it. But my brothers do.

"Hey, baby," Gianno says. "What've you got beneath that bonnet?"

Aedry slips from my hold, dragging my brothers forward. "Don't make me kill you in front of all these witnesses," she tells them, putting as much distance between them and the girls as she can.

I follow behind them, chuckling into my fist as my brothers gripe about Aedry destroying their chances at finding a nice Amish girl.

She ignores their comments, leading them past that man we met when we came in, the one who breeds Labrador Retrievers. As much as she's fussing over my brothers, I don't miss the way she glances at the dogs by his side. They wag their tails, remembering her, too, and probably the way she fell all over them when she stopped to pet them. The dogs are from a champion line and weren't for sale. I asked the man for his card when she slipped into a small tent that sold spices and he mentioned he breeds them.

I know she still misses her dog, the one from her childhood. With the way my brothers went nuts over the dogs, I'm thinking about buying her one and having them help her take care of it. Gianno could use a running partner and Apollo could use something to keep him out of trouble and make him more responsible.

I've never wanted a dog, but if it makes Aedry happy . . .

Shit. Gianno's right. I am a pussy.

I catch up to them as they reach a stand selling potato pancakes and soup. "Be respectful before you get us chased out of here by men wielding pitchforks," she tells my boys when they return the smiles of yet another group of girls who pass them.

"I've got this," I say, when she reaches into her purse and pulls out her wallet.

She crinkles her brow. "This day was supposed to be my treat," she protests.

I shake my head. "You don't pay for anything when I'm around," I remind her.

"That's how it should be, miss," the old man at the stand says when Aedry tries to argue. "It's only proper for a good man to take care of his lady."

I wouldn't call myself a good man. But I would call Aedry one fine lady.

The man fills four giant bread bowls with rich stew, its thick and hearty scent instantly making my mouth water. I take my and Aedry's servings, following my brothers as they plop down on one of the outdoor benches. The sun's out today and even though it's only about twenty-eight degrees, I can't deny it's a beautiful day. I've never been out to the boonies of Pennsylvania, except once to bury a body (yet another of Vin's mistakes), but we won't go there. Not today.

Out in the country, it almost seems like life is too good to be true. Everyone here greets us with a smile, a "yes, sir" or "no, sir," appearing to mean what they say and how they come across. It's strange for a city boy like me to find peace here, but if there's such a thing as heaven on earth, I find it here among the quiet surroundings, the snow-covered trees, but mostly the company.

Apollo and Gianno wolf down their food like they haven't been stuffing their faces all day, before diving into the potato pancakes and homemade applesauce like they're starving. "Can we get some of this stuff to take home?" Apollo asks, pointing to his food. "And maybe a couple of those fresh pies we passed, too?"

"Of course," Aedry says, sighing when I shoot her a look that lets her know no way is she shelling out the bills for it. "You're impossible, you know that?" she tells me, leaning in to kiss my cheek.

I tilt my head so she meets my lips, making her grin. My brothers take it as their cue to leave, stopping only to toss their garbage in a rusty old barrel. I expect her to call to them to not wander far, or to ask them if they need any money, that's what she always does. Instead, she keeps her focus on me, her large blue eyes shimmering with a sense of sadness that makes me frown.

I stroke her face. "What's wrong?"

She opens her mouth as if to deny that anything is, only to quickly close it and briefly glance away. "Can I ask you something?"

I already don't like where this is headed, but she doesn't give me a chance to respond, forcing the words out as if she's afraid to speak them. "Why won't you make love to me?"

I drop my hand away, returning to what remains of my lunch. "Salvatore," she begins.

"You want to discuss this here?" I ask.

My excuse that we're in a public place is a pathetic one at best. There's no one near us. Those bustling around are gathered near the food and craft stands or hurrying toward the folk band taking stage at the center of the make-shift village.

"Maybe this isn't the best place," she admits. "But you don't ever want to discuss this with me anywhere."

I take a few pulls of my water and work on finishing my stew and bread. It's a good meal. But I can't enjoy it. Not with what Aedry wants to talk about. Every time we mess around, it takes all I have not to slide inside her and take her hard.

Hard. That's exactly how I want to pound into her. That final claim I alone can perform to prove to myself, and to the world, that she's mine. But I can't do that to her. Someone like Aedry doesn't deserve a good fuck. She's entitled to the lovemaking she's asking me for and that I'm incapable of.

I have sex with women in a way that would scare an inexperienced and sweet woman like Aedry, ramming my hips with the force of my anger and sin. I've never hurt a woman with the way I've taken her, nor have I ever forced one. But with Aedry, I'd be forcing my dark side into her, poisoning her and ruining her innocence.

I've tried to explain my reasons as best as I can. She doesn't believe me or understand what I'm saying. That doesn't mean *I* don't understand why she's asking. The last few times she's begged me for it, I've flipped her onto her back, shoving my face between her legs and finishing myself off as she comes. It's not that I don't want her to touch me—hell, she drives me crazy when she does. But when she does . . . shit, I *can't* do that to her.

"Is there someone else?" she questions.

Anyone else would freeze at my scowl. She doesn't. "Someone else meeting your needs in a way I can't?" she presses.

She's using her counselor voice. The one that's non-judgmental. Yet, I can sense the lingering hurt behind each syllable.

"Is that really what you think?" I ask.

She shakes her head. "Don't do that," she tells me.

"Do what?"

"Answer by asking a question and turning it back on me," she explains. Again, her voice stays gentle, confronting me in a way that doesn't challenge, but expects the truth.

I don't respond, returning to my water. "I don't want to be your second choice," she says. "Or the good girl you think you should hang onto if there's something more you want."

I crush my plastic bottle in my hand and return her stare. She thinks there's someone else. I can't deny she isn't right. Vin's world, the organized crime lifestyle I'm a part of, *is* my mistress—the one that spoils me for Aedry. I can't tell her that, so again I put it back on her.

"Then what do you want to be?" I ask, alluding that maybe we shouldn't be together if what I'm giving isn't good enough.

I don't know if it's the force behind my voice, the severity of what I'm implying, or maybe it's that Aedry isn't as tough as she wants to be. Whatever it is has her glancing down and away. I want her to keep her gaze averted—and hope she'll drop the subject so we can hang on to what we do have and make the most of the day. But she doesn't. As tough as she's finding it to be—especially with me acting like a total ass—like always, she digs deep for courage and meets my face. "I want to be your everything," she whispers.

I've been stabbed, shot, and kicked in the liver. But nothing has ever caved my chest in like her words or her beautiful pleading face. She means what she says. She wants to be my lover and friend, and the mother to my boys—everything I never realized I needed or wanted until she walked into my life.

For what seems like too long we watch each other, trying to gauge what the other is thinking. When it becomes too much for me—and, hell, maybe for her, too—I give her an answer neither of us wants to hear. "No," I say, rising.

Her lips part. I don't miss the pain flashing across her delicate features. "No, to what?"

I toss my waste and hers into the garbage. "To all of it," I answer.

I wait for her anger, for her to finally snap like all the crazy bitches I've fucked—to tell me off and walk away—*something*. Despite that I think I'm doing the right thing by her, that doesn't make me less of a dick for how I do it.

She stands slowly, clutching her purse against her like it's going to shield her from what I say or halt the tears welling her eyes.

"I love you, Salvatore," she says, the words lodging my breath brutally in my chest. "I only wish you would let me."

She walks away, wiping her eyes as she heads into a quilt store.

Never in my life have I hated myself more.

"Hey, Aedry," Apollo says from the back of my ride. "Do you think you can make us Ma's lasagna tomorrow night? It will go good with the pie, don't you think?"

That's another thing Aedry's done for me and my brothers, brought a little of our mother back to us. Apollo found our great-grandmother's recipe for lasagna in an old cookbook, the same recipe my mother made that she'd learned as young girl. It was written in Italian and it took some doing, but he and Gianno painstakingly translated the recipe so Aedry could make it.

No one told me what was going on. I came home one night following a hell of a day dealing with Vin to the smell of "home." It was my birthday. I didn't care enough about it to mention it to anyone. But my brothers remembered and told her ahead of time.

Instead of spending money on something I didn't need, she prepared the lasagna, gravy, and garlic bread exactly like my mother once had. That was her gift to me, to us. I swear, I've never been given a gift with so much heart.

We ate in silence, my brothers and me remembering a time when the woman we all loved was still with us. I don't think Aedry realized the impact this gesture would have on us. Or maybe she did. Apollo ate with one hand shielding his eyes and me and Gianno savored every bite like we were scared to let the moment pass.

That was the night I realized I'd found another woman to love in a way a man like me never thought possible. It should have made me feel good. But it didn't. If anything, it was a reminder that she's with the wrong man and how much of a coward I am for keeping her with me—how selfish I'm being for wanting her as much as I do, and not letting her find someone who deserves her.

I couldn't find the words to thank her for that meal and for all the good memories it brought. Instead of getting pissed, she smiled, kissed me, and wished me a happy birthday. I didn't feel enough like an asshole, I suppose I needed reminding she's always been too good for me.

"We'll see, honey," she answers Apollo.

I take the exit ramp into Jersey City. She's been quiet since our talk. A and G noticed and they have been talking up a storm since we left Pennsylvania, making up for the uncomfortable silence between us.

"You want to watch *Big Ass Spider* tonight?" Apollo pushes, trying to keep her talking.

She releases a small breath. "I won't be staying over tonight," she responds quietly.

My attention cuts her way. She keeps her focus ahead. That's not what we planned. She was supposed to stay with us all weekend.

I work the muscles of my jaw. I shouldn't be pissed. After how I treated her and what I said, what did I expect—that she'd come home to me, to my bed? But I am pissed, at myself.

I take a sharp right at the last possible second, surging the tension thickening the air.

"What—"

"I'm dropping you off first," I tell Gianno, cutting him off.

Aedry's place is on the way to our apartment. I'm going completely out of the way by going back to my place first. That doesn't raise suspicion or anything or bring the silence around us down like an ax.

I pull into our parking space about fifteen minutes later, setting the SUV in park. "Let's walk them up and get them settled, then I'll take you home if you want."

She doesn't move. She's not coming up, likely guessing I'm trying to keep her here. Again, my brothers don't miss a thing.

"Don't God damn bother," Gianno snaps, throwing open his door.

Any other time, I'd rip into him and tell him to watch his mouth. But he and Apollo are furious, knowing I screwed up with Aedry. She slips out, hugging them close like it's goodbye. It just about tears me apart.

What the hell is wrong with me? Didn't I practically give her an ultimatum? Tell her I didn't want what she was offering? If she wants to walk away, she should. It would ease my fucking conscience for keeping her with me and from a man who deserves her love.

It's what I believe. So why does it I feel like I'm losing my right arm in one slow torturous pull?

Because she's a part of you, asshole, I tell myself. No matter how many times I remind myself that I'm nothing but toxic to her, there it is. I don't want to be without her.

She slides back in, reaching for her seatbelt and snapping it in place without a glance my way. If she was anyone else, I'd call her an Uber. No way would I drive her home. But she's not some skank who's trying to take a swing or asking me to buy her shit. She's Aedry. A woman who deserves respect.

She wants to be my everything, she claims. She can't see she already is.

I ease out of my spot carefully and pull onto the main road. Again, we drive in silence. Again, it eats at me all the way to her neighborhood. I find a spot almost at the end of the block. The minute I set my ride in park she opens the door, walking toward the front of her building without saying goodbye or bothering to see if I'll follow.

I cut the engine, flinging the door shut behind me and stalking forward. I slow my steps when I realize she's not in a rush. She unlocks the door as I reach her, allowing it to fall behind her as she steps inside the foyer.

I catch it before it closes. She didn't exactly hold it open, but she didn't slam it behind her, either. I'm not sure what she's up to. All I know is that I'm getting pissed.

"You can stay here if you want," I tell her. "But I'm walking you to your door."

She strolls ahead as if I didn't just growl at her. "Suit yourself."

I storm forward, following her as she hops up the steps. Any other day, I'd have my arm around her and she'd be glued to my side. I force myself to keep my stride relaxed, even though by now I'm ready to rip someone's throat out.

With her carefree pace, and the way she neglects her environment, anyone could attack her. Safe neighborhood or not, she needs to be careful.

"You need to watch your surroundings. Anyone can come up and grab you," I snarl, angry that this is what she does when I'm not around and even more furious that I won't be at her side anymore to protect her.

She glances over her shoulder as she reaches her apartment, her gaze indifferent as it passes along my form. "Oh, I doubt that," she says, turning back to unlock the deadbolt.

"I mean if I weren't here," I say, trying to keep from yelling. "Decent area or not, we're a short drive from a city infected with pervs and maniacs waiting for the opportunity to assault you."

"Mmm," she says, nodding.

It's as if what I'm saying isn't important. I follow her inside, throwing the door closed behind me and flicking the lock. "Look, Adrianna. You can be mad at me all you want for speaking the truth. That doesn't mean you get to be careless, or that I want anything to happen to you."

She places her keys and purse on the counter and shrugs out of her coat, hanging it on the hook by the door in this tiny-ass apartment. "Is that what you were doing?" she asks, slipping out of her boots, and socks. "Speaking the truth? Like you always do, right?"

My muscles tense as she throws what I said in my face. I don't know if she's seen through all the lies I've told her about Vin, or the lies I told her today about how I feel. But when she pulls her sweater over her head, I still for different reasons. Her dark hair brushes against her shoulders as she wiggles out of her jeans and her hips swing as she strolls into the bathroom.

She's wearing those shiny brown panties she just bought, the ones that are nothing more but a strip of cloth across her ass. They give a glimpse of her sweet body, especially when she bends—*shit*—like she's doing now as she flips on the water to her shower.

"What are you doing?" I rumble, feeling myself get hard.

She keeps her back to me as she unsnaps her bra. "Getting a shower," she explains, like I'm a moron.

I pinch the bridge of my nose and scrunch my eyes closed. I all but shoved her away today—gave her every reason to walk away when she told me she loved me and I didn't say shit back—rejected her as if she hasn't been good to me—as if she didn't turn my world upside down—or become the woman I'd cut my own heart out to protect.

My hand falls away in time to see her panties drop to her ankles. She pauses as she pulls aside the transparent curtain. "If you want to leave, *leave*," she says, her voice tight. "Lock the door behind you and toss your key in my mail slot. I won't make you stay if you don't want me."

She steps into the tub, the cascade of water soaking her naked form as steam rises to the ceiling. I stand there, taking in what she tells me and mesmerized by the way she passes her hands along the skin that felt like silk beneath my touch.

I did this to her. I denied everything she offered, including her love. This is what I told her I wanted, right?

I replay every damn detail of our time together, knowing that life without her is the last thing I want. She's telling me to walk, giving me an out, because this is the hand I forced her to play. But as much as I think I should, I can't leave her.

Just like I can't keep my hands off her.

She steps out of the shower like I'm not there and no longer exist, passing a thick white towel along her face, hair, and curves before wrapping it around her body and edging toward the sink. She pauses in front of the mirror.

At first, I think she's going to say something, but instead she reaches for a comb to pass through her thick hair.

Like I said, I don't know what she's up to. All I know, is that I'm done watching.

She finishes combing her hair. I march forward and lift the bottle of lotion she reaches for out of her hands. The hitch of her breath when I nip her neck is her only acknowledgment of me, that and the way her eyelids lower as I glide the lotion across her skin.

My hands . . . they're not as fast as I want to be. They pass along her shoulders and arms like a slow dance between my palms and her skin. I fall to my knees, feeling the muscles of her toned legs tense as I massage up, and down, and further up until my spread fingers cup her ass.

Part of me thinks I should stop, that she may not want what I'm doing to her. But the soft moan she releases as I slip my hands beneath the towel and knead her ass tells me that at least for now, she doesn't want me to leave. I yank the towel off her in one hard tug. It falls in front of me as she grips the edges of her sink, her body shuddering as I pry her legs apart and take my first lick.

My face buries deep and my tongue probes, thickening my staff so it bulges painfully against my jeans. She gasps with each flick I give her throbbing center, each pull of her sweet flesh, her hips circling as I spread her thighs further.

Her increasing moans and the way her thighs tremble tell me she's peaking, she's almost there. I go faster, needing to hear her release. I expect her to come in that way she always does for me, with her back and neck arching, and her screams of pleasure releasing through clenched teeth. Just as she starts, she stumbles away from me and into the hall.

I clasp the edge of the sink, gliding my tongue over my lips. "Where are you going?" I ask, my voice as rough as crushing stone.

Aedry's eyes glaze with lust. She clutches the counter behind her, appearing to struggle to keep her balance. Her breath releases in short bursts and her skin is flushed. "What are you trying to do to me?" she asks.

I rise arduously, my erection stabbing and clenching my pelvis. But I don't answer.

She shakes her head, the motion batting her small breasts and drawing attention to their tight centers. "If you didn't want me, I'd understand," she says, her voice quivering and her focus lowering to the large mass behind my zipper. "But you do—"

I don't feel myself move, I'm just suddenly there, my body shoved against hers. "It's not that I don't want you," I tell her. "And you know it."

She tilts her chin, capturing my gaze. "Then prove it," she says.

I know what she's asking. I'm ready to tell her no, point out all the countless fucking reasons I shouldn't rip off my jeans and push inside her. But before I can ease away, she wraps her arms around my neck, kissing me softly and in a way that makes me feel every bit of her pain, fear, *love*.

"Make love to me," she begs between kisses. "*Please.*"

She should be reaching into my jeans or rubbing herself against me to get me to give her what she wants. But what she's doing to me—everything she's making me feel—makes me want her more.

It's like all the hate and anger leaves me at once, all the poison infecting my body dripping from my pores and vanishing into the air. But it's the guilt over everything that I've seen and done since working for Vin that stays, keeping me from acting.

My fingers fasten against the counter on either side of her as I struggle to stay in control. "You don't want this," I bite out. "Not from me."

I try to keep my face averted. But Aedry's done with my excuses and she's done waiting. She nibbles her way along my jaw. "You're wrong," she whispers, slipping her tongue in my ear.

I don't stand a chance, not with how she's holding me like I might break.

"I love you," she says, clutching me tighter. "Show me you love me, too."

I shouldn't. But I do, losing my mind to everything she's making me feel.

I lift her into a straddle and carry her to bed, kissing her hard.

We flop onto the mattress with me on top of her, my hips grinding against hers as my clothes are flung on the floor. I reach between us, rubbing my thick head along her slick center. But as I start to push in, I hesitate and ease away from her.

She clasps my shoulders, her pleading expression holding me in place. "Don't," she says, "I need to feel close to you."

Every tendon in my body constricts against my frame as reason and desire fight it out. I jerk my chin, looking away from the woman I'd give my life for. "I'll ruin you," I say, speaking through my clamped jaw.

She caresses my face, drawing my focus. "You've only ever made me better," she tells me quietly. "Help me make you better, too . . ."

God help me, I do.

My chin dips to her neck, my tongue trailing along her throat as I carefully make my way inside her. Aedry's knees fall open, helping to ease the agonizing push of my hips. Her body seizes mine, clenching me tighter and thickening the lust heating the air.

I want her so much, but I take my time, advancing and stretching her slowly, kissing her softly and gently passing my hands through her hair, along her breasts, and back to that face that always finds its way into my dreams. Her body fastens around mine, grasping me as if afraid to let go. She's perfect . . . so damned perfect.

I'm not even halfway in when her head lolls to the side and her brows knit taut. "Am I hurting you?" I murmur, kissing the spot behind her ear.

"I'm all right," she bites out.

"I can stop," I answer, withdrawing gradually even though every pull away from her kills me.

"No," she says, her voice barely audible as she pulls me to her. "Please don't."

Her mouth finds mine, keeping us joined. I hover over her, torn by what to do. But as she relaxes beneath my touch, I tilt my hips, rocking forward until she and I become one.

She grunts as I withdraw, my thrusts gradual as I take her with care. She's my beautiful Adriana, my star, my love. I can't tell her, so I whisper the words in a way she can't understand.

"Mia bella Adrianna . . . mia stella . . . mia amore."

I've fucked a lot of women. I've never cared enough to make love to any of them. Until tonight. Until Aedry. Until everything in my world changed when she told me she loved me . . .

Chapter Seventeen
Aedry

I'm not sure what time it is. All I recognize is that it's pitch black, I'm in my bed, and I hear Salvatore's voice.

"I'm staying at Aedry's tonight," he says, his deep vibrato like a soft echo in the darkness. "If you're hungry, get some cash from my drawer and order food . . . No—*no* . . . no parties, no guests . . . I swear to Christ I'll beat your asses if I find out you had anyone over . . . What? . . . Yeah, we're still together . . . She's fine . . . Apollo, don't worry, everything's all right."

It's what he claims, but I catch the worry in his voice. I blink my eyes a few times, trying to shake the sleep as my vision adjusts to the darkness. It's funny how everything can change in a matter of hours. At the festival, we were having so much fun, until Sal pushed me away.

I spent the rest of our trip in absolute misery, doing my best to keep my smile for the boys and my distance from Salvatore. He gave me space, but he wouldn't leave me completely alone. He'd stand outside each makeshift shop I visited, waiting for me to finish browsing, despite how I barely looked at what was in front of me.

He realized I needed time, and maybe he did, too. But that wedge that grew between us devastated me. He didn't make an effort to reach for my hand, nor did he speak directly to me. It was as if he'd already moved on, and I was nothing more than a woman he was obliged to take home.

Although I blame myself for discussing such a sensitive subject in public place, I didn't expect his response. But the way he regarded me when he stroked my cheek, I've never felt so adored. I hadn't been certain about Salvatore's feelings for me, but I was then, until he once more erected those proverbial walls I'd worked to push through.

My first reaction was hurt at how easily he seemed to dismiss me. Without actually saying the words, he told me to leave if I wasn't happy with the way things were. But I am happy. I love him and I told him so. I could have chosen better circumstances, but the more I felt him shove me away, the more I needed him to know what he means to me.

My virginity was my gift to him, that final demonstration that he's who I've been saving myself for. A small smile plays along my face as I realize how different he is from the man I'd envisioned myself falling for.

I'd convinced myself my "first" would wear polos and slacks, or perhaps a conservative suit. I was sure he'd be a professor or possibly an attorney, likely because that type was always my draw. I never expected someone so strong, sexy, and dark to fill my heart and make me feel beautiful. Perhaps, that was his gift to me.

I shift beneath the sheets, allowing my hand to skim along my belly. I'm not sure exactly what I expected sex to give me, but I honestly thought it might change me, even a little. But I'm still Aedry and no matter how much I've learned over these past few years, I'm still that young woman who drove to the big city from North Carolina.

My hand trails down my belly as I remember how it felt to have him push inside me. He kept each press gentle despite the lust sizzling in his eyes. He wanted to go harder, I could tell by the way the muscles of his shoulders strained as he passed his hands along my body. But he took his time. And that flash of tenderness that lit his eyes when our bodies joined . . . God, it was like a glimpse into his soul.

I tilt onto my side as I hear his fingers tap along his cell phone, my hand stroking his back. He pauses from where he sits naked on the edge of my bed before glancing over his shoulder.

"Hi," I whisper, so filled with emotion my voice quakes.

He rolls over, the edges of his features wrought with concern as he cups my face. "You okay?" he asks, his thumb sweeping away a tear that escapes.

"I'm fine," I answer.

His gaze drops briefly as he speaks. "You don't seem fine," he says, his frown deepening.

He's worried he hurt me or that I have regrets, but that's not case. "Sorry," I say, swiping another tear. "It's just . . . I waited a long time for you."

The way he melds his gaze with mine, I'm unable to draw my next breath. "How do you do that?" he asks.

"Do what?"

"Say all the right things."

Before I can deny it, he pulls me to him for a long, lazy kiss. As he inches away, I smile against his lips. "How do you do all the right things?"

My words aren't meant to upset him, but as I watch, his features turn to stone. "I don't," he responds.

I press my palm over his heart, feeling it beat beneath the thick wall of muscle. "You do with me," I whisper.

"That's not what it seemed like today."

"Today wasn't easy," I confess. "You made it better by staying with me." My eyes burn with the words that follow. "But you have to stop pushing me away. I don't like feeling like I'm someone you can easily discard—"

"You're not," he says. He forces a curse through his teeth as he jerks his attention away. "I should have let you go today. But I'm selfish as hell when it comes to you, so I couldn't, and I did something I maybe shouldn't have done."

"Why did you want to let me go?" I ask, my throat tightening. I clasp his shoulder when he tries to ease away. "And why do you regret what we did?"

He squeezes his eyes shut, bowing his head. "Because you're too good for me," he bites out, returning the force of his focus on me. "You always have been and you always will be."

For a brief moment, I can't move, the weight of his words holding me in place. "I don't understand why you think that. I only know I don't like you believing it. You're my world, Salvatore. I wish I could make you see what you mean to me."

I don't wait for him to argue like I know he will, kissing him deeply. For a moment, I'm sure he'll wrench free from my hold. Instead he gathers me to him, his lips hungry for mine. I surrender to him, ingraining his taste and the feel of his skin into my memory.

His thick staff extends along my belly, making me groan. Yet as I reach for it, he clasps my wrist, keeping me from him. "Did I hurt you?" he asks. "Tell me the truth," he says, making it clear he won't let me stroke him until I answer.

"No," I respond, but my answer comes too quick. Doubt spreads along his features.

I slide my wrist free as he loosens his grip. "The way we made love wasn't what I expected," I begin.

My voice trails as his fingertips skim around my breast to circle my nipple. "I was hoping after all the times I made you come with my fingers that it wouldn't be so bad."

The centers of my breast stiffen as I try to find my words. "It was uncomfortable, not painful, but so beyond perfect it felt more like a dream."

His features continue to reflect his doubt. But it's the truth, and I need him to believe me. "I didn't want it to end," I admit. "You took your time, using care, and the way you held me, it's like you never wanted to let me go."

"I don't want to let you go," he says, his rumbling voice appearing to fade in the darkness.

"Then don't," I say, kissing him once more.

His bare skin encompasses mine. I don't dare tell him how embarrassed I was to simply lay there holding him against me. Aside from encouraging him with the sway of my hips, I wasn't sure what to do. My fear was he wouldn't be able to finish, that my lack of involvement would prevent his release. But when he did, and as he filled me, we locked eyes in a way that proved his love.

He may not be ready to tell me and I'm not sure he ever will. But that didn't make the moment any less sacred.

Sharing intimacy is hard for Salvatore and it's taken a lot for him to let me in. Sex . . . it wasn't solely about me giving him my virginity. It was about him accepting he was deserving of something he felt was so pure.

I shudder as his erection grows against my belly. When I reach for him, he clasps my wrist, pulling my hand and the one under me. He pins them over my head as his tongue glides along my throat. I like what he's doing, his nibbles causing me to writhe and slide my nipples against his chest.

Yet I'm so desperate to please him, I can't simply lie there. "Are you sore?" I ask, my accelerating pulse and tightening center make me daring. I push up on my legs, causing the thick head of his penis to press harder between us.

He averts his head, growling. He's turned on, but once more he's holding back. "Do you want me to kiss it?" I ask, my comment more of a plea.

"Aedry . . ." he says.

"Please let me," I say.

He takes several deep breaths before releasing me and rolling onto his back. His hands sweep along my spine as I draw an invisible line of kisses from his throat to his hard stomach. I pause as I reach his hardness and flick the tip. I may not know what to do when it comes to sex, but by now I know what he likes when I taste him.

He bites back another swear, rushing to push up on his elbows and cup the base of my neck. But when he grips himself and leads the head toward my open mouth, he takes his time, teasing my lips before feeding me his fullness.

His head lolls back, the muscles along his throat and chest contracting with his increasing breathing. He shifts beneath me, threading his fingers through my hair and lifting the strands away from my face so he can watch. I smile bashfully as I glance at him, stirring a groan as he pops free of my mouth. I smile again, this time more playfully, deepening my tastes and savoring his expanding flesh.

I love having this control over his pleasure and the sounds he makes as I take him further. It's almost a challenge, to see how far I can go and how tight the cords along his throat will constrict beneath my touch.

When he bucks beneath me, I almost think he'll let me finish him this way. But these last few hours have changed everything between us.

He gathers me in his arms, lowering me onto my back. "Are you ready for me, again?" he asks against my ear.

I nod and spread my legs. Despite his careful strides to penetrate, I can't deny I'm tender. That doesn't make me want him any less.

I've never felt so close to anyone. It wasn't just what we did, it's how he made it all about me, how those rough hands passed over my body as if I were a delicate rose he was afraid to crush.

He rubs his erection against me, searching for his way in as he murmurs in my ear. "You're so beautiful," he rasps, tugging on my lobe and speaking quietly in Italian.

I'm not sure what he says. That doesn't stop each syllable from etching into my soul and melting me against him.

I tilt my chin, wanting to see him. Agonized euphoria encompasses his features as he slides inside me. I crane my neck, exposing my throat for him to kiss. There's pressure, lots of it. I can feel his entirety as he withdraws and advances. But this time, it doesn't hurt. This time, it feels good . . .

A whimper breaks through my throat, followed by a lustful groan. Salvatore's head falls beside mine. "Am I being too rough?" he murmurs.

"No," I gasp.

He holds his position, his warm breath teasing my shoulder. He doesn't believe me, so I tilt my hips, encouraging him to move. I expect pain. My thighs quiver when it doesn't come. The tightness and pressure remain, but the sensation stirs unexpected jolts to shoot into my center, causing us both to swear.

My chest rises and falls, making it hard to speak, each inkling of movement electrifying the nerves along my throbbing flesh. "What was that?" I stammer.

Salvatore pushes up on his elbows, fervor encompassing his strong features. "Me teasing your G spot."

"Oh." I bite my bottom lip and shift my weight, his thick head skimming the spot again and causing my eyelids to flutter.

"*Fuck*," he groans, almost falling on top of me.

He shakes with desire. But when he speaks, I'm the one who can't seem to move. "I'm going to go harder," he says, swallowing with great difficulty. "If it's too much, tell me to stop, and I will."

I barely manage a nod as he withdraws. When he thrusts, I practically claw my way through the mattress.

"Too much?" he asks, stopping in place and balling the comforter in his fists.

"No," I whimper.

"You sure?"

"I'm sure," I say, slipping my tongue into his ear.

Salvatore abandons his restraint, proving how much he wants me, and maybe how much he's longed for me, too …

Chapter Eighteen
Aedry

Making love with Salvatore is as amazing as it sounds. My problem is that as the weeks pass, it's clear he's doing most of the work. My movements are awkward at best, despite his insistence that I'm doing everything right. I find it hard to believe, especially knowing that the women he's slept with were far more experienced than me.

Research nerd that I am, I start surfing the net for erotica sites. All in the name of science, of course.

I turn my head to the side as I stare at my computer screen, and a little more when I can't figure out whose arm is where and what body parts I'm looking at. I want to be a better lover. When we're alone, I often ask Sal what he likes and if what I'm doing is right. He's patient and sweet, guiding me and teaching me what to do with his body. As much as I try, I often feel like a total klutz.

I want to be more for him and I am determined to match his past lovers in skill and endurance. So, here I am, dressed in flannel pajamas and hopping from one website to another as the deep cleansing mask on my face dries, trying to figure out what the hell I'm looking at so I can do it.

Maybe.

Good Lord, she's flexible.

A knock on my door interrupts my very important study time. I think it's the Thai food I ordered and skip to the door, giggling when my stomach gurgles in anticipation.

I open the door, leaving the securing chain in place. You can't see much. But Sal sees enough.

His eyebrows slowly crawl up his forehead. "Aedry?" he asks.

My fingers pass along the hardened goo covering my face. Weeks. I've spent weeks dressing in sexy clothes and lingerie, only for him to find me like this.

He said he wouldn't be able to see me tonight. He said—

"You on your way to clown school, baby?"

Oh, God. I flick the chain off and let him in, narrowing my eyes at the sight of his smirk. "This is a new look for you, hot," he says, laughing.

I lunge at him when he lifts his phone and sets it on my face. "Don't you dare," I say, trying to snatch it out of his hands.

He keeps it up and away from me. "I need a new shot for my wallpaper," he says. "This is perfect."

He's playing dirty. Well, so can I. I reach around him and tickle his side, that one spot on his body where he can't handle being touched. I catch his phone when he drops it, backing away from him as he charges.

"Give me back my phone," he says, his features growing playful.

"You can have it after I wash my face," I say, running into the bathroom and flicking the lock.

I turn on the water and scrub my face at Mach 1 speed. I manage to take the mask off, but now my skin is blotchy from the cold water. I remove the towel from my head. My thick hair is still wet and the strands stick to my face.

"Adrianna," Sal says, his voice rough. "You coming out?"

My hands fall to my sides. "Yes," I mumble, humiliated that this is the condition he found me in.

I try fluffing out my hair, but all that does is partially push it away from my face. I give up, expecting to find him either in the kitchen or the living room.

Wrong again.

My stomach bottoms out when I find him sitting on my bed . . . next to my open laptop. I curse the day I adjusted my screen saver to kick in after ten minutes. I edge closer, dropping my hands against my sides when I realize I'm wringing them.

Sal scrolls his finger down to toggle, his eyes skimming over the images. It's not until I'm almost to him that he glances up. "You're watching porn," he says slowly.

I freeze in place, hating the way my voice cracks. "It's not porn. It's, uh, erotica."

He raises a thick brow. "It's the same thing," he says. "Erotica is just a term used by women, so they don't feel guilty about watching porn."

My entire body heats. "I was doing it for you—"

"While wearing your clown make-up?" he asks, chuckling. "I didn't realize you were into the kinky shit."

"It was a deep cleansing mask," I insist.

"Sure, it was," he says. "All you were missing was the squeaky red nose." He hooks his finger into the waist of my pajamas and pulls me to him. "So where do you keep it? In here?" he asks, sliding his hands into my pants to caress my bare cheeks.

I jump away from him. "I'm trying to be a better lover," I say, pointing to the laptop.

He shakes his head, taking another look at the screen. "I don't know, Kansas, this chick is pretty damned flexible."

"You're impossible!" I say.

"Is it the suit?" he asks, parting the jacket open to expose his light blue silk shirt. "Not enough polka dots for you?"

He cracks up when my face reddens. "You think you're so hilarious, don't you?"

"Maybe not as funny as you, but I can't juggle or wear pointy hats."

"Salvatore!" A knock to the door gives me an excuse to turn away. I only manage a step before he snatches me in an embrace.

He pulls me against him, trailing kisses along my neck. "You expecting more of your friends to shove in your little car?"

I try to bat his hands away, but I'll admit, now I'm laughing. "It's my food, I ordered Thai."

"Here. I got it," he says, releasing me to reach for his wallet.

I whirl around on my way to the door just to point at him. "You're not paying for me, when you weren't even supposed to be here."

"Aedry? You in there?"

My steps slow as I recognize Donnie's voice. I glance at Salvatore, who frowns.

"Aedry?" she calls again.

"Yes, I'm coming," I tell her.

She greets me, holding the bag of food in her hand. "He said it was for you," she says in the way of a greeting. "I hope you don't mind."

"Um. No. Of course not."

I lift the bag from her hands and allow her through. But while Salvatore is surprised to see her here, she doesn't react the same way. "Hi," she tells him.

"Did you follow me here?" he asks.

"I've been here before," she slips out of her coat and lowers herself to the couch. "Hasn't Aedry told you we've been shopping?"

She fails to mention that while she's dropped me off and picked me up outside, that she's never actually been inside my residence. But the way she takes in my small apartment, lets him know enough.

He meets her with a hard stare that softens as he takes her in. I'm not sure what's happening, or why she's here. She's been very needy. I've invited her out with us a few times, worried about how she's doing. But I didn't invite her tonight.

Instead of standing there watching them, I move into the kitchen and place the take-out on the counter. "Would you like some dinner?" I offer.

"What are you doing here, Donnie?" Salvatore asks, not giving her time to respond.

"Your brothers said you weren't home," she responds. "I thought I'd find you here." She glances my way, forcing a smile despite how her stare seems to take in my flannel pajamas. She's in Chanel. I recognize the dress from our shopping excursion. Her long blonde hair is brushed to perfection and her make-up is flawless.

I don't think there's ever been a time I've ever felt unwelcome in my home, but that's how I feel then. She's not here for me, she's here for Salvatore.

"I guess I was right," she continues, fixing her smile on Salvatore.

I walk out of the kitchen, refusing to hide while they continue like I'm not there. "You didn't answer my question," he reminds her.

Instead of joining her on the couch, he edges to my side, although I don't feel like he's entirely with me. "That doesn't tell me why you're here," he reminds her.

Her smile dwindles. "You were supposed to be at my place yesterday, today, and the other night. And you weren't."

"You need to take that up with Vin," he says.

I think he sounds angry, but there's more in his features than frustration. He's concerned about her.

"You were supposed to be there with me, Sal," she says, her face splintering. And as quickly as she arrives, she picks up her coat and leaves.

"Donnie," he calls to her. She doesn't stop, causing Sal to hurry after her.

I stand there for a few minutes, expecting him to return. When he doesn't, I head back into the kitchen and lay out the containers of food. But as I reach for plate, I find I'm no longer hungry.

I bristle when I hear the key slip through the deadbolt and the door open. I don't bother to look up, knowing it's him and wishing it wasn't.

"Hey," he says.

He wraps his arms around my waist, the care he uses causing my head to lower. I don't want to be hurt, but that's exactly what I feel.

"You're not going to eat?" he asks.

I shake my head. It's all I'm capable of then.

"What's wrong?" he asks, pressing a kiss to my temple.

I turn to face him. "I wasn't sure if you were coming back," I tell him honestly.

"There's nothing between me and Donnie. She's upset and she needed someone to talk to. It's the only reason she came to find me here." His thick brows draw tight when I don't answer. "You know that, don't you?"

The disappointment I feel causes me to shift my gaze. Donnie came, because she needed Salvatore specifically, not me and certainly not us. All the things she managed to say in the short amount of time she was here will stay with me. She reminded him about the days he was supposed to be there for her and wasn't, demonstrating how much she needs and wants him.

But I need and want him, too.

I don't mean for my insecurities to spill like a dam, but they do anyway. "She's gorgeous," I remind him.

"I don't care about her, not like that," he says.

"I wish I could believe you, but sometimes it's really hard."

"You have nothing to worry about," he insists.

"I think you're wrong." The lump in my throat tightens. "Remember the other week, when Donnie accompanied us to dinner? Everyone assumed she was with you."

He rights himself, releasing me from his grip, but I'm not done. "The hostess asked how long you'd been together and the waiter held out a chair so you could sit beside her, complimenting you for having such a 'fine lady' at your side." My voice quivers with my final words. "That was hard to take, so don't judge me for what I'm feeling, especially when she comes here to my home looking for you."

I'm not exaggerating. That's what happened the last time Donnie was with us. Despite my close proximity to Salvatore, everyone stopped to look at him and Donnie as they passed, assuming they were the perfect pair. I probably would have assumed the same thing and, because of it, did my best to dismiss the experience with a smile. It beat finding the nearest hole to crawl into.

It wasn't anyone's fault, but that didn't mean I wasn't hurt or offended.

I lower my chin when he takes my hand and leads me out of the kitchen and across the living room. He sits on my bed, holding my hips and positioning me in front of him when it's clear I won't join him.

"I'm sorry," he says.

He told me the same thing that night, after he made a point to tell the hostess and waiter that he was with me. He also spent the rest of the night with his arm around me, showing anyone who noticed that I was the woman he was with.

It was sweet. But the blows to my ego left an impact that was hard to shake, more now following Donnie's appearance.

Even as his fingers stroke my hips, the humiliation I felt that night resurges.

"Remember that idiot you were talking to. Sam?"

My brows raise, both because he catches me off guard and I don't know where he's headed. "You mean Max, the part-time counselor?"

He nods, though it seems to annoy him when I say his name. "Want to know what I thought when I saw you with him?"

"That you wanted to pound him to a bloody pulp?" I offer, although I'm not joking.

"Yeah. I did. There stood the perfect guy for my woman." He pauses. "Someone you'd probably go for, if you weren't with me."

I realize what he's saying. But Max isn't who I want. "Salvatore," I begin, only for my voice to trail when I catch his expression.

"I wear a suit," he says. "That doesn't make me a professional, or a man someone would picture you with. I'm not clean cut. I didn't go to college. And I'm nowhere near where I want to be for us." He glances briefly toward the picture of my dog, Moonlight. "That doesn't mean I'm not trying. And it sure as anything doesn't mean I want anyone else. *You* have the power to destroy me, Adrianna," he says, stroking a strand of my hair away from my face. "*You're* the one holding all the cards and you don't even fucking know it."

My hands slide over his shoulders as I search his face, my heart clenching over what he tells me.

"I wish you could feel everything I feel when I look at you," he says. "I wish you could understand how alone I am without you. If you did, you'd never doubt who you are to me."

His large hand smooths along my cheek to gently hold my face. I mean to say something, so he knows that I feel the same way. But as quickly as my thoughts come, so does his mouth against mine.

"I'm sorry," he says once more, his breath a sweet whisper along my cheek. "Please, *mia bella*. Let me show you what you mean to me."

He pulls me in to straddle him, his tongue eagerly welcoming my taste. My hips instinctively shift against his lap, rubbing hard. He scrunches his eyes closed and his head lolls back, exposing his throat.

I nip his chin and slide my tongue along his ear, adding more pressure to his lap. I expect him to flip me over and yank off my clothes, but he allows me to play and take control. As I nibble his neck and rock my pelvis, I pop the buttons loose from the front of my pajamas. When I reach the last, I pull his head forward, and offer him a breast to suck. My taut nipple skims over his lips just once. He cups the swell, his tongue flicking greedily.

My head snaps back and my hips grind harder when his pulls turn deliciously aggressive. He tugs off my bottoms as I free his erection, my body anxious to receive his.

My movements are clumsy, not as smooth as I'd like. But as I fall onto his lap and join our bodies, I tap into that wild side that wants nothing more than to please her lover. He groans as I increase my speed, alternating between bouncing and gliding. Our gazes lock as he continues to touch me.

"That feels so good, baby," I whimper, biting down on my lip when my core tightens and grips him further.

It doesn't take me long to peak, not with his lustful stare upon me, not with how his hold on my hips helps me go faster. Our lovemaking is loud, sinful, *powerful*, and he likes it. No, he likes *me*. I orgasm two more times before he finally releases, his body bucking beneath mine.

I smile as he fills me, rocking slowly and holding him gently. Yet when his stare drills into mine and his fingers tease the points of my breasts, I'm not sure either of us is ready to stop.

He rolls me onto my back, pushing up to stare at my face as his hand glides between my breasts. "I'm going to pull out, okay?" he says, his quick breathing making it hard for him to speak.

I edge up on my elbows, shifting my hips to draw his attention and keep him in place.

He lowers his lids and releases a curse. "Aedry, I'm not supposed to be here. Don't make it harder for me to leave you than it already is."

I gasp when he pulls out. Again, he curses, falling beside me. "You're leaving?" I ask, tilting to face him.

He opens his eyes then, but only partly, stroking my face. "I'm supposed to go round with Vin. But I couldn't stand the thought of not seeing you, even for a little while. Lucca is covering for me."

"You're going to watch Vincent as he visits his other establishments?" It's something he hasn't done, or at least mentioned, in a while. I was hoping that after the last incident, someone else would accompany him. Or that Vincent would request a police escort.

"The businesses he's checking in on are in a better area," he assures me, likely reading my thoughts. "It should be fine."

"But you don't know for sure, do you?" I ask.

He strokes my hair. "If he didn't need a security team, he wouldn't have hired me. North Jersey, it's getting worse when it comes to gang violence and people desperate for money. I have to make sure someone running a business and trying to stay ahead like Vin succeeds. You understand?"

"I suppose," I say. "I only wish it didn't have to be you."

"It's either that or strip for money," he adds, smiling. "Both pay about the same. If you prefer, I'll consider switching professions."

"That's a great idea," I say, beaming. "Maybe I'll do the same. Ripping off my clothes in front of a room filled with lonely men has to pay more than counseling."

I crack up when he scowls. "What's the matter?" I ask. "Can't the brooding wall of muscle take a joke?"

"You're lucky I like you," he says, adding the smirk that makes my toes curl.

Our humor dwindles as we both remember he needs to leave. My arms encircle his neck, anyway. "Can you encourage Vincent to hire police protection, or perhaps use Lucca more frequently?" I don't know Vincent, and this is my first time hearing Lucca's name. The idea of anyone getting hurt, even people I don't know, upsets me. But the thought of anything happening to Salvatore terrifies me. When I think about what happened the last time he rounded with Vin, I just want to hold him against me.

"There's a reason Vin hired me to look after him and those he associates with. I'm good on my feet and even better with my hands. It's my job, Aedry. Lucca . . . he's still new. He's learning, but Vin still wants me to handle the majority of his security." He shrugs. "As far as the cops go, there's a lot of shady shit going on within the county. Nothing ever came of the police report we filed last time, so Vin doesn't feel cops are people he can count on."

"Oh," I respond, not bothering to hide my disappointment.

"Give me time, okay?" he asks. "I'm trying to figure out a way I can do something else. Believe me, I don't want to keep doing what I'm doing."

I nod. Although he doesn't discuss his work much, I know he's not happy at his job, and that it's not something he looks forward to.

"I have to go," he reminds me, although I'm still not ready to let him go.

"Will you at least stay for dinner?" I ask. "I ordered a lot of food. I was really hungry."

"I noticed," he says, watching me carefully. "Do you think you're pregnant?"

My body warms. "No, just hungry. I skipped out on lunch to check on a student."

He frowns. "You went to someone's house? I don't like it," he says, before I can answer. "Anything can happen to you."

"It was at a shelter where she's staying. I'm trying to keep her in school."

"I still don't like it," he says. "Nothing can happen to you, ever. Understand?"

"I think I do," I say, returning his focus so he'll see I worry about him, too. "Please be careful tonight. And call me when you're done so I know you're okay."

He nods, as if he doesn't want to think about things, but then his stare skips to my alarm clock. "Shit," he mutters. "I have to go."

He shuffles to the edge of the bed, fixing his pants. Sometime during our lovemaking, my laptop fell to the floor. I didn't notice until he lifts it and places it on the mattress beside him. He glances over his shoulder, giving me a wry smile. "You know you don't need that, right?"

With the exception of my pajama top draping my arms and shoulders, I'm completely naked. I know I shouldn't tempt him, but it's hard to watch him go. I crawl across the bed on all fours, straddling him before he can protest.

He hauls me close, kissing me hard. I moan, the crotch of his pants pressing against my tender folds in a way that both aches and entices. I bite down on his lip in a way that drives him wild.

"Are you sure you have to go?" I say, gasping as the throbbing in my core accelerates.

He spits out a curse and drops his gaze. But when he returns his focus on me, I know I'm not the only one who craves more. "I don't want to leave you or the sight of this face," he tells me.

His words cause me to smile, even though they're not the ones I long to hear. I try to make a joke, realizing I'm making it harder for him to leave and hoping to alleviate some of the growing strain between us. "Even when this face looks like this?"

He doesn't return my smile, cementing me in place with the power of his stare. "This face is the one that haunts my dreams and lures me to your bed. I can't be without it, and I especially can't be without you." He releases a heavy sigh. "It's taking everything I have to leave you, Adrianna. I don't know how the hell I ever lived without you . . ."

Chapter Nineteen
Salvatore

I walk into my apartment to find my brothers and Aedry dancing in the living room. The TV is blasting with some shit that can't possibly be real music. Aedry is in a red dress that looks painted on, giving me a view of her perfect curves as she moves. Her dark hair sweeps along her shoulder blades like a silk sheet. She hasn't cut it since I told her I like it long. And the way she looks . . . damn, she's gorgeous.

My shoulder falls against the wall as I watch her shake, bulging the jewelry box stuffed in my coat. I dropped a few bills on it and I still think it wasn't enough, not for what she means to me. The thing that's eating at me is it's not the ring I want to give her—the one where I ask her to be my wife.

Lies. All I've fed her is lies about what I do when I'm away from her—telling her anything to make her think my work with Vin and everything he's a part of is legit. I painted him to be a victim, an honest businessman fighting for the little guy. It's a hell of a task. Everything he does makes me sick.

My only cure from it all is Adrianna and how I feel when I'm with her.

Christ. How many rings did I look at before settling on the bracelet? Hell, I don't know. That gnawing feeling, and the way my gut clenched when I realized I might be making a mistake, shifted my attention to the other side of the store. It's not that I don't want her to be my wife. It's more like I'm afraid she'll say yes.

I want a big house with a big yard for her, my boys, and whoever else comes along. But until I save enough, the only way to have the cash I need is to move up the ranks the way Vin's expecting. But I can't.

As much as the world will be better off without some of the scum he deals with, I don't want those same tainted hands that pull that trigger or dig that knife to touch the beautiful woman dancing in front of me. No, I can't soil her with my sins any further. And I can't look my brothers in the eye, and tell them to be good men, when I can't even manage to be a good man for them.

When it comes to my future, I do a lot of thinking, but my thoughts always return to Aedry and how much I want to marry and make babies with her. But each time I deal with Vin's shit, I'm reminded that I can't bring a child into the world knowing that from one breath to the next, I could leave this world and Aedry to raise our babies alone.

I shove the velvet case deeper in my pocket, knowing that for now, I'm making the right choice by waiting to give her that ring.

I push off the wall and step forward as the three of them spin to whatever the hell they're dancing to and see me standing there. Aedry squeaks and stumbles back in surprise, while my brothers scramble to the couch, like I didn't see them shaking their asses to that stupid song.

"Hi," Aedry says, smiling brightly and hurrying into my arms. "I didn't see you there."

My eyes cut to my brothers as my hands glide along her bare back. "I can see that," I say. "What'd you do? Lose a bet?" I ask them.

"Leave them alone," Aedry says, kissing my lips. "We were just having a little fun."

"It looked it," I say.

My brothers smirk, but they can't hide their reddening faces. They always act tough, except around Aedry. Like with me, she has a way of drawing out their not-so tough sides.

"Ready to go?" I ask.

"Yes. I just need my shoes." She walks back to the side of the couch, lifting a pair of spiky black platforms from a box beside a pair of silver stilettos.

My brothers couldn't figure out what to get her for her birthday. She seems to like shoes, so that's what I suggested. Damn fine choice by the way her hips sway when she walks toward my brothers after slipping them on.

She bends to kiss Apollo on the head. "Happy Birthday, Aedry," he tells her, swinging his arm around her.

"Thank you, cutie," she says, turning to hug Gianno. "And thank you both for the shoes."

"Yeah. Thanks," I say, as she strolls back toward me.

Gianno frowns. "You're the one who picked them out," he points out.

"Only 'cause I knew she'd look hot in them," I say, nibbling on her ear when she reaches me.

"Behave," she murmurs.

"Only because we have company," I murmur in return.

I pull away and help her with her coat. "Don't stay up too late," I tell my brothers.

"What time will you be home?" Gianno asks.

He lifts the controller to his PS5, trying to act casual. He's slick, but the shift in Apollo's posture gives him away. "Soon," I respond.

"Soon?" he questions.

I smirk. "Soon enough to catch whoever you plan to sneak in," I answer.

They grumble as I lead Aedry out. Yeah, I know them a lot better than they think. I stop to kiss Aedry for real as we wait for the elevator.

"Happy Birthday," I tell her, holding her close. I reach beneath her coat, pressing my palm on her lower back, my lips passing along her crown. "You look beautiful."

"Thank you," she says, sighing softly.

"You okay?" I ask.

She starts to nod when I peg her with a look that tells her I know she's lying. "Rough day. It's better now that I'm here."

I keep my arm against her as we step into the elevator. "The kids at school giving you shit?"

"No, but because of budget cuts, I maybe out of a job," she says.

I clutch her hand and lead her out, trying to keep my voice steady. Aedry wants to save the world, one kid at a time. And some of these kids need serious saving. To hear she won't have that opportunity seriously pisses me off. "Why you?" I ask, opening the door to my ride for her. "You're the best counselor they have."

She doesn't answer until I slide into the passenger seat and lock my seatbelt in place. "No, I'm the newest full-time counselor they have. The principal is trying to see what he can do to help, but it doesn't look good."

I try to keep my face relaxed as I pull onto the main road, aware that I'm frowning. "All those kids you're seeing? What's going to happen to them?"

"They'll be divided among the part-time staff they keep," she answers, trying to keep her composure.

These kids count on Aedry in ways that extend past her duties. I get that they need to let people go. It's happening everywhere. But she's the one the staff should be fighting to hang on to.

"Have you thought about going into private practice?" Not that it's something I want. I don't like the idea of her being alone with someone who could hurt her.

"It's not something I can afford to do at this time." She slips off her coat. Now that it's late March, it's not as cold. But there's something in the way she wriggles out of it that catches my eye.

"What aren't you telling me?" I ask.

"I don't want to talk about this now," she says, her voice growing sad.

I shake my head. "Aedry, you can't say something like that and expect me to let it go."

She rubs her hands against her thighs. "Even if the principal comes up with more money, it will only be a part-time position at best. I can't make my expenses on such a small salary. He said . . ." She gives herself a moment. "There's a chance he might have to let me go before the school year ends."

"The fuck?" I say. "How can they do that to you—and these kids?"

At first, I don't think she'll answer. "There have been some expenses they hadn't counted on, including damage to the roof following that bad snowstorm in February and some vandalism that occurred over Winter break. He has to make some difficult choices and, in his mind, it's easier to lose one counselor than one teacher."

"Quit," I say. "If this is the way they're going to treat you, leave."

"Salvatore . . . I can't."

I pull onto the road leading to the restaurant. "Move in with me or not. Either way, I'll support you until you can get a better job and less misery."

Her hand finds its way to my lap. "I can't leave those kids until I'm asked," she says.

And I'm not moving in, she doesn't bother saying.

We don't talk the rest of the way to the restaurant. But maybe it's better. She's heartbroken over the possibility of leaving a job she loves and is committed to. Me, I'm pissed they broke her heart.

She pauses when the valet opens her door. "Let's forget about what I said, okay?" she pleads. "I just want to have a good time."

I throw my door open when she steps out, dropping the key in the valet's hand. I don't say anything as we make our way into the restaurant. If she were my wife, I'd support her, take care of her, and that's all there would be to it. But she's not and there's not a damn thing I can do about it. Not now.

Shit.

We sit in a quiet booth away from the noise of the main dining area. But when the waiter spouts the special and leaves to put in our drink order, she places her menu down and reaches for my hand. "Don't be angry, love," she says.

My thumb swirls over her knuckles. "I'm not mad at you," I say. "That doesn't mean I like how you're being treated."

"It's no one's fault," she says. "Not really."

I'm ready to argue, but as the candlelight shimmers against Aedry's deep blue eyes, my anger rights itself and only she remains. Her day sucked. That doesn't mean her night has to.

Something in my features causes her to smile. She slides closer, leaning her shoulder against me. "I love you," she whispers.

My chest tightens in that way it always does when she speaks those words. She doesn't tell me she loves me much, but every time, it causes me more pain than pleasure. Maybe she guesses as much, which is why she limits how often she says it. I wish she didn't have to, just like I wish I could say it in return. I feel it. I know it's real. But if I tell her, I'll never be able to let her go. Even though one day I may have to, just to keep her safe.

The knowledge that I may one day leave her drives a chisel through my heart. But I can't think that way, not tonight. Tonight, she's still mine.

I rummage through my pocket and place the velvet box in front of her. She lifts her head. "What's this?"

"Your present."

"I thought dinner was my present." She laughs. "That and the tiny piece of fabric you called a negligee."

"You called it a negligee," I remind her. "I call it something small enough to snap off with my teeth."

The waiter returns with our drinks. I put in an order for shrimp cocktails and crab cakes, knowing both are Aedry's favorite. "You know me so well," she says.

"We'll see," I tell her, motioning to the box.

She waits for the waiter to disappear before carefully lifting the velvet case. But when she opens the lid, all she does is stare, her eyes widening in her shock.

She glances from the box, to me, back to the box. "Salvatore . . . this is too much."

I kiss her head. "Not for you."

The way her face lights up, I regret not getting her that ring—the platinum one with a two carat square cut diamond in the center with another carat of diamonds surrounding it in an antique setting. She would have loved it and maybe even would have said yes.

"Thank you," she says, kissing my cheek.

"It's just a bracelet," I tell her.

"I mean for being so good to me," she whispers.

Her comment gives me the barest pause. Damn, I love her so much, it sometimes hurts. But tonight, that pain is even more severe.

"Will you help me put it on?" she asks, sparing me from having to say something more.

She carefully lifts the bracelet and places it in my hand like she's afraid to break it. I clasp it around her wrist, lifting her hand to kiss it. "You like it?"

"It's stunning," she answers, mesmerized by how the row of diamonds and sapphires sparkle in the candlelight.

Dinner is good, even better than I expected, but mostly because of the company. My woman is happy, smiling, making me forget everything that's wrong with my life until I catch sight of Vin and Donnie on our way out.

I clutch Aedry against me, trying to shield her more by instinct. Son of bitch. What is he doing on this side of town?

If we weren't walking straight toward them, I'd edge us back to the bar and try to give them the slip. But he's already seen me and so have the two men watching his back.

I force a smile and keep going. "Hey, Sal," he says, grinning like an old pal. He leaves his men behind. Donnie stays glued to his side, pretending she's not high and that this isn't the first time in weeks that Vin's done more than fuck her.

I see right through her and him. I don't like it, and I don't like the way his attention drifts toward Aedry.

I shake his hand. "Hey," I say. "Just on my way out."

"Who's this?" he asks, tilting his chin toward Aedry.

"Sal's woman," Donnie chimes in.

Donnie answers before I can respond with something vague that won't fucking give away Aedry is more than a one-night stand. My anger flares, feeling betrayed. If Donnie wasn't high, she'd know better than to tell Vin who Aedry is to me.

If that's not bad enough, she rushes forward, slinging her arm around Aedry and kissing her cheek. "Hi, sweetie," she says, making it clear they've spent time together. "I've missed you!"

"Hi, Donnie," she answers, carefully returning her hug.

When she'd showed at Aedry's, she'd hit rock bottom. I hated how she made Aedry feel, but as messed up as Donnie was, I couldn't just let her walk out. I needed to make sure she wasn't going to do something to hurt herself before I returned to Aedry.

The day after, me and Donnie had a long talk. I told her to keep her distance from Aedry and that if she needed a friend, to come to me and leave her out of it. She agreed, only because she didn't want it to hurt my relationship with Aedry. But the way she's clinging to Aedry now is stirring things up in a way I don't need.

Vin's shit-eating grin widens, irritating me more than it should. I'm ready to walk out, let him believe Aedry is just one of Donnie's slut friends I'm fucking, and hoping Donnie will sober up to tell him as much. But Vin, for all he does a lot of stupid shit, picks up on more than I want him to.

"Your woman?" he says, his focus on Aedry as she returns to my side. "I didn't know you had a woman."

Aedry straightens. I need to get her out of here, but I'm too slow.

"I'm Vincent," he says, offering his hand. My back stiffens as he turns her hand beneath his grasp and kisses it. "Sal's boss."

Aedry blinks back at him. "Oh, hi," she says, her smile wide, yet unsure. "It's nice to finally meet you."

"Finally?" he asks. He keeps his grin, but a lot of words go unsaid behind those teeth. "How long have you been together?"

"Not long," I say, before either woman can answer.

Based on my gruff tone, Donnie's common sense pokes through her haze and she realizes her mistake. Too bad it's too little, too late. She quiets, but so does Aedry. In trying to protect her, I disrespected her, which is the last thing I want.

"This is Adrianna," I say.

"Lovely," he says. "So, you have yourself a woman."

The change in who I was during dinner to who I am now doesn't go unnoticed. Aedry looks to me, appearing confused. I want to take her hand, assure her she's safe, and avoid embarrassing her any more than I already have. But Vin already knows there's something different about Aedry. I don't need him to realize how much or that I'd bleed for her without thinking twice.

I clamp my mouth shut as Donnie leans in to say something to him.

Vin cuts her off. "You like Italian food, Adrianna?" He smirks. "Or should I call you Aedry?"

"Italian is my favorite," she answers, smiling politely. "And please, call me Aedry."

He points at her. "Then you need to come to our house for dinner. My woman makes the best gravy in Jersey."

She clasps my hand, looking hopeful. "We'd love to," she says. "That's so nice of you to invite us."

Vin's full attention bounces to me. "Then we'll see you tomorrow at eight," he says, making it clear he's not asking.

"Vin, our table is ready," Donnie mumbles.

He smiles at Aedry, making like he's this Boy Scout, instead of the guy who was wiping blood off his face just two days ago. "All right. We'll see you then."

I watch him and Donnie step toward the dining area, followed closely by his men. I put my arm around Aedry and lead her away, pretending like Jersey's biggest crime boss didn't just invite us to dinner at his place.

Vin turns around, his stare meeting mine briefly before it skips to Aedry.

It's then I know I can no longer keep my two worlds from colliding. And that I can no longer shield the woman I love from their darkness.

Chapter Twenty
Aedry

Salvatore jogs toward me when he sees me edging out of my building trying to hang on to my food, purse, and the gift bag. "Hi, love," I say.

I steal a kiss as he reaches for my tray of baked rolls and pie. Tonight, he's wearing a new black suit and gray dress shirt. His focus travels down my figure, taking in the sleeveless pink dress he likes. My kiss, or perhaps my dress, draws that sexy half grin I can't get enough of.

Until he frowns. "Why didn't you wait for me? I would have helped you carry this stuff out."

"You're so cute when you brood," I tell him, easing his frown and causing his grin to return.

I slip my arm through the crook of his elbow and carefully walk down the small set of stairs. I'm wearing the silver shoes the boys bought me for my birthday, and have long since determined fashion can be deadly. I keep my eyes on my feet until we reach the walkway. "We're already running late," I remind him. "With Donnie going out of her way to make dinner, I didn't want to waste any time." I snuggle closer to him. "When you texted me that you were almost here, I came down to save us some time."

Sal has been working out in the gym a lot lately. Even when he's relaxed, his muscles bulge. Yet, it's the added tension my words cause that has me looking up. "What's wrong?"

He places the pie over the rolls long enough to open the driver's side door and pop the trunk. "Donnie isn't making dinner," he says.

Instead of slipping into the front, I follow him to the back, watching him as he sets the food down and secures it with a net.

"Is she ordering food?" I ask, aware I'm not getting the whole picture.

He slams the door closed. "No," he answers, placing his hand on my lower back and leading me to the front. I pause before slipping inside and securing my seatbelt, eyeing Sal as he walks around the front of his SUV.

He slides in, keeping his focus away from mine.

"Is she sick?" I press.

"No." He rubs his jaw, appearing irritated as he pulls onto the main road. I wait for an explanation, but instead he motions to my gift bag on the floor. "What is that?"

"A house warming gift for Donnie and Vincent. I hadn't realized they'd moved in." It's how I answer, because it's what I believed. But now I know it's not true. I glance at the bright orange bag with the glittery white tissue paper poking through, feeling foolish.

"Salvatore, please tell me what's going on."

He takes his time answering, as if attempting to spare me from some awful truth I don't need to hear. "We're not having dinner with Vincent and Donnie," he says. "We're having dinner with Vin and his wife."

"What?" I squeak, certain I misheard.

He pulls onto the highway, his expression rigid. "Donnie is Vin's *gumad*, his mistress. Rita is his wife." His eyes slant my way. "I take it Donnie never bothered to tell you."

"No," I say, my voice tightening. "She—" I cut myself off, feeling my skin prickle with heat.

I have to admit, it takes me a long while to answer. "She always referred to him as the love of her life, and spoke of their relationship as if they've been together for a long time. When she said he wouldn't commit to her, I didn't realize it was because he was already committed." My attention wanders around the cabin, as if searching for something that would have clued me in long before this. "Why would she date a married man?"

"Because of what he gives her," he replies, although by now I figured it out.

"It's not that I know these things don't happen," I say, trying to clarify what I'm feeling and work through how blind I've been. "But Donnie can have anyone. Why would she settle for being second best when she's capable of so much more?"

He shifts in his seat. "For Donnie, being second best to Vin is better than being nothing at all. She's been with him a long time, even longer than Vin's been with Rita."

"Donnie came first," I say.

"Yeah. She did." He sighs. "The thing you have understand about Donnie is she always wanted to be a kept woman. When she saw Vin, she saw her chance. She expected him to marry her, but then Rita came along. Vin married her, instead."

"But he didn't let Donnie go."

"No," he answers. "And Donnie didn't want to walk away."

I start to speak, but my thoughts return to the previous night. When Vincent said "our house" and "my woman," I thought he was referring to Donnie. It's no wonder she didn't text me back when I asked her what to bring or why Sal was so tense during our encounter. That *bastard* invited us to *his* home, to *his* wife, in front of *his* mistress!

"I don't want to go," I tell Salvatore. "I don't want to be a part of these lies."

He curses under his breath and rubs at his jaw. "We have to. Otherwise Vin will take it as a sign of disrespect. According to him, Rita's been cooking the gravy all day and is excited to meet you."

"I don't like this," I insist.

"I don't, either. But even if it's just this one time, we have to be there."

"Oh, my God," I say, pushing the hair out of my face. "Does Rita know about Donnie?"

"It's not our business, Aedry."

It's not, but . . . "Why didn't you tell me?"

"I thought you were trying to be nice to Vin, because he was my boss. It was your birthday. When we got back to your place, I wanted to make it and keep it about you—not this shit he pulls all the fucking time."

I never understood why Sal was so tight-lipped about who he works for. But now that I realize what kind of sleaze his employer is, I can't blame him.

"I'm going to tell you something about Vin," he says. "Something I don't usually talk about."

I expect him to tell me something worse, or that Donnie is one of many women he keeps around. But what he says makes me realize how complex his relationship with Vin really is.

"I wasn't winning the case against the state for guardianship over my brothers," he says. "I didn't have the age, degree, or occupation to be considered an appropriate guardian. It didn't matter I was the only family willing to step up. Or how much I love them. The court saw what they wanted to see, and it sure wasn't anything that worked in my favor."

The way he speaks reflects his frustration and likely the bitterness he experienced.

"Vin and me, we'd been friends for a long time. I'd helped him out when we were kids. He remembered and helped me when it mattered most." He glances at me. "He paid for that big shot attorney and he gave me a job. If it wasn't for him, Apollo and Gianno would have stayed in the system and been split apart."

And likely molested and abused, he doesn't mention. But he doesn't have to. I'm familiar with the child welfare system, and I recognize how badly it's broken.

"I had no one to turn to. All I had was Vin and he came through." He shrugs. "I owe him, Aedry. I wish I didn't, but I can't forget what he did."

"I'm sorry," I say, not only for what he's feeling now, but also for everything he went through.

He seems to realize, lifting my hand when I place it on his lap and squeezing it gently. I don't like Vincent and I'm not certain Salvatore does either. But we both know what could have happened if Sal hadn't been granted custody of his brothers.

As much as I'm grateful for what Vin did for Salvatore, and Gianno and Apollo, too, I can't excuse his treatment of Donnie or his wife.

"I still don't like this," I say.

"I know. I don't, either. We'll go. We'll play nice. And we'll leave."

"I don't have to see him again?" I ask.

He looks at me then. "No. I swear to Christ, I'll never let you near Vin again."

We remain quiet the rest of the ride to Bergen County. It takes roughly half an hour for us to reach the gated community. I expect the security guard on watch to step out with a machine gun, or at least demand identification. But all he does is nod Sal's way before the gates part and we're allowed through.

The entire development is packed with opulent homes surrounded by even more gates. It's all too much. No sense of community or home. This isn't a place where a neighbor would knock on another's door to borrow a cup of sugar, or where block parties would take place.

"I didn't expect him to live like this, especially with the types of small businesses he owns." My voice trails. "Sal, how does someone who owns the shops you described in the locations you mentioned live here?"

"Vin comes from old money," he says. "And all those businesses add up. He has investments all over the country."

"He does?"

"Yeah, but it's the places here in Jersey that give him problems based on where they're located."

What he says makes sense. But I can't shake the feeling there's more to it. "This place is so over the top," I say, when we pass another immense estate. "What kind of people live here?"

"Celebrities, people with money to throw around," he answers.

"More businessmen like Vincent?" I ask.

He pauses before answering. "That's right."

He doesn't seem affected, appearing relaxed. I can't say I feel the same way. My parents' house is sweet, and encompasses the certain warmth every home should have. Everything here seems sterile and cold. "Have you been here a lot?" I ask.

"A few times. For their house warming, engagement, and Christmas party. That sort of thing."

"Christmas party?" I ask.

He rolls to a stop in front of a gate with a large white mansion perched on a hill, angling in his seat to face me. "Yeah," he says, stroking my jaw with his finger.

When he told me he couldn't come to North Carolina for Christmas because of his work schedule, I didn't press, recognizing the hours he keeps. Perhaps I should have asked. "Is this the reason you wouldn't come home with me?"

"I didn't choose Vin over you," he says. "I was only trying to spare you from all this." He leans in for a kiss, trying to reassure me. But it's not enough to squelch the horrible churn in my belly when the gates clang open. "We won't stay long?" I ask.

"Dinner, dessert, and we're out," he promises.

He pulls ahead, stopping in front of a large circular driveway. I almost expect a butler to rush through the double doors. But when they open, Vin steps through, followed by a young woman who reminds me of Amy Winehouse.

"Hey, Sal," Vin says, shaking Sal's hand as he shifts the food he's carrying beneath one arm. I try not to cringe when he kisses my cheek or think about where those lips have been. "Aedry, nice to see you again."

I nod in a way I hope appears polite and perhaps shy, instead of what I'm really feeling. Without meaning to, my thoughts wander to Donnie. She's no innocent lamb for choosing to be with a married man, but I can't help feeling sorry for her. She's miserable during the best of times and so lonely when he's gone. And Vincent's wife . . . I don't even know her and my heart breaks for her.

Salvatore keeps me close to him as he bends to kiss her cheek. "Hi, Rita," he says. "Good to see you." He draws me to him. "This is Aedry."

Rita's smile is wide and she immediately throws her arms around me. "Hi, Aedry. So good to meet you, sweetie."

"Hello, Rita," I say. I return her hug. Like with Donnie, I sense her underlying loneliness, making it hard to keep my smile. "Thank you for inviting us to your home."

"Of course!" she squeals. She turns to Sal, smiling as if she approves. "This is who you've been hiding from us? She's gorgeous—*gorgeous*," she emphasizes in her thick Jersey accent. She lifts the tray of rolls and pie from his hands and leads us into the house. "Come in, come in, I'm dying to get to know her."

I hold tight to my smile. I don't want to be rude or take my tray of rolls and smack Vincent over the head with it. Oh, wait. I do.

The house-warming gift I purchased is going back to Macy's tomorrow with the hopes I can exchange it for a castration set, or perhaps something with metal teeth I can rip Vin's balls off with.

"You all right?" Sal whispers in my ear.

I nod and lie. "I've been fighting a migraine all day."

He knows I don't suffer from migraines, but he runs with what I'm trying to say. "If you start to feel worse, let me know and I'll take you home."

"Rita sometimes gets migraines," Vin interjects.

I'll bet she does being married to you.

"She can probably give you something she takes," he offers, helping me out of my coat.

"That's not necessary. Thank you," I say, watching him place my coat and Sal's in the closet.

As I feel my temper surge, I remind myself of what Vincent has done for Salvatore, his brothers, and the community. But a man who mistreats women isn't one I can like or respect.

My heels *clip-clop* across the white and black marble tile as I try to relax. "You have a lovely home," I say. It is beautiful and modern, but almost too perfect. There's no personality, only a reminder of the wealth within it.

Rows of oil paintings and artwork take up every few feet. The expanse of foyer and hall are not overcrowded, but it's clear each one cost a small fortune.

"Thank you," Rita responds, motioning to the food in her hands as Vin escorts Sal into another room. "What have you got here?"

"Just dinner rolls and an apple pie," I answer. "I didn't know what I should bring and I was too intimidated to make anything remotely Italian."

Her laugh lifts my mood, but only slightly. "You're a doll. Why don't you go into the parlor? I'll be in soon with some hors d'oeuvres."

"Oh, no. Please, let me help," I tell her, hurrying behind her as she walks into an immaculate gourmet kitchen. I would have offered either way, but I'll admit there's a huge appeal in keeping my distance from Vincent.

The hem of her tight black dress skims just above her knees. She's my height, but tiny, with perfect round breasts I'm assuming Vin paid for.

My eyes scan the large kitchen. I've never seen wealth of this magnitude.

"What does Vincent do for a living?" I ask, wondering briefly if she'll tell me something different than what Sal has. I shouldn't doubt him, but this . . . this so much.

"You don't know?" she asks casually.

"Salvatore doesn't really discuss work much," I answer, which isn't far from the truth.

"Oh." She bends to remove a tray of tiny quiches from a large industrial oven. "He owns several businesses, hardware stores, diners, things like that."

It's what Sal had said. But being here, I can't help wondering how much money can be made from screws and Taylor ham sandwiches. "He's also part owner of a few casinos," she adds.

I'm almost relieved to hear the news. *Okay. That makes sense.* "I'm surprised you don't live closer to Atlantic City," I comment.

Rita raises her brows. "Ever been to Atlantic City?" She laughs when she catches my grimace. "Yeah. It's nicer being close to New York, don't you think?"

"It is," I agree. I wash my hands and dry them on a towel. "How can I help?"

She gives it some thought. "I have tomatoes, fresh basil, and the best *mutzadel* here in Jersey. Would you prepare it and add some balsamic and oil?"

She doesn't tell me how to prepare it exactly, assuming I know. I can't help wondering if she's testing me. But if this test is about food, I might actually pass. "Of course," I reply.

She lays the items out in front of serving plate, but as she turns to the stove to stir a large pot of pasta sauce, my eyes travel to a box of toothpicks.

"Do you mind if I use these?" I ask, when I realize that it's cherry tomatoes and mozzarella balls I have to work with.

"Use whatever you'd like, Aedry," she answers, without turning around. "This is your house."

"Thank you. You're very kind," I say, reaching for the small box. She's trying to be nice. I need to do the same.

I spear a cherry tomato, add a ball of mozzarella, a bent leaf of basil and repeat the process until I have what resembles a pretty flower. I place it on the plate and reach for another toothpick.

"So . . . how long have you and Salvatore been together?"

"A few months," I answer, curving another leaf of basil.

Her frantic stirs to the sauce slow. "As in *three* months?" She taps the spoon against the pot. "Or more?"

I reach for another cherry tomato. She doesn't know anything about me, but she wants to, even though I'm not certain Salvatore would approve of how much I'm telling her. "I was trying to spare you," he'd said in the car.

"We've been dating since the fall," I answer, hoping I'm giving her enough, yet not too much away.

"It's been a while," she says, her voice trailing.

"Mmm," I answer, hesitating when I realize she's giving my answer a great deal of thought.

In the silence that follows, I prepare another stem of basil, tomato, and mozzarella. I'm hoping she'll move on or tell me more about herself. When she says what comes next, I almost fall to the floor.

"Have you met her yet?"

I place the stem on a plate, trying hard to keep my motions casual, even though I already suspect whom she means. "Who?"

"Vincent's whore," she answers.

In growing silent, I tell her exactly what she wants to know. She laughs without humor. "Come on, Aedry. I'm not blind. And I assure you I'm not stupid."

I turn slowly in her direction, my voice as leaden with sadness as my expression. "I don't think you're stupid, Rita."

She straightens, keeping her back to me from where she was placing my rolls in a wire basket. "She was here before me. So, she stays. But men don't marry whores, do they?" She glances over her shoulder at me. "They marry good women like us. Those who cook, who wait for them to come home, those they're not embarrassed to bring to church when they confess their sins, right?"

I don't answer, because she's not really asking. She's telling me how she feels.

"Have you met her? Donatella?" She huffs when my expression gives the truth away. "I know her name and I know what she looks like. I followed them once, right before we got married." Her voice cracks. "I wanted to see what she could give Vin that I couldn't."

"I'm sorry," I tell her, meaning it down to my soul.

"Don't feel sorry for me," she says, despite how her lips press together in her attempt to hold back her tears.

I abandon my station, walking slowly to her side. Out of instinct, I embrace her, gathering her carefully in my arms.

She stiffens against me with so much resentment, I'm sure she'll push me away. But then she returns my embrace and tells me something I don't expect to hear. "Thank you," she says, sniffling. "I promise to be there when it happens to you."

I break away, taking a step back. She was crying on my shoulder seconds ago, but now those tears are nowhere in sight. "What?" I ask.

She cocks her head, scrutinizing me closely as if I can't possibly be this naive. "Come on, Aedry. Salvatore and Vincent are cut from the same cloth. Do you think your pretty eyes will spare you from the control over women men like them crave? It won't be long before he leaves your bed for someone else's." Her irises sparkle with anger. "If he hasn't already."

"He wouldn't do that to me," I say, hating the sudden doubt that quivers my voice.

"Why?" she asks. "Because he tells you he loves you or swore before God that he wouldn't?" She lifts the back of her hand, twiddling her fingers to draw attention to the large engagement ring and wedding band. "That doesn't mean anything when power means more."

She motions to my side. It's not until I glance down that I realize she's pointing to my bracelet. "Did Salvatore give you that? What did it cost you? A night alone? Maybe more?"

My mouth is closed so tightly, my teeth ache. She strolls toward me, her hips swinging, and her steps barely registering over the increasing pounding in my ears.

She stops directly in front of me, sighing softly and shaking her head. "Whether you believe me or not, Sal will eventually get an extra friend to play with. Maybe more if he stays as tight as he is with Vincent." Her voice is casual. But she laughs when she catches a glimpse of my face. "Don't look so sad, Aedry. It's all a part of the game."

She may have gone from tears to laughter, but I don't find anything she says amusing. "What if I don't want to play?" I ask her.

"Ah, but you will play," she tells me. Her smile remains, yet it's not enough to hide the flickers of misery plaguing her face, and the sorrow lingering so close to the surface.

Her attention fixes on the bracelet Salvatore gave me. I don't fight her when she lifts my hand, not when I see how fast her light brown eyes pool with tears. "You'll play, because you love him . . . tut-tut-tut," she says when I open my mouth to deny it. "You know you do, despite knowing there's more to Sal's work than what he tells you."

My spine grows rigid enough to crack.

"You'll play the role of his devoted woman, you will," she tells me. "Just like you'll keep your mouth shut for pretty little things like this." The tip of her long red nail taps over my bracelet. "In exchange, he'll give you a nice house, his name, and babies. Those are good things, Aedry. There's no shame in that."

Slowly, she lowers my hand, her hips swaying as she returns to the stove. I barely move, a feeling of dread tightening my chest hard enough for me to clasp it.

As I watch, she opens the oven door and removes a covered dish. "Be a dear and finish up," she says, blindly staring at the wall. "Vincent's hungry. I don't want to keep him waiting."

Chapter Twenty-One
Aedry

Vincent entertains us with stories all through dinner. Rita enthusiastically and repeatedly jumps in, adding to Vincent's conversation in that animated way of hers.

Vincent is very funny and a natural storyteller. Strangely enough, neither his ability to spin a tale nor his quick wit squelch my urge to nut punch him.

This lying and cheating snake supports two women, lavishing each with gifts in exchange for their silence and obedience. He doesn't care whom he hurts, turning a blind eye to the tears they shed for him. And for what? To feel more like a man?

Bastard.

Sal sweeps his thumb over my hand beneath the table. I don't realize how hard I'm squeezing it until then. I glance down to see our interlaced fingers, hoping to find some comfort in the way his large hand presses against mine. On a different occasion, maybe his gentle hold would be enough to soothe me. Not tonight and definitely not here.

I smooth my free hand over my skirt. This should have been a fun night out. The meal was delicious and

Vincent and Rita went out of their way to make us feel at home. Rita bustled about, rushing to make certain everyone had everything they needed and more.

"Sit, Aedry. You're doing too much," she said after I helped lay out the food.

Vincent's gestures were more showy. He opened a bottle of wine I couldn't pronounce, nor was familiar with. The way Sal leaned back on his heels made me think it was outrageously expensive. And now, following the decadent dessert Rita spent hours preparing, they share a bottle of Scotch twice as old as I am.

"And that's when the little prick valet runs off," Vincent says, laughing as he finishes his story. "But I don't give a shit. I'm introducing myself and shaking a *legend's* hand."

Rita rolls her eyes. "Aedry, I didn't know what was happening. I'm like, where the hell is he going? I don't watch football. I don't know who this guy is."

"How could you not know him? He did that Nike commercial. The one with the puppy you like," Vin adds.

I'm barely listening to Vincent's tale about how a parking valet brought him a famous athlete's Jaguar, mistaking it for his. I'm so done with playing nice and I just want to go home.

They laugh when he motions back to the picture of Vin with the guy at the Super Bowl. Sal chuckles, but I can only manage a weak smile at best.

On the surface, Vin and Rita seem like such a happy, loving couple. It's almost easy to forget that they're willingly living a lie. But I'm just as bad, indulging them by keeping my mouth shut. And when it comes to Salvatore, I don't know what to think. Regardless of how tight I'm clinging to his hand, I can't help but be upset at him for accepting and being a part of this lifestyle.

He knows I'm not happy. I can tell by the way his thumb continues to stroke my hand. I all but sigh with relief when Rita stands to clear the table. I rise with her, carrying my plate and Sal's along with the tray of leftover pasta.

"That's a good woman you have there, Sal," Vincent remarks as I walk away.

Fuck you, I obviously don't say, even though I can feel his seedy stare crawling along my spine.

I'm rinsing the plates and setting them in the dishwasher when Rita sweeps in with the remains of our dinner. "Aedry, leave them. The maid will clean up in the morning."

"It's okay," I say, moving fast.

I don't like this dysfunctional relationship. In a way, I'm angry at Rita for putting up with it. Yet, I do feel sorry for her and for Donnie, too, despite her part in this. So, I fill the dishwasher and scrub a few pans. It's all I can do for her.

I'm drying my hands after wiping down the counter when Sal and Vincent step into the kitchen.

"Aedry, we should go," Salvatore says.

Rita throws her arms around me. "I wish you didn't have to," she says.

I think she means it. Maybe she sees a shared camaraderie with me. If so, she's wrong. No way would I put up with this *arrangement*.

"Thank you for a lovely dinner," I manage.

"You're welcome, sweetie." She hugs me again, this time tighter. "Let's get together for lunch next weekend. We'll make a day of it—get our nails done, do a little shopping." She whirls me around to face our men. "Vincent's treat. Right, Vin?"

Vin nudges Sal and motions to us. "See what having such a fine woman at your side is going to cost me?"

"I'll cover Aedry," Sal assures him, glancing my way.

He steps forward and into Rita's outstretched arms to thank her for dinner. But when Vincent reaches for me, I can't help recoiling from the reek of too much scotch on his breath and the way his kiss to my cheek lingers more than it should. The move is subtle, yet I don't miss the intent or the offer behind it.

And neither does Salvatore.

Salvatore hauls me to him before I can completely break away from Vincent's embrace, tucking me behind him. The two men lock eyes, their expressions tight, their stances rigid.

For a moment there's only silence and the promise of pain.

Sal's glare is as lethal as it was that night in the club when those men cornered me . . . seconds before he made them bleed and drew his gun.

I don't realize I'm not breathing until the air trapped in my lungs releases in a brutal rush at Vincent's laugh. He takes us in, the way Salvatore shields my body with his, and the way Sal's unyielding stare grinds a hole into Vincent's face.

"Never thought I'd see the day this would happen," Vincent says, continuing to watch us.

Sal's only response is to ease his hand away from his hip. Unlike Vincent, Salvatore isn't smiling.

Rita steps forward, her hands clasped in front of her as her attention skips between us. She realizes a great deal went unsaid in Sal and Vincent's tense exchange.

"It's late," I say, my nails skimming along Sal's back as I look up at him. "And we've troubled our hosts long enough." My words are only partially true. I want to get out of here before something happens that we'll regret. "I'm tired," I add, when he doesn't move, my voice pleading with him to walk away.

Salvatore stays fixed on Vincent when he answers. "All right," he says. "Goodnight."

As simple as that, it's as if nothing had occurred. Vincent laughs again and Rita starts yapping about this bistro she's dying to try in the city. They walk us out as I hold tight to Salvatore. It's taking everything not to sprint to the SUV and drag him with me.

Rita waves as we pull out of their long driveway. "I'll call you about lunch," she yells.

It's not until Sal turns onto the main road that he acknowledges anything close to what happened. "I'll leave you some bills for your time with Rita. If it's not enough, keep the receipt and I'll reimburse you—"

"I'm not going out with Rita."

"Vin won't be there," he responds in a way of an answer. "And that shit he pulled? It won't happen again now that he knows who you are to me." He keeps his attention ahead, but I notice his hands tighten on the wheel as if he's remembering how Vincent touched me. "Rita's different. She's not like him. She's just trying to be nice."

I don't agree. She plays this game as much as Vin. I'm ready to take my toys and go home. "Rita is lonely. She wants a friend who'll quietly support her lifestyle." My voice drops. "But I'm not her."

"If you shun his wife, Vin will see it as a sign of disrespect."

"Really?" I swivel in my seat. "So, it's okay for him to disrespect his wife by sleeping with Donnie and God only knows how many other women? But if I say no to lies and the lunches, and disapprove of all this, *I'm* the one being disrespectful?"

Sal cuts his stare my way. But it's not just my words or my tone that alerts him of my anger. "It's cultural," he says. "A man of Vin's status and position is expected to take other women *and* to have the means to maintain a mistress."

My face heats. "And as his friend, as someone in your position, is that expected of you, too?"

Sal stops the car at the light and turns to me, his gravelly voice as inflexible as his features. "Yes."

His admission is like physical blow. My first instinct is to scream at him. But the hurt overtaking me is so crippling, it's like a dam bursting. It's all I can do to beat back my tears.

"Adrianna," he says, curling his hands tighter around the steering wheel. "I would *never* do that to you."

"Is that what Vin told Rita?" I ask, my voice quivering as my tears release.

He doesn't answer me, kindling my sorrow, but also my anger. "In working for Vincent, you're around him a lot. Are you also there when those women he cheats with arrive?" Again, he doesn't respond, which tells me more than his words can then. "Salvatore . . . have you been with them, too?"

For the longest few seconds of my life, he remains quiet. When he answers, it's as if he brings down an ax on my heart. "Not since you," he tells me.

I turn to stare blindly ahead, breathing so hard, I swear I'm going to lose it. Damn it. God *damn* it.

I open my mouth, ready to demand that he tell me what exactly he means, only to shut it. As much as I feel I should know, the thought of some woman fondling him and expecting everything he does to me in our bed destroys what's left of me.

I should never have been with him. But now I know I'm in too far.

Chapter Twenty-Two
Salvatore

Aedry won't look at me, won't talk to me. What I said, about not being with anyone since her, is the truth. I meant to make her feel better—to reinforce who she is to me. But in admitting my past deeds, I fed her more of my poison and now she's dying before me.

She shrivels in her seat, like a wilting rose that once bloomed before I came along. I should let her go, back into the sun where she belongs and away from the damage I alone cause. But I can't. I may be her poison, but she's the one who gives me life.

When I pull in front of her building, I know she's going to run. This time, she's not going to slam that door in my face. I hit my seatbelt release before I finish pulling to the curb. I barely shift my ride into park before she storms away. I don't bother reaching for her. Instead, I move quickly, around the front of my SUV, hitting my key fob just as she bounds up the stairs to the main entrance.

My hand shoots out, blocking the door when she tries to swing it closed. She doesn't turn back, hurrying up the stairs. She knows I'm right behind her, keeping pace even when she pushes faster. At the top is where she flat-out runs, reaching her door and unlocking it. I'm not running, but I am hauling ass. I catch the door before she can shut it and prowl inside, slamming it behind me.

She whips around, backing away as I flip the deadbolt. "I'm not okay with this," she says.

Her eyes widen as I shrug out of my coat and jacket and toss them over the back of the bar stool. "Not okay with what?" I ask, loosening my collar.

She knows what I want and what I'm after. I tug the buttons of my dress shirt open, popping one off with the speed and force I'm using to peel out of my shirt. "I'm not okay with you being with other women," she stammers. She jerks her chin as I expose my bare chest. "Salvatore . . ."

I strip out of rest of my clothes, growing harder with each step I take toward her. She edges away, through the small living room, through the opening in her sheer curtains, and around the bed. I follow close, my steps relaxed, my posture easy, despite the heat searing its way through my groin. Her back smacks against the corner. There's nowhere else for her to go.

The shit Vin pulled sparked a possessive trait fierce enough to make me want to tear his throat out. That lingering kiss was meant to tempt her into his darkness and to give her a taste of what he wanted to do to her.

He doesn't get to have her. No one does.

I'll destroy anyone who tries to hurt her.

"Sal . . ." she says, as I draw closer.

Her tone drips with sex, the same way it does before I make her come.

A primal need to claim her overrides my senses, blurring my vision in a lust-filled haze. I need her legs wrapped around me and her begging me for it, just like I need to pump into her deep and fill her.

My hands slap against the wall on either side of her. "I won't be with you if you're with someone else," she stammers. "Do you hear me? I won't put up with that."

I take her hand in mine and kiss it, then slip it between us, gliding it over my stiff length. "Does it feel like I want anyone else?" I ask, my voice a hungry growl.

She trembles, but it's not out of fear. As much as I need her body and as much as it's killing me to wait, I'll never force her. She knows it.

Again, she trembles when my lips pass along the curve of her neck. "You're who I want. You're who I need," I whisper between flicks of my tongue. "Can you feel it, Adrianna? This is what you do to me."

My hold is loose enough for her to break away, she doesn't, keeping her strokes steady.

My hand leaves her, once again slapping against the wall as my head falls forward and my body curls around her. "I want you," I grunt against her ear, as her grip tightens and her speed increases. "I want you forever . . ."

I grit my teeth, gasping when she abruptly releases me. "I'm sorry," she says, her fingertips grazing along my chest, luring my focus toward her face. "I'm so sorry . . ." Her expression is stunned as she searches my features.

It's what she asks that nails me hard in the gut, knowing that if I answer there's no going back.

"Did you say 'forever'?" she asks, so softly I barely hear her.

I struggle to speak, every breath I'm taking burning with how bad I need to be inside her. "Don't you know what you mean to me?" I ask.

She shakes her head slowly, biting down on her bottom lip. My fingers smooth across her jaw line as I tell her the truth, feeling each word down to my soul. "I love you, Adrianna," I rasp. "You're my fucking world."

Tears flood her eyes, shimmering her dark blue eyes like jewels. "I love you, too," she whispers.

Her arms coil around my neck as my body and lips meld with hers. We're only kissing, but already she's whimpering the way she does when she starts to peak. She wants me. But I need to prove exactly how much I want her.

She breaks our kiss as I grind against her, her head falling back against the wall as she shrugs free of her coat and she hikes up her skirt. My mouth lowers to her neck and my hands seek out her breasts, pulling down the front of her dress to expose the tightening tips.

Aedry jolts as I suck. The wait has been too much for me and for her. She moves the crotch of her panties aside and reaches for me, rubbing the thick tip of my erection against her folds. But for what I want to do to her, I need her panties off. I tear them from her hips in one quick motion and haul her up to my waist.

I rush us to the bed, tossing her legs over my shoulders as I lower her to the bed. Any other night, I'd fall to my knees, dip my tongue between her legs, and play. But tonight is not the night I can take things slow. I slide into her in one easy motion. But when I thrust, it's deep, fast, and feral.

Aedry writhes beneath me, her body sliding against the sheets with each slam of my hips, swearing—screaming—moaning my name.

My hands grasp her ankles tight, carnal hunger increasing my speed. Each orgasm I give her causes her body to grip me tighter. I'm no match for the spasms clenching me. In one ruthless explosion I succumb, falling forward into her embrace.

I clutch her against me. "I love you," I gasp, kissing her face, lips, throat. "I swear to Christ, I'll never let you go . . ."

Chapter Twenty-Three
Salvatore

The night we had dinner with Vin and Rita was a turning point in our relationship. It could have ended badly and I could have lost Aedry forever. Instead, it bonded us and we spent the rest of the night making love.

I fought to keep from telling her how I feel, believing I'd somehow finish ruining her. Months later, we're still going strong.

Things aren't perfect. Not by a long shot. That night at Vin's solidified Aedry's suspicions that Vin isn't the respectable business owner or philanthropist he pretends to be.

The cash she's seen me carry, the gun I don't leave my place without, and the bruises I've come home with following sit-downs, are putting a strain on our relationship. While I'm not lying to her, I'm being far from honest.

"Are you involved with drugs?" she asked me.

"No. I wouldn't do that to you or to us."

"Prostitution?" she asked, in a way that seemed to kill her.

"No," I answered, putting enough force behind my words that she'd realize I'm not a part of that shit.

"What about weapons trading?" she pressed. "Sal, you need to tell me what Vincent does."

"Vin is a man with questionable morals and legitimate businesses." I snagged her waist and pulled her to me when she tried to walk away. "But I swear to you, I'm only in charge of security, making sure no one hurts him or Donnie."

Yeah. Donnie. She got back on his good side, not that it's going to last.

Aedry relaxed in my arms. She needed to hear that all of us, me, her, and my brothers, are safe.

They are. I'm not. But I couldn't exactly tell her that. I make it like the people Vin associates with and encounter are the problem. She doesn't know he's Mafia. If she did, she'd walk away, taking my soul with her.

For now, though, she's with me. And I'm going to make every day count.

The breeze sweeping in through the open taxi slaps against our faces, filling our noses with salty air mixed with the aroma of tropical flowers. To our right, the sun's setting on the horizon, casting light along the clear blue water. Jesus, the Cayman Islands are like heaven on earth, almost too beautiful to be real. Very much like this woman in my arms.

Aedry pushes her dark hair away from her face and looks up at me, smiling. "Great day," she says.

"Perfect," I agree.

She, my brothers, and me, along with Aedry's friend, Autumn, spent the day taking a private tour of the islands. When I asked Aedry what she wanted to do for Spring break, she said to spend time with me, Gianno, and Apollo.

"Let's celebrate with them. They've worked so hard."

She was talking a nice dinner out, maybe even a movie. I was talking a serious getaway. We did it my way, and we snagged Autumn along so she could watch my brothers, so Aedry and me could have some time alone. Aedry misses her friend, and for all she's "quirky" like Aedry describes her, she's a good friend to Aedry. Not like those skanks I saw her with at the club.

My hand sweeps over Aedry's golden skin. Her tan isn't as deep as mine, Apollo's, or Gianno's, but she's surprised me by managing some decent color, considering how light her skin is. Autumn is a different story. That redhead has to be the whitest person on this planet. And don't forget that she's spent the two days we've been here lathering her skin with SPF 100.

I didn't even know they made that shit.

"Laugh all you want, but I'm thwarting premature aging and skin cancer," she insisted when me and my boys cracked up following Gianno's offer to buy her a Mumu.

"Jesus, you look like a redheaded snowman with glasses," Gianno told her. "If you're 'thwarting' anything, it's a chance to get laid."

"Nah, some men like that igloo shit," Apollo countered.

We all lost it on that one. In fact, we've laughed a lot, which is good. When Vin offered up his secluded vacation home, I didn't want to take him up on it, sure there was a catch.

"Why are you looking at me like that? Can't a guy do something nice for a friend?" I didn't answer. Vin doesn't do something for nothing. "Come on, Sal. I didn't mean any disrespect. If I knew who Aedry was to you, I never would have put the moves on her. Let me make it up to you and your woman."

Me and Vin, we're all right. Not great, not bad, just all right.

He's tried to make amends with this trip and by leaving me to solely guard Donnie lately. But I can't let go of the shit he pulled with Aedry. He crossed a line that night. I can't forget it and I can't forgive.

"You okay?" Aedry asks, tracing my jaw with her fingertip.

"Fine. Just thinking it's good to be here."

"It's *amazing* to be here," she emphasizes. "Thank you for all of it." She looks behind her. "And for inviting Autumn. She never gets to have fun."

"She's going to have fun tonight."

"Why?" She tilts her head. "What are you up to, mister?"

"Mister?" I prompt. "What does that make you?"

"Someone who's happy to love you," she says.

My smile eases. I wish I could sit back and enjoy everything she gives me, but there's that part me that knows this woman is too good for me, and that what we have can't last. No matter how much I need it to.

Instead of complimenting her in return or maybe spewing some of that lovey-dovey crap pussies would say, I clasp her knee and rub it. It's my way of feeling close to her and letting her know I like her with me. "I'm sending them to swim with dolphins."

"Are you serious?" At my nod, she beams, but then she frowns. "Wait, then what are we doing?"

"You get to skinny dip with a shark."

"A shark?" At my nod, she starts laughing. "Does this shark's name happen to be Salvatore?"

"It's like you can read my damned mind."

I kiss her temple when she shakes her head. "They get dolphins and I get a naughty shark?"

"A naughty shark who has something nice planned. Trust me," I add, when she tries to argue.

She leans against my shoulder. "I do trust you," she whispers.

I know that. Which is why if she ever knew the type of man I worked for, it would be over between us. But I don't think about that now. I glance over my shoulder to where Autumn and Apollo are having it out over who made the best Spiderman.

"Christ," Gianno mutters. "It's like I died and went to Nerd Hell."

He slips out first when we reach the villa. Aedry stays with me as I pay our guide. As much as we're in paradise and have our own suite, our alone time hasn't been enough and I'm finding it hard to keep my hands to myself around my brothers.

I lift her for a kiss as the driver pulls away, lowering her slowly before leading her down the brick walkway. She glances around the garden as we step onto the front porch. "This place is so beautiful. I wish we could stay here forever."

To think what's waiting back for me in Jersey, with how bad Vin has screwed up, I can't say I don't wish the same damn thing. We step into the tile-covered foyer. Goosebumps spread along her arms as the air conditioning hits us hard.

She huddles closer to me, shuddering. "I'll admit, I miss the heat down South."

I almost suggest we move back to where she's from. Damn, I'm so tired of Vin and all the shit that comes with this lifestyle. But for now, the best thing I can do is keep putting money aside and investing like I have been.

In another year, I'll have enough in Gianno and Apollo's trust funds to get them through college. And the way my investments are taking off, one day, I'm going to take her and my brothers far away and open up my own MMA gym. But one day is still far away. And Vin isn't letting anyone leave. For now, I have to keep doing what I'm doing until I figure a way out.

The family room opens up to a wall of glass leading out to the lanai. Her eyes widen. The crew I hired already placed lit candles to float around the pool, and set a table of with white linens with fine china. Two chefs, one preparing appetizers and the other the main course, are already working hard to finish the elaborate dinner, while a server rushes to fill glasses with champagne.

"Hey," I call out when Apollo and Gianno head for the table where an older woman is placing jumbo shrimp cocktails on a tray. "You're taking your stuff to go."

Autumn pauses in the middle of reaching for a glass of champagne. "What's up?" she asks, looking at Aedry.

I motion with a tilt of my chin, so she can tell her. She grins at Autumn. "Salvatore arranged for you and the boys to swim with dolphins."

A round of "omigods" from Autumn follow a slew of "holy shits" from my brothers. They might have seemed hungry, but they scramble out the door when their cab arrives.

"Let's play Star Wars trivia on the way down," Autumn suggests when I tell them it's going to be an hour's drive.

"Nerd," I mutter.

"Devirginizer," she fires back, skipping past me.

I smirk. Like Aedry, Autumn doesn't take my shit. But it's Aedry's laugh that causes me to turn back toward our suite. She steps out in a strapless white dress that hugs her small curves and shows off her tan.

"I don't usually wear white," she says, her cheeks flushing when all I do is stare.

The dress falls above her knee, looking more bride than girlfriend. It's something I shouldn't like or want so damn much. But I do, even though every part of me that's still reasonable warns me against it.

"What's wrong?" she asks, softly.

She smooths her palms over my chest when I avert my gaze. The longer we're together, the more I know she's the one. I want to marry her. But while I told her I'd never let her go, I'm not sure how long I can keep her with me, even with what I plan to do tonight, and especially not with everything that's going down with the bosses.

"Salvatore?" she says.

"You look beautiful," I say.

"Thank you," she says like she doesn't believe me, like I don't mean every damn word. "You look really great, too."

I showered after making sure everything I planned was in place. It's hot outside, but I wore a long-sleeved white shirt, knowing it's a look she likes on me.

In the distance, thunder crashes, but it doesn't draw her attention. She walks slowly toward me, realizing something is messing with my head.

"What is it, love?" she says.

She had to go and call me that. I press a brief kiss to her lips. "Nothing. I just need to eat."

She nods and allows me to lead her to the table. She does a double-take when a local band is led into the lanai. I pull her against me. "I told you I don't dance. But tonight, I'll make an exception."

She beams through her shock. I pull out her chair, but just as she sits, Devan, one of the staff members approaches. "Sir, you have a phone call."

There's a hint of urgency in his features. I already know who's calling, but I don't let it show. "Someone's calling you here?" Aedry asks.

Rather than give some lame excuse or flat out lie I say, "I'll be right back."

I try to keep my pace steady as I follow Devan into our suite and take the call.

"Salvatore," I say as a way of a greeting.

The unsteady breath Vin releases warns me I'm in a shit ton of trouble even before he speaks. "You alone?"

Hell. What did you do?

"Yeah. What's up?"

"We have a situation."

He says "we." Like always, Vin makes his problem, my problem.

"What situation is that?" I say, already assuming I'm flying out tonight to fix whatever Vin fucked up this time. As much as I'm usually ready for anything, I'm not prepared for what he says next.

"Lucca is on the other side of the island, taking out Bianchi. Him, Encacio, Carlo, and two locals already wasted his first on the beach, and a couple of men, but there was another boss we weren't counting on being there, along with a few of his boys." He lets out another breath like he's taking a drag. Like the first, it comes out ragged. "Lucca's the only one left. He needs you to take out the other targets."

Rage unlike anything I've ever felt roils my stomach like lava. "You're telling me you sent me, my woman, *and* my family to the same fucking island where two mob bosses were meeting?"

"It wasn't supposed to go down like this," he says, his voice rattling.

"How the hell was it supposed to go down—when you're pitting every last boss against you?"

Vin pauses. He knows I'm pissed. That doesn't stop the words that shoot out of his mouth. Because he's scared and because he's not God damn here to take care of his own business—because he fucked up yet again—he plays the boss card, and he plays it hard. "Devan has the jeep for you. Ammo and the pieces you need are in the glove compartment. You're going to go to the compound, you're going to back-up Lucca, and you're going to take care of whoever threatens my position. Do you understand me, Sal? You *need* to do this."

"You mother*fucker*," I bite out.

The silence on the other line is like a death warrant itself. He didn't just set me up, he put everyone I love in danger. If Vin was standing in front of me, I swear to Christ I'd choke him with my bare hands.

"I'm not asking you," he says, making like I didn't call him what I did. "I'm telling you, do this."

He disconnects. It takes all I can not to tear this room apart.

He wanted me here for backup. He knew—*knew*—I wouldn't just hop on a plane and leave the country. So, he sweetened the opportunity by inviting my family.

Rage quivers my hand. It's Aedry's sweet voice that forces me to get it together. She knocks lightly on the door. "Salvatore? I'm sorry to interrupt, but the appetizers are ready."

I don't answer, wrestling with whether to snag her and my boys and get the hell out of here or do what Vin asks. If I try to escape, Vin will put a hit on me to keep face. No, that asshole won't do it himself. He hasn't got the balls. But the shit he's sending me to do . . . no way in hell will I get out of this alive without blowing someone's head off.

"Salvatore?" Aedry calls once more.

I swipe at my face, not realizing how bad I'm sweating until then. "Give me a minute, babe," I tell her. From the years and shit I've been handed, I shouldn't be surprised how steady I keep my voice. It comes with practice. But with Aedry and my family in danger . . . that's trouble I never counted on—not out of the country—not away from where I can protect them.

Right now, I don't have a choice. Right now, I'm Vin's bitch and he damn well knows it.

Chapter Twenty-Four
Salvatore

I open the door, expecting Aedry to be standing there. As I look out to the lanai, she's back in her seat and turned to where the band is playing a calypso version of a modern song. She looks . . . happy, sitting there with a tray of fresh oysters at the center of the table and two large shrimp cocktails placed at each setting.

Her smile fades as I approach.

"Is everything all right?" she asks.

I kneel in front of her and place her hand in mine, taking in her soft, beautiful features and recognizing I'm waiting too damn long to answer. "Aedry," I finally say. "You know I love you, don't you?"

Slowly, she clasps her mouth, her shock evident in her soft voice. "Oh, my God . . . *Sal.*"

The stress brutally clenching my gut twists harder. She thinks I'm proposing! "I have to go out," I say quickly.

"Oh," she says, her face heating. "Wait, you're going now?"

"I have something to take care of."

"Um. Okay." She glances at the food. "Let's have a quick bite and I'll go with you."

"No. You stay here," I say, rising. "Enjoy the meal, the band, it's all for you. I'll be back as soon as I can."

What I tell her isn't an explanation. It's nothing more than a bunch of lame-ass comments thrown together. When it comes down to it, I have nothing to say—nothing that will explain why I'm leaving her, by herself, after setting up this surprise in the middle of paradise.

My vague comments do jack to console her. She averts her chin when I try to kiss her, keeping her attention away from me when she speaks. "Where are you going?"

"A friend of mine is here on the island. He's in trouble and he needs me to go find him."

Her expression crumbles as she tries to understand. "But then why can't I go with you?"

"There's a storm coming," I say. As if on cue, thunder crackles in the distance. "I don't want you out with me if the weather gets bad."

She drops her gaze, but then meets my eyes. "Is this friend really a man?"

My stare hardens. I'm not pissed she asked. I'm angry at myself for giving her a reason to doubt me. "Yes."

She doesn't answer, releasing my hand and shifting her body to face the food. "I thought you were hungry," she reminds me.

I don't respond in the way that she wants or in the soft voice she deserves. My fury at Vin keeps my tone sharp. "I'll be back soon," I say.

I want to tell her that I love her. I don't want to walk away with her mad at me, especially if I don't make it back. But I can't. I don't tell her I love her much. If I do now—soon after I already said it—she'll know something's wrong.

I kiss the top of her head and make a silent vow, for her and for my brothers, to make it back.

Devan, he's one of those men paid well to keep his trap shut and his employer happy. Don't know if he's ever killed. Don't care. But this isn't the first time he's done shit that maybe he shouldn't. He steps around the jeep, moving like a shadow. "The items requested are in the glove compartment as promised, and the navigation system is set, sir."

I try not to take it as sign as the breeze picks up and the sky darkens. In the distance, and a hell of a lot closer than before, thunder booms. I look Devan square in the eye. "No one but my brothers, my woman, or her friend steps foot on this property, understand?"

At his nod, I slide into the jeep, making quick work of checking the Sig, two 380 autos, and a few daggers with enough jagged teeth to shame a shark. But it's the bulge at my hip that draws my attention.

The ring, the one I'd planned to give Aedry tonight, pushes against my leg.

I pull it out. I want to look at it and pretend for just one God damn minute that someone like me can have a real future with someone like her. Instead, I drop it in the console and use the ankle strap in the kit to secure my knife in place.

Given the arsenal at my disposal, Vin doesn't want anyone walking away. If he gave me this knife, it's to make a statement. What the fuck's wrong with him? I'm not one of those mindless sheep of his, willing to cut anyone he points to. But if I stand a chance at getting through this mess alive, I'll need every weapon I have.

"Is there anything else, sir? Devan asks.

He takes a step back and drops his eyes when I face him. No. This man hasn't killed. But he thinks I can. "If I'm not back by morning, get my people out of the country by any means necessary."

"I will, sir," he says. "And if you wish, there are men who can protect them for a price. You want them here?"

"No," I say, cutting him off before he can continue. "Just you."

"Very well, sir," he says. He seems to understand what I'm telling him, that I don't trust anyone and that my family needs to stay safe at all costs. For everything he's doing and how easily he agrees, Vin must have dropped ten to twenty grand in his lap.

I tilt my chin and start the navigation system. From Aedry's side to the time it takes me to pull onto the dirt road is maybe three minutes tops. Each of those minutes is long and I change my mind about grabbing Aedry and finding my brothers about half a dozen times. But once more, I have to do what Vin says.

Except, as far as I'm concerned, this friendship is long over.

My debt will be paid in blood tonight.

The drive to Bianchi's estate should only take thirty minutes. With the rain causing mudslides all over the island, it's been an hour and change, and I still don't know how close I am. I swerve all over hell, working out a plan. Lucca should be calling me and he's not. Either he's dead, hurt, or running for his life. I find out which it is as I round the bend.

My lights strike Lucca staggering down the road, illuminating his pale face and the blood streaming down his body. He lifts his piece and fires. I swerve out of the way, narrowly missing a tree as I skid off the road.

I roll the window down when I catch sight of Lucca in the side view mirror. He stumbles forward, his gun out.

I crouch low. "It's S!" I call to him, careful not to reveal names. "I'm here to get you out!"

The other family probably knows who he is by now. That doesn't mean I need to announce him. And as much as I think his head's not clear in the condition he's in, I'm hoping he can recognize my voice and hear it through the rain.

When he doesn't answer, I ease up in my seat in time to watch him collapse. Every instinct tells me to get out and haul ass—that he's done. But Lucca, he's young, smart, and, to some extent, a friend. I can't leave him.

I throw the door open, my feet kicking back the mud as cold rain comes down on me in waves. I roll Lucca over from where his face is buried in a puddle. He coughs up a bunch of brown shit as I haul him into a fireman's carry.

"God damn," he groans.

He's hurt and I'm making it worse. I don't care. I move fast, the rain pelting me hard in the face as I rush back to the jeep. I throw open the rear door and toss him in the back seat, shoving him forward. He crawls across, swearing until he slumps onto his back.

I jump into the driver's seat, ready to stomp on the gas and get my family out of the country. But there's a job to do and I need to finish it.

How the hell am I going to get us through this?

"Who's left?" I yell.

Lucca speaks through his teeth. "No one. Me and Carlo got the last three." His breath hitches. "Carlo didn't make it."

I grip the back of the seat. "You sure?"

His face is pinched tight, blood seeping through the fingers pressing against his shoulder. "No one's left. No one."

This should give me some relief, but if Lucca is this messed up, the whole thing was a bloodbath. "What about the staff?"

"No one will be here until the morning," he says, his breath releasing fast.

Based on what he's telling me, there must have been a plan. But that plan was blown to shit, given Lucca's condition. "We have to get out of here," he slurs. "Tonight. There's a plane at the airport ready to take us."

I crank the engine and peel out. "Not without my family," I tell him. We skid back onto the road, the navigation system spouting directions. As I straighten the wheel, I take the ring I'd planned to give Aedry and fling it out the window.

I spend the next thirty minutes hydroplaning through the mud smeared roads, almost crashing twice and barely able to see more than a foot in front of me. I was a fool for thinking I could ask Aedry to marry me. How could I give her a good life when my own life has turned to hell?

I barrel across the villa's front lawn, plowing over a couple of bushes when I lose control.

Lucca's in the back, quiet. Too quiet. I need to stop wherever he's bleeding from or he's never going to make it. I drag him out, throwing his arm over my shoulders. The moment I heave him onto the porch, the front doors fly open and we're hit with a wash of light.

"Sal—" Gianno's voice cuts off when he sees me carrying Lucca. "Holy *shit!*" he yells.

Apollo backs away, his face turning as white as Lucca's. "Aedry," he calls. "Aedry!"

She and Autumn race toward us as I cross into the foyer. Aedry screams when she sees us, stumbling to a stop.

Autumn charges forward, lifting Lucca's opposite arm only to freeze.

"He's been shot," she says, at the same time Aedry asks me what happened.

"You've been shot?" Aedry says, rushing toward me.

I looked down, realizing I'm soaked with Lucca's blood. "I'm fine," I say, my gaze shifting to my brothers. "Pack your suitcases. We're leaving now."

"But . . ." Apollo begins.

"I said *now!*" I snap.

"Let's go," Gianno tells him tightly. He hooks his arm, leading him back to their room, meeting my face with anger and fear.

"What happened?" Aedry asks again, her hands skimming all over my body.

I drag Lucca to the couch, speaking fast. "Lucca works for Vin. Vin gave him a vacation just like he did us." I lay Lucca across the leather sectional with Autumn's help. "He went out, broke down, and was attacked. I found him like this when I drove out to help him."

Autumn takes off into the kitchen, rustling through drawers.

"You found him like this?" Aedry stammers.

I look up from where I'm putting pressure on Lucca's shoulder. Her voice is barely audible. She doesn't believe me. I try to make her. "I swear to Christ this is how I found him."

"I was robbed," Lucca mumbles.

I thought he was unconscious, but he heard enough.

Autumn returns with towels and a first aid kit. Strands of her hair fall away from the make-shift bun held together with a pencil at the top of her head, and her glasses are dangling on the tip of her nose. But her voice is steady and so are her motions.

She shoves a folded towel against Lucca's shoulder and gets to work on unbuttoning his shirt. But as she runs her hands down his thigh, she freezes.

She lifts her blood-soaked fingers, ignoring the smears coating her light blue dress. "Sal, your friend has been stabbed and shot in the leg. He needs a hospital and emergency surgery."

"No," Lucca bites. "We need to get the fuck out of here."

"You're not going to make it to morning unless you're treated," Autumn insists. "You're losing too much blood."

Aedry's hand cups my shoulder. "Sal," she says. "We have to get him to a hospital."

She barely gets the words out when the side door whips open. In one motion I stand, my piece out, pointed, and ready to fire.

Aedry and Autumn scramble to stand as Devan stills in place with his hands out. "The main roads are flooded," he says. "There's no getting to the airport or the hospital tonight."

"Then call for help," Autumn snaps, showing me a side of her I've never seen. "This man needs treatment."

Devan's gaze passes along Lucca before returning to me. "There's no getting out," he repeats.

I house my piece. "He was attacked when his car broke down," I say. "They took his money and left him on the road like this."

Devan doesn't miss a beat. "There is a local gang responsible for attacking tourists. The police don't do anything. Half their profit goes to them."

It's bullshit and I know it. Neither Aedry or Autumn appear to notice. Aedry kneels in front of Autumn as she resumes her inspection of Lucca's injuries. "Do you think you can help him?"

Autumn works fast, cleaning Lucca's wounds. "Not with what I have." Her eyes widen when Lucca removes his hand from his shoulder and a gush of blood seeps out. She slaps a fresh towel against the wound, ordering Aedry to keep the pressure on it.

"What do you need?" I ask, trying to keep my voice even.

"What?" Autumn asks like she didn't hear me.

"What do you need to help him?"

"Medical instruments, intravenous fluids, stitches, antiseptic . . ." Her eyes travel back to his face. "And blood. He needs a transfusion."

I turn back to Devan. "If she gives you a list of what she needs—pictures, things like that—can you get them?"

"My cousin owns a medical supply store," he answers. "It's only a mile down the road. Show me and I'll get it."

More bullshit. If there is a supply store, he's breaking in and breaking out. Devan has been paid a lot of money to be the go-to man.

Apollo and Gianno wander back in, both looking sick. This whole scene is reminiscent of our parents' death. Jesus Christ, I would have done anything to spare them from this shit.

"Get your phones," I order. "Autumn is going to list off everything she needs. Find pictures and give them to Devan."

They inch forward, like they're afraid to get too close. "Sal," Autumn says, her voice soft. "It may not be enough."

Lucca's unconscious again, his skin sweating and his pallor worsening. "Autumn," I tell her. "It's going to have to be . . ."

Chapter Twenty-Five
Aedry

Sal keeps me close against him as we step onto the runway. Puddles litter the tarmac, the leftover rain giving it an added shine. It's cool, but not so much to make me shake. Yet that's precisely what I'm doing.

I glance behind me to make sure Apollo and Gianno remain within reach. They look as bad as I feel, the lack of sleep and the stress from the night ringing circles around their eyes. Ahead of us, Autumn follows closely behind Devan and his "cousins," as they carry Lucca toward the private plane.

Lucca backed Salvatore's story, as did Devan and his family to some extent. I should believe them, but I can't. I don't believe anything he tells me anymore.

When I saw Salvatore last night, covered in blood . . . every fear about losing him came crashing around me in one horrible rush. I was beside myself, hurrying to gather our things, and helping Autumn with Lucca's care.

Autumn was a Godsend. She took control in a way I've never seen, and that I am completely incapable of. My knees buckled when she located the bullet and dislodged it from Lucca's thigh.

"It was only imbedded in the muscle," she said, as if it was the best news ever. Perhaps for Lucca, it was.

The supposed good news didn't stop poor Apollo from vomiting in the sink. Lucca, who only received a local anesthetic and Tylenol for pain was (understandably) out of control during the procedure. Sal, Devan, and Gianno held him down, but it was Autumn, *all* Autumn, who calmed him with her voice. She was more than the mother hen I'm used to, the person who used to insist I wear a scarf in the winter and who fed me chicken soup when I didn't listen and caught a cold. She was . . . *amazing*. Salvatore noticed it, too. And he wasn't alone.

After an hour or so of sleep, I woke to find Autumn curled up next to Lucca, trying to keep his body warm. He spoke softly to her as he gently stroked her face. Lucca is rough and startling like Sal, but in many ways more dangerous. The look he gave Autumn was one of awe, as if this angel who found him was the one he'd been waiting for.

"Get in the plane and get settled," Sal says, his expression so laced with ire the ground crew passing him gives him ample space. "I have to take care of business before we can take off."

A few weeks ago, I would have questioned him, but today I don't. It's not that I'm weak or too tired to argue. It's more like I'm afraid, not of Salvatore, the man who shields me with his body as he walks beside me, but of the secrets he shields himself with.

He bends to kiss my cheek, but I withdraw, my reaction stinging us both. But I don't pause to apologize or to offer a reassuring smile. Right now, there are others who need me more.

I reach for the boys, wrapping my arms around their waists and hurrying them along. Apollo wraps his arm around me, too, needing comfort and someone to soothe his lingering fear. Gianno surprises me by draping his arm around my shoulders, as if to assure himself we're all still alive.

An odd sense of doom churns my gut, but it's the foolishness I feel that keeps my head lowered. Just hours ago, when I thought Salvatore was proposing, I was out of my mind with joy. There's nothing more I wanted than to tell him yes and promise him forever. And now . . . now I'm not certain we'll make it to next week.

Whatever he really went out for risked our safety. Not just mine and his, but Autumn and the boys. I can't spend my life with a man who'd risk so much, so easily.

"We're going home?" Apollo asks me, his voice oddly vacant.

I stroke his arm. "Yes, sweetie. We're going home."

We reach the steps to the private jet and it's all I can do not to freak out. We rode a commercial airline to the island and now we're on a luxury plane, yet another red flag signaling Sal's lies.

Apollo hesitates, stopping at the base of the metal stairs.

My instinct is to haul him forward, to where the first step toward safety lies. But his pallor and features keep my motions gentle. "Apollo . . . what's wrong?" I ask.

His weakened expression stays ahead. "We didn't get to swim with the dolphins," he answers.

The place that conducts the dolphin excursion shut down shortly after they arrived due to the approaching storm. But that's not what he means. He's telling me his vacation was not what he envisioned, and it became something out his worst nightmares. It's too reminiscent of what his life was supposed to be, back when his mother was still alive and he felt safe.

"I know," I tell him, acknowledging his fears. For now, it's all I can do.

Gianno glances my way, recognizing how close Apollo is to losing his composure. "Let's just get the hell out of here," he says, leading him up. He freezes at the top, before rushing back down and dragging Apollo with him.

"What's wrong?" I ask, readying to run for our lives.

"Lucca—he's freaking out," he says.

It takes me a moment to digest what he's saying before I race up the steps. The jet is large. A row of seats takes up the right, but it's the sofa running along the opposite side that holds my attention. Devan and his men are struggling to hold Lucca down.

Lucca is flailing wildly, swearing and flinging his fists. I rush forward as his hand punches out and strikes Autumn across the face, sending her flying and her glasses shooting to the floor.

I expect her to react with shock or to edge away in fear. But before I can reach her, she's already to her feet and back at Lucca's side.

She leans over him, grabbing his face as he continues to fight the arms trying to pin him down. "Lucca, it's Autumn," she says, her voice soft, yet firm. "You're safe. Do you hear me? You're safe . . . I'm not going to let anything happen to you."

She turns to the men. "Let him go," she tells them.

They exchange glances. Like me, they think Autumn has lost her mind. She levels her gaze at them. "I said, *let him go*," she repeats.

Lucca's body is so rigid, he appears more statue than man. His glare travels to each of the men holding him as he eases his frantic flailing. One by one, their hands drop away.

"Thank you for your help," Autumn tells the men. "You can leave him to my care."

Her palm is pressed against his shoulder, holding him in a way those strong men failed to do.

Lucca fixes his livid stare on the men, watching them pile out. It's not until their voices echo away from the plane that his attention returns to Autumn.

"Did I hurt you?" he asks her, speaking through his teeth. His eyes widen as they fix on her swelling cheek. "*Shit*," he says. "I'm sorry."

Autumn shifts her position from where she's kneeling on the floor. "I'm all right," she assures him.

Lucca's timbre is so edged with anger, it's all I can do not to haul Autumn away from him. Unlike me, she's not afraid. She smiles softly, appearing relieved that the immediate threat is over. "The morphine I gave you made you relive the attack," she explains, her gentle voice growing sad. "I'm so sorry. I only meant to soothe your pain."

Her voice trails as Lucca lifts a strand of her wild hair and tucks it behind her ear, his fingertip dragging along her jawline to hook beneath her chin. "I would *never* hurt you," he rasps.

The gesture is innocent enough, but there's so much sex behind his tone and touch, he appears seconds from peeling off her clothes. Autumn's face flushes, her full pink lips parting as their gazes lock.

I back away, realizing I'm intruding on their moment only to ram into Salvatore. He catches me. I didn't even know he was behind me. Apollo and Gianno must have alerted him there was trouble. As it is, he's looking past at me to Lucca, his frown revealing his concern and his surprise.

Autumn reaches for her discarded glasses and quickly covers Lucca with a blanket. By the time she tucks it around him, he's already sound asleep.

"We're taking off soon," Sal says. "Are you okay if I leave you?"

I think he's talking to Autumn until he leaves when I nod. Apollo and Gianno slip into their seats, tossing me worried glances. Autumn continues to skitter around the plane until she finds another blanket to place over Lucca, who's begun to tremble. I'm hesitant to interrupt her care, waiting until she heads to the rear of the plane to speak with her.

There's a small eating area in the back. I find her at the sink washing her face. I touch her back gently, gasping when she turns and I see how swollen her cheekbone is. "Oh, my God, Autumn."

"I'm all right," she says, when I continue to gape at the swelling. "He isn't the first patient to lash out at me and he won't be the last."

"He seemed so out of control," I say for lack of anything better.

Her demeanor dwindles, growing sad. "I gave him morphine for the pain and so he'd sleep, but what he really needs is blood. He lost so much, the small dose was enough to trigger hallucinations." She shakes her head. "Whatever happened . . . Jesus, Aedry, he was fighting for his life. If Salvatore hadn't found him, he wouldn't have made it."

"Do you think he'll make it now?" I ask.

"I don't know. I gave him the antibiotics Devan brought, but the surgical procedures I performed weren't sterile or under the best conditions. We'll need him transported to the nearest hospital when we land. Can you look after my bags? I won't be able to take them with me in the ambulance—"

"You're going with him to the hospital?"

Her eyebrows knit as if she's confused by my question. "I have to. He's my patient."

"Is that all?" I find myself asking.

Her blush tells me more than she actually says. "What else would he be?" she asks. The sadness returns to her voice, despite her small smile. "Did you *see* what he looks like, Aedry? No way would someone like him fall for me."

Which is the same thing I said when I met Salvatore.

Autumn didn't see the way he caressed her when she slept beside him. The way he looked at her was as if she reminded him of someone he's been searching for, or lost, long ago. Not that it's necessarily a good thing.

Lucca doesn't come across as the warm friendly type. Like Sal, he strikes me as someone unaccustomed to kindness and familiar with how cruel life can be. Despite his critical condition and agitated state, he recognized how tirelessly Autumn cared for him and her efforts to help him.

I take in my friend, her beautiful flawless face, that long mane of red hair, and her heart. Someone like Lucca could very much fall for someone like her.

I don't tell her. While Lucca didn't intentionally hurt her, this is a man capable of harm. A hard body, quick hands, and a tough life are not qualities Autumn needs in a man, and neither are the lies he helped spread last night.

I try not to think about how smoothly Salvatore spoke and how easily each excuse came, not when I'm feeling so fragile, and not with Apollo and Gianno so close.

Without another word, I return to my seat, ignoring that nagging feeling which warns me those lies are just a few of many since I first met Salvatore. I wanted to trust him and believe he's a good man. But after all this . . .

I click my seatbelt in place and look out to the tarmac, my breath catching when Sal passes Devan a thick roll of bills. I close the shade, blinding myself to what's in front of me.

The last thing I ever wanted to say to Salvatore was goodbye.

But now, I no longer have a choice.

Chapter Twenty-Six
Salvatore

I grind my hips against Aedry, every pound forward bowing her spine and lifting her breasts closer to my face. I pull one of her nipples into my mouth to suck, prolonging her orgasm. Each thrust, each stroke, each kiss makes me feel close to her. The problem is, this is the only time I feel close to her.

Since we returned from the island, nothing has been the same between us. Vin has me watching his back or someone else's almost every night—his way of punishing me for grabbing him by the throat and slamming him against the desk the minute I got a hold of him.

"You fucked me and my family over," I told him, squeezing his throat tighter.

"You're wrong," he said, gasping and batting at my hands. "I'm the one saving them."

I released him only because I wouldn't walk out of the building alive once his men found him dead. He claims to be the one saving my family, but he's wrong. His idiotic strategies, his ineptness with being a leader, and his increasing incompetence are slowly killing everyone under him. Where will that leave my brothers? Shit, where will it leave Aedry?

His shock and fear when I attacked him quickly dissolved, turning to anger and reminding me how deeply screwed I am. "What are you going to do, Sal? Leave? I'd like see you try." He slides away from the desk, brushing himself off, like he almost didn't piss himself when I had him by his scrawny neck. "The only way you leave me is in a body bag. Friend or not, no way in fuck do you leave alive."

My hips slow as I finish filling Aedry and lean down to kiss her. Our quick breaths don't allow my lips to linger, but that doesn't stop me from meeting her face. For a brief moment, she stares back at me like she's done a thousand times, with nothing but adoration and love. But it doesn't last.

She averts her gaze. "I need some water, okay?"

In other words, get the hell off me.

I roll to my side. She shifts to the edge, reaching for her silky robe. That's the other thing she does, cover herself around me. Instead of watching her walk naked to the kitchen, all I see is her trying to shield herself from me.

She fills a glass at the filtration system in her refrigerator and takes a few sips. She then fills another one and returns to bed, passing the glass to me. "Thank you," I tell her, drinking it down.

I place the half-empty glass on her nightstand and slide beneath the covers, waiting for her to join me. God damn it, it's been a week since I've been able to spend the night—to do more than kiss her in passing.

Instead of losing the robe and crawling back to my side, she sits quietly at the edge of the bed. I hate feeling like she's so far away, but what I hate more is the feeling I'm losing her.

My arms slide around her waist as I lower my chin to kiss her shoulder. She sighs like she's sad, placing her glass beside mine. I think she's going to stand or find some excuse to get away from me. Instead, her arms hold mine, keeping me close to her.

"I miss you," she tells me.

I still, knowing she means more than the nights we've spent apart. She misses what we had before our trip, before I almost got us killed. "I miss you, too," I say, resting my forehead against her shoulder.

Part of me wants to tug down her robe, drag my tongue along her delicate skin and spend the night inciting her passionate screams. I want to feel close to her. Jesus, I *need* to feel close to her.

"I know I've been working a lot. I'm hoping that'll change," I tell her, despite knowing there's little chance in the near future. "The summer's coming up. Maybe we can take a few days and go to the mountains. If not, maybe this winter, we can try skiing during one of your breaks from school."

There's more I want to say, but her stiffening posture halts my thoughts. "What's wrong?" When she doesn't answer, I straighten, turning her so she faces me. "Aedry, what is it?"

She purses her lips as if wrestling with what to say. "My lease is up next month. I'm not going to renew it."

I want her to tell me it's because she wants to move in with me. Based on her tone and the way she seems to slip further away, I know that's not it. "Why?" I ask, pulling her closer and scared out mind over what she's about to say.

She doesn't look at me when she speaks, something's she's been doing a lot lately and that kills me every time. "I was given notice last week," she says. "All the counselors, with the exception of Jalisa, were let go. The principal said he was sorry, but there was nothing he could do."

"You have to be fucking kidding me. What about all those kids you see?"

"They have volunteer counselors and students earning their masters lined up for the fall—" She releases a breath when I curse. "It's okay. I knew it was coming."

"Move in with me, until you get a new job."

I'm spitting out the words, despite what remains of her disappears within my grasp.

"I'm not moving in with you, Salvatore." She swallows hard. "I'm moving back to North Carolina."

I'm barely breathing, waiting for the next blow to come. All that follows is a heavy silence that pries us further apart.

The air in my lungs turns to liquid cement. "What about us?" I ask, unable to take it anymore. I stroke her back gently when she doesn't answer, ignoring the way it's shaking. "Adrianna . . . what about *us*?'

My question causes her to crumble. I hate how defeated she seems. But I hate that she's not answering me.

She closes her eyes, like what I say causes her pain. When she opens them, they give away her misery, as does her tone. "I can't stay with you. Not with what you do, and who you work for."

If I were anywhere else, I'd be sure there was a bug and that she was baiting me to give her information. But this is Aedry being honest and calling me out on my lies.

My hand falls away from her back. I don't even try to deny it. "How long have you known?"

She clasps her hand over her face and leans forward, stifling a sob. I guess she expected me to pretend I didn't know what she was talking about—or convince her she's wrong. But I can't. I can't do this shit to her anymore.

"I had my doubts early on. But you were so sweet, I thought I was reading too much into it." She wipes her eyes. "It's when we had dinner with him and Rita that I finally realized what was happening."

"Why didn't you say something?" I'm not accusing her of burying her head in the sand, but I know her and can see what this is doing to her. I don't understand why she didn't confront me before.

"I wanted to, but I kept . . ." She gasps, as another row of tears trickle down her face. "I kept wanting to believe in you, believe in the good man I know. But when we went to the islands and you returned covered with blood, I couldn't believe in you anymore."

Each word she says pounds my skull, but it's the disappointment and pain claiming her small form that rips me apart.

"You held me in your arms like I could somehow break," she tells me. "As if you would do anything for me."

"*Because I would*," I grind out, my voice harsh with how much it hurts to look at her. "I would do *anything* for you and my family."

"If that were true, you wouldn't be where you are, Salvatore." Her face crumbles like she's trying not to cry, but she doesn't manage. "I don't understand how you could be so kind and good to us, while belonging to something so horrible." Her hands slap against her lap in frustration. "Tell me why you did this. Please, I need to know how you can be a part of that world."

Words jumble in my mind like a traffic jam. She needs and deserves an explanation. Except what comes out isn't planned, but maybe I don't need it to be. Maybe for once in the God damn time we've been together, I need to come clean about who I really am.

"I did what I had to do to survive. But I'm not what you think I am, not entirely." Her lips part, her shock as obvious as her pain. "I'm not a made man. I've never hurt a woman or a kid, and I've never killed . . . but I've seen and done a lot of bad shit, protecting Vin."

I'm ready for her to tell me to walk—to get the hell away from her and not look back. What she says is worse and laced with everything that makes me love her.

"Come with me, you and the boys. Come with me to North Carolina."

Everything she said, from her first tear to the last hits me like a row of linebackers. But it's her last few words that finish bowling me over. I throw my legs over the bed, pulling on my briefs and shoving into my discarded pants.

Her voice breaks. "Where are you going?"

I finish buckling my belt. "Not to North Carolina," I respond.

She scrambles to stand beside me, clutching my wrist when I reach for my shirt. "Don't walk away. Come with me and we'll start fresh far away from here."

"I'm not leaving. This is my home." It's a lame excuse and yet another lie, and we both damn well know it. But after hearing that she's leaving—that's she's not willing to stay anywhere near me—*shit*—she might as well have belted me in the stomach with a sledgehammer.

"So, that's it?" she asks me, the agony in her voice freezing me in place. "It's over?"

Those lies—every last one I've fed her— those times I brushed her away to keep my secrets—morph into a noose, fastening around my neck and pulling tight. I'd fucking kill for her, die to keep her safe, rip out my soul and hand it to hell itself to save hers. I would do anything for this woman, but I can't do this.

"Stay with me," I say. "*Here,* in Jersey."

"No," she says, taking a step back. "Not like this."

My shoulders rise and fall with each tortured breath. I knew the day would come when Aedry would call me out. But I didn't expect it to be today. And I sure as shit am not ready for it.

The weight of her disappointment clouds her features, threatening to split her in half. "My parents have a house we can stay in," she says. "We can live there until we both find jobs—"

"*I have a job*," I snap, my fury at Vin, at myself, and every piss poor decision I've made since deciding to work for him burning its way through my veins.

Menace unleashes like venom through my pores. Anyone else would bolt. But this is Aedry, the one person in this world who doesn't fear me. She closes the distance between us, cupping my face with so much tenderness, I practically melt against her palms.

"This isn't a job," she says, struggling to speak. "This is a death warrant. You said you haven't killed. But I *saw* what happened to Lucca and I know what he did to stay alive. Leave with me before you finish killing the man that I love."

When I meet her gaze, everything I kept from her releases in a few simple words. "This isn't something I can walk away from alive."

My words are like vicious blows I can't spare her from. Her hands fall away from me as she edges away from my reach. I follow her, wanting to take it back—to spare her from the truth and shield her from the monster I sold my soul to.

She knew. Since learning Vin was Mafia, she fucking knew he'd order my kill if I left. But it took me telling her for that dam of lies to break and crush her, and for her to accept there's no getting out.

I expect her to scream, to hit me, to run away in fear. I don't expect the heartache that claims her features or the betrayal that trembles her voice when her face meets mine.

The tears she beat back release at once, spilling like raindrops across her paling skin. "I love you, Salvatore. I do," she adds, when I clench my jaw in disbelief. "Prove to me that you love me, and that you're the good man I believe in." Her words claw at my insides as she embraces me with her slender arms. *"Please*," she says, weeping. "Let's leave all this behind."

What I do next doesn't come easy. It's the hardest fucking thing I've ever done. I clasp her wrists and pull them down carefully, breaking her hold and keeping her in place. "I *can't*," I answer, the words burning like acid down my throat.

She doesn't move, her tears drying as numbness claims her. "You promised never to let me go."

I did. But it's because I love her that I do.

I step away from her, my chest throbbing in agony as I reach for my clothes. I march across the room, barely feeling the floor beneath my feet. I make it to the hall, slamming the heavy door behind me.

It's not enough to muffle Aedry's sobs.

I walk down the stairs, my vision blurring as my eyes burn. She was *everything* to me. Now the only thing I can make her is a memory.

Chapter Twenty-Seven
Salvatore

I keep my eyes ahead, toward the door and away from Donnie. She's sitting at her vanity, putting on her makeup like she isn't too fucked up to focus, like she isn't so wrecked her hand doesn't shake. Two lines. That's how much she already snorted.

That door leads out to her living room. The next leads me out of her apartment. The minute Vin steps through, I'm out and on my way back to my brothers. But, I'm sure as shit not back to anyone else.

Two lines, I repeat in my head. But it's been *two months* since I last saw Aedry, last held her, last touched her. I sent her a dog. That's right, a black Lab puppy. It was supposed to be something to make her smile, knowing how much she loved the last dog she owned.

I never intended it to be a goodbye gift, but that's what it became. It took everything in me not to see her. I ignored her texts, her calls, her pleas, until she finally stopped reaching out. That didn't mean I wouldn't give my life to hear her voice.

When the breeder called me to say the puppy was ready, I couldn't bring myself to tell him I didn't want it or give up one last opportunity to show Aedry I love her. I had him send the dog to Aedry's parents' home, something sweet to give someone sweeter, and maybe something to show her how sorry I am.

She called Gianno and Apollo to let them know she received the dog and to tell them she loved them. She also told them that she wasn't coming back. Apollo . . . God *damn it*. He broke down, losing his shit like he was losing our mother again. But, it's what he did when she disconnected that I can't get past.

He charged out of his room, nailing me square in the face. "What did you do?" he demanded when I shoved him to the floor. Vicious tears streamed down his face. "What the hell did you do, Sal?"

When I eased off him, he just lay there, releasing his grief as Gianno lowered to his side. Gianno . . . you can say he was pissed, meeting my eyes with enough hate to rip my insides out. I could tell he wanted to lash out, take a swing, destroy some shit. Hell, he still does. Apollo, too, based on how they're behaving—getting in fights, mouthing off.

Their hearts are broken. They don't realize mine is, too.

"What will it take for you to kill?" Donnie asks, yanking me back to reality where my head should be and away from the memories that haunt me.

My stare fixes blankly on the door. I don't answer, knowing she's trying to bait me.

She laughs in that way she does when she's high. It's not her real laugh, the one I used to hear when we were kids. The one she used to mean. No, that real laugh is dead, just like she feels on the inside. I can relate, seeing how part of me died when I walked out on Aedry.

Shit.

"I know you haven't killed. Vin's told me you always leave it for someone else." She stares at her reflection, like she's someplace else. "He says, 'Sal will make pussies bleed, but he's too much of a pussy to make them stop breathing.' You know what I think?" she doesn't wait for me to answer. "That killing means you're finally his, and what's left of your soul is gone."

I push off the wall, not bothering to argue. She's right. She's smart. But like me, Vin's ruined her.

On her vanity, between her sixty-dollar lipsticks and hundred-dollar perfumes, lie small empty vials of blow. Tina, the new girl Vin's been keeping on the side, isn't into this shit. At least not now. I know, because I've started watching her. I give it another month, maybe less, and Donnie's out.

Donnie's a friend. But I can't help her like she needs me to. That doesn't mean I don't care what happens. "You need to get out of this," I tell her.

She laughs again when I loom over her. But while she's playing it off like she's in control, I know she's not and I don't stay quiet. "You're beautiful, Donnie," I say. "You're young and you still have a chance. Get out and have the life you're meant to."

The tears that follow give away everything she's trying to hide. "Where will I go? And who will I go to? You?" She reaches out, huffing when she cups my groin and I wrench away from her. "No. This belongs to someone else, doesn't it?"

Her stare returns to the mirror like she can see something beyond it. All that's there is the shell she's allowed herself to become, the one she paints in pretty colors, hoping Vin will still want to stroke it.

"You haven't touched another woman since Aedry, have you?" she asks. "You haven't let Vin's whores blow you or get you off."

No. I haven't. That doesn't mean I answer.

I edge from her reach. Donnie's been asking about Aedry and I haven't told her shit. But she knows I'm not over her and that I never will be.

"Did you love her?" she asks, her voice a shadow of what it once was. A tear streams down her face, cutting a line in all that makeup caking her skin. "Did you want to make babies with her? Did you see yourself growing old with her—being buried in the same damn grave as her?"

Again, I don't respond, her words slicing me like razor blades. Everything she said is everything I wanted with Aedry, everything that's tearing me up when I think of her. Two months of not waking up with her beside me—of not seeing that smile that made me whole—it's a wonder I can still function.

That emptiness I feel deepens which each breath I take. I know Donnie's messed up and wants to mess me up with her. I put it back on her. Unlike me, Donnie still has a chance.

"Leave, Donnie. Sell everything you have and get the hell out of here. I'll give you some bills—enough to start fresh. But you have to leave. You hear me? You *have* to get out of this."

Anger finds its way into her tone as another tear falls. "You tell me to go. You tell me to leave. But you won't go yourself, because he won't let you. *No*," she says. "He won't. He may not need me. But he sure as hell needs you. Doesn't he, Salvatore?"

Again. She's right. But again, I don't tell her. No, I don't have a choice. But she needs to believe she still does.

Before I can argue, her front door opens and a pair of feet stomp inside. "Sal?" Vin's voice calls out.

I take one last look at Donnie. "It's not too late for you," I tell her, my voice whip sharp.

"You're wrong," she says, her odd tone halting me by the door. Her eyes glue to her worn reflection, agony practically aging her as I watch. "You're *so* wrong, Salvatore."

There are so many things I can tell Donnie—too many words to remind her of what she once was. But with Vin here, I can't. Like I said, he's ruined both of us.

I step out to of her room and around the corner into the living room. Vin and Lucca are standing by the white leather couches, Lucca's expression tight. Vin meets me halfway, keeping his voice low. "Tomorrow night, we're taking out Liberella." He laughs when I just look at him. "What? Do you think I can continue to allow his disrespect?" His smile erases. "I want you at the house with Rita starting at dawn. No one gets in, you hear me?"

Just when I think Vin can't dig his grave deeper into hell, he does this, target New York's strongest boss. What's the master plan this time? Storm his house—his business? Poison his damn food? Whatever it is, if he fails, it ends for all of us.

Our numbers are few, and most of his men are ready to jump ship to the other side, seeing how many he sent to war to die on his behalf. He's thinking go big and go strong. I'm thinking he's lost his damn mind. I don't tell him. I don't say anything that might spare his life—not after what he pulled on me and my family.

"You think the remaining bosses will come after Rita?" I'm not really asking, more like clarifying what I've wondered about. Family is supposed to be off limits. That's the rule. But Vin has done too much shit and lost too much honor, and now, his wife is at risk. Hell, we all are.

When he doesn't answer and reaches for a smoke, I ask, "What about Donnie?"

He takes a long drag and blows it out slowly. "She's out. I already stopped paying for this place. She's got maybe another two weeks here if that."

Every muscle in my back tenses in time with my clenching fists. "Are you going to tell her?"

"She'll find out when the eviction notices start piling up." He shrugs. "The other one," he adds, referencing Tina or whatever the hell her name is. "She'll be your regular watch once I'm sure Rita's safe."

A small creak behind me tells me Donnie was at her bedroom door and that she heard every word. I don't react. I can't.

Vin doesn't notice, edging toward Donnie's bedroom as Lucca makes his way to my side. I shouldn't be shocked that Vin's here to fuck her, even though he's already fucked her over.

"What?" Vin asks, laughing when he catches my glare. "She still gives the best head in the Tri-states."

He's saying that shit to look strong, not that he'll deny Donnie when she falls to her knees.

I glance at Lucca when I hear Vin close the bedroom door behind him, realizing he's watching my every move. Since the island, he kept trying to figure me out. I can't shake the feeling there's more to him. But, it's what I catch in his dark stare when he shifts his focus in the direction of the bedroom that halts me in place.

Holy shit. Lucca *hates* Vin.

Can't say he's alone.

He notices me watching him. The lethal stare he pegs me with almost has me reaching for my piece. "What the fuck are you doing here, Sal?" he asks, his voice barely audible.

He's not asking me why I haven't left. No, there's more to his question. But I'm not telling him shit.

Shots fire, causing Lucca and me to dive on the floor.

My sig is out as I army crawl along the floor and squat on the wall beside Donnie's door. Lucca's on the opposite side, his piece tight in his grip. In our brief exchange, I know he's thinking the same thing I am: someone followed them here to take Vin out.

It's Vin's voice and tone that bottom out my stomach and tell me more than I want to know.

"Fuck," he says. "Holy fuck."

My head falls back against the wall and my heavy hands lower to the floor. No, baby girl . . . no.

It takes me too many long seconds, but I eventually stand.

I house my piece and slowly open the door.

"Sal?" Lucca asks.

I know what I'm about to see. That doesn't mean I'm ready to see it.

Blood seeps from what looks like a flesh wound on Vin's shoulder, staining his dress shirt. His pants are down to his ankles and his body shakes as he cowers on the floor.

I wonder briefly how many sucks Donnie got in before she snagged Vin's gun. It couldn't have been too many. But it was enough to shoot him before she turned the gun on herself.

Lucca steps in behind me. Unlike me, his piece remains drawn. "*Jesus*," he says.

Donnie, the girl from the neighborhood, the one I grew up with, the one *all* the girls wanted to be, lays sprawled across the floor, her blood-soaked hair covering her once beautiful face.

In a thousand years, I'll never erase that moment from my mind. I don't deserve a reprieve or mercy. Donnie did.

"Crazy bitch fucking shot me," Vin says, like it's not obvious. He's shaking hard, from pain, fear, and God only knows what else. "If I hadn't moved, she would have nailed me in the chest. I need a cleanup crew now—and the doc. Have them dump the body upstate—"

"Go fuck yourself," I tell him. I feel wobbly as I rise, but when I face him, my features harden along with my stance.

"What did you say to me?" Vin asks, scorn halting the quiver to his voice.

I don't feel myself move. From one second to the next, I'm hauling Vin up against the wall by his throat. Lucca's hand goes up, his piece aimed at my head, but my focus is all on Vin and his reddening face. Vin slaps at my wrists, trying to talk. I don't let him.

"I'm out," I tell him.

Drool spills from his mouth. He tries to argue. I give another squeeze. Donnie was a friend. *My friend.* Lying there like she is, she could have been Aedry, or my brothers. When it comes down to it, Vin has never given a shit about anyone but himself, not even a woman who would have killed for him.

My eyes sting briefly for who Donnie was—that girl from the block who didn't want to be poor, who wanted to be something better, who just wanted Vin to fucking love her.

I can't mourn for who Donnie was or what she became. Not now. Just like I can't stay in this world any longer.

"I'm not asking you," I say. "I'm telling you. I'm out. And if you come after me, or anyone that's mine, you'll fucking wish the bosses finished you off."

I drop him like the trash he is and storm away, his mangled chokes the only sound I hear until I reach the front door and Lucca calls out.

"Sal . . . I can't let you leave."

Maybe he saw me reach for my Sig as I stalked out or maybe he didn't. I don't have to turn around to know his gun is out and ready to fire.

I grit my teeth. "I'm done, Lucca. I'll fight Vin and I'll fight anyone he sends after me, but I don't want to fight you."

I don't hear him so much as feel him approach. I whip around, my gun out.

Something in his stare keeps me from firing. Slowly, he lowers his gun. "You want out, go," he says. "It's not too late for you."

I watch him, unsure if he's lying. "What was your woman's name—Aedry? It's not too late for you and Aedry."

Maybe it's hearing Aedry's name or the way that he says it that makes me believe him. "It's not too late for you, either," I tell him, remembering the way he looked at Autumn. "Walk away. Give yourself a life away from this shit."

"You little bitch!" Vin calls out. "Kill him, Lucca. Kill him now, God damn it."

Lucca shakes his head, slow and purposeful. "I'm not done. Not with Vin or the rest of the bosses," he says.

I freeze in place, taking in what he tells me. "Go," Lucca says, his tone more of a growl.

In the brief flash of Lucca's eyes, I see everything he's about to do. I rush to the door, careful not to make noise.

Lucca's fast. The shots fired through his silencer are seconds apart. "That was for my sister, motherfucker."

I shut the door behind me. I don't have to be in the room to know he's talking to Vin's corpse. Yeah, there was more to Lucca than any of us could have known. A lot more.

Epilogue
Salvatore

My new Range Rover eases down the county road as the air conditioning streams along my arms at full blast. A hundred degrees. That's how hot it is in North Carolina.

"You sure we're going the right way, G?" Apollo asks from where he's sitting in the back.

"No. Siri's not answering shit out here. But that guy at the market said this is the right road," Gianno tells him. "Right, Sal?"

I nod, but I don't say much, my head racing with too many thoughts. The last thing I heard before we left Jersey is that the remaining bosses are battling it out for Vin's territories. The shit-storm he started caused a lot of bad blood. Every boss wants more, and everyone is willing to kill for it.

Fine. Let them. It's no longer my problem. And I swear to Christ it never will be.

Days. That's all it took us to sell our place, pack our shit, and move out of the state. We were ready to leave the area and all the bad memories behind.

We've been here almost a week, in the town next to where Aedry is supposedly living. The realtor Gianno found online has been showing us around. There's a long list of places we like, close to the MMA gym I want to buy.

It's nice here. Good schools. Quiet. Lots of land, and close to outdoor malls more akin to Rodeo Drive than anything I pictured in the south. Although we're here, I can't be sure we'll stay.

Not if Aedry doesn't want me.

I pass my hand through my short hair. I stopped shaving my head the night Donnie killed herself. It sounds insane, but the hair marks my rebirth—and one of many steps I'm taking to what I hope will be a better life. I'm not sure Aedry will like it. I'm not even sure she'll like me—not after everything I put her through.

Hell, who am I kidding? For all I know, she hates me.

It's the reason I've been dragging my feet trying to find her. It wasn't until this morning that I finally worked up the courage to go to the little cottage she's renting and knock on the door. I stood there waiting, only for the little old lady watering her lawn next door to call to me.

"Hey, there," she yelled. "Y'all lookin' for Aedry?"

"Yes, ma'am," I answered.

"She's at her folks place a few miles past the farmer's market."

She made it sound easy, but we're still looking for her, even with all those people we asked for directions.

My ride kicks up more dirt, slowing when Siri finally decides to make an appearance. "You have reached your destination," she tells us.

"Is she serious?" Apollo asks.

To our left is a huge field, extending to a hilltop lined with trees. To our right is pretty much the same, except for an old barn near the road. I roll to a stop and set my ride in park, trying to figure out what to do, just in time for the barn door to swing open.

"Holy shit," Gianno says, slowly. "Look at Aedry."

My world grinds to a halt. Aedry steps out, carrying a basket tucked under her arm. The puppy I sent her bounces loyally beside her, wagging its tail.

"Good girl, Midnight," she tells it.

Aedry's dark wavy hair is longer, brushing against the tie of her red bikini top as she closes the door with her foot. She doesn't bother to glance our way, walking down a small path, her tiny denim shorts clutching her ass as her cowboy boots dig into the mud.

Apollo shoves himself between our seats, trying to get one last view of her as she disappears behind the barn.

"What the hell are you looking at?" I snap, pushing him back.

"Sorry, Sal," he says. "But damn. Did you *see* her?"

I let out a breath. "Yeah. I saw her."

Gianno whips his head toward me, his eyes wide. "Don't fuck this up, Sal."

"Yeah. Don't fuck it up," Apollo agrees, staring back to where she disappeared.

I swing open my door, muttering a few swears and forgetting the flowers I brought. I move fast, prowling forward. For all I thought I was ready to see her, I'm not.

She looks . . . *beautiful*. What kicks at my gut is that she also looks happy. This isn't the first time I've wondered if she's better off without me, or if she's found someone else—someone who makes her smile, draws her laughter, and fires her passion—someone who didn't make her cry like I did.

My feet stomp as I steel myself for what she may say or do. If she tells me to leave—if she doesn't want to see me—I'll go. I won't like it, but I'll respect it. Even if it finishes killing what's left of me.

The moment I clear the barn, a large white house with a wrap-around porch comes into view, a sprawling pasture just behind it. The whole place resembles a painting, too perfect to be real.

It doesn't hold my attention. Aedry does.

Her hair flutters behind her as a warm breeze coasts along the field. I'm not sure if I should yell her name, wait to get closer, or—*fuck*—I don't know what to do. All I know is the need to have her in my arms.

Her dog whips around, barking and growling, alerting her of my presence. She turns, slowly, her eyebrows lifting when she sees me. I stop a few yards away from her, staring at the way her hair flows around her.

I'm dressed in dark jeans and a tight black T. With my hair growing out like it is, at first, it's almost like she doesn't recognize me.

But then she does.

The basket falls at her feet when she clasps her mouth, the motion revealing the depth of her shock. I don't think she wants me here, but from one breath to the next she takes off, racing toward me.

I charge forward, lifting her when she throws herself into my arms and straddles me. My lips find hers, seeking her out as my hands sweep through her hair and along her back, clutching her tighter against me. Christ, it's like we've never been apart—my body, my mouth, my damn *heart*, as hungry for her as she is for my touch.

I don't want to let her go, kissing her until she finally pulls away.

Her soft smile warms me, but it's the tears shimmering her blue eyes that remind me how much I hurt her. Her fingertips trail along my jaw and her gaze sweeps along my form.

"You're here," she says, hardly believing it.

"Yeah, I am." I ignore the dog continuing to circle us, my voice breathless. "I went to your house. Your neighbor told me where to find you."

She motions behind her to the field. "They needed help milking."

"I don't know what the fuck that means," I tell her honestly.

Her laugh stirs my smile and squeezes my heart like only she can. "The dairy cows," she reminds me. "The ones my parents bought."

She quiets then, pressing her forehead against mine, relief and maybe a little pain, too, flooding her small features. Our closeness allows me to feel her body heat and bask in everything I've missed about her. That perfume, the flowery one she wears, seeps into my nose, and her hair feathers against my cheek, reminding me of all those times she fell asleep against me and how easily she stole my heart.

I stroke her back in the silence that follows, wondering how I ever survived without her and assuring myself that, at least for the moment, she wants me with her.

"You're safe?" she asks, her gentle voice cutting through the sounds of the birds singing and her dog panting at my feet. At my nod, she glances over my shoulder. "And the boys?"

"The boys" she says, that familiar sweetness reminding me of everything that makes her Aedry. "They're good," I answer. "In my ride waiting for me."

I lower her to the ground, but maintain my grip on her hips, trying to speak.

Shame born from my sins forces my gaze briefly away. But when I meet her face—*God*, that beautiful face—my words are strong. "I'm out," I tell her. She lowers her head in a way that tells me she understands. "I'm not a part of it—and I won't be anymore."

When she doesn't say anything, I spill the rest. "I moved here a few days ago." She jerks her chin up, her eyes rounding. "For you . . . for us. I don't want to be without you. But if you don't want me, I promise I won't stay."

Tears spill down her cheeks, driving that spike deeper into my chest. My fingers glide along her hips. "I love you," I tell her, pleading with her to believe me. "And I'm sorry for everything—every last lie and everything I've done to hurt you." I all but fall to my knees when she remains quiet. "*Please*, Adrianna . . . give me another chance to love you."

Her expression crumbles as tears drench her face. "Do you have any idea how much I've missed you?" she asks, her voice breaking. "Do you know how hard I've cried being without you?"

My throat tightens. "I lost my soul when I lost you," I confess, everything I'm feeling slicing into each word. "You're my world, Adrianna."

She chokes back a sob, nodding like she understands what I'm feeling. "No more lies?" she asks. "No more secrets?"

"No," I rasp. "I know I messed up. I know I've hurt you. But if you let me, I promise to spend the rest of my life making it up to you."

I fall to one knee, pulling the small velvet box from my pocket. This isn't the ring I tossed, the one from that man who wasn't good enough for her. It's the antique one I found on her birthday, the one that made me want to be that better man for her.

She takes in the ring, her cries hard enough to rock her shoulders, but not enough to stop her smile. "Forever?" she asks.

"Forever," I promise.

Let Me

An O'Brien Family Novel

by Cecy Robson

CHAPTER 1

Finn

I see the strike coming at me a split second before it connects with my skull. My head snaps back from the force, the crowds' hollers resonating like a muffled cry in the distance. It was a good punch—lightning quick with enough impact to knock most guys on their asses. But I'm not most guys.

You hit me, I'm only going to hit you harder.

My right hand shoots up, blocking and smacking away the kick gunning for my ribs. I pivot out of the way, again, and again, and again, avoiding Easton's arms and legs as they come at me. He's fast, strong, with a six inch reach advantage. But he's too eager to take me out and not pacing himself like he should. Already he's breathing hard and it's just the start of the second round.

I take my time to figure him out, planning each move, searching for that opening I need. Do I take a few bashes because of it? Sure. It's part of the job. But believe it or not, it's part of the job I look forward to.

Those punches and kicks remind me that I still *feel*, that I'm still human. And that for now, I'm still alive.

"Oh!" some drunk behind me yells when my

uppercut finds Easton's chin.

He staggers back, swiping the blood oozing from his lip, yet he keeps his grin. He's trying to make like it was a lucky shot. That it won't happen again.

Like me, Easton needs to win this match. And if he does, he'll move up to the top ten, making him a contender for the UFC Lightweight title.

Talent aside, the guy's a raging asshole, and so are the idiots in his training camp. They've been trash-talking since the moment I agreed to this match. I didn't really care and laughed most of it off until they got personal and took it a step too far.

Again he nails me in the head. It's not as hard as it was last time which tells me he's getting tired. Does it hurt? I guess.

But let's say I'm a guy who's used to pain.

Easton grins. He thinks I'm afraid of him. He thinks he has me where he wants me. But fear is an emotion I don't allow myself to entertain. Fear gets you hurt and rips you apart till you think there's nothing left.

I dodge out of reach. He scowls and takes another swing. This one gets close enough to my jaw to create a breeze that whips across my skin.

"Finn," my brother Killian barks from the side. "Take him out *now*."

He's worried about me. So is my family. But now's not the time to think about them. I keep my hands up as I edge away, letting Easton think I'm backing down, that I'm tired and need to catch my breath.

I sidestep when he lunges forward, avoiding his next swing and use the momentum to drop my head and nail him in the temple with a roundhouse kick.

Like I said, Easton's fast.

Too bad for him I'm a little bit faster.

The kick is my signature move, as natural for me as the next breath. He goes down like I planned. But in the

Octagon you don't stop just because your opponent collapses like timber. You charge forward. You show him what you're made of. And you prove just how tough you really are.

That muffled screaming, isn't so muffled anymore. The crowd loses their shit as I pounce, my blows nailing Easton in the face until the ref's arms hook beneath mine as he hauls me off. I back away, my fists up because I already know I won.

I should do a back flip or some crazy shit to incite the crowd. This is it. My time has come to own it. But the good things aren't as great as they can be. Not with the memories that haunt me. And not with the anger they stir.

Killian rushes in as the medic wipes down my face. I'm bleeding from the punch Easton caught me with at the beginning of the round. I didn't think it was that bad, but the way the ringside medic is pressing the towel against my head clues me in the gash isn't closing like it should.

"I'm going to have to stitch you up, Fury," he mumbles.

"I figured," I tell him.

Kill pats my back. "Good job," he says.

Maybe he believes it, but I don't miss the concern in his voice. He thinks I took too many unnecessary hits. I can't really argue, seeing how it's true.

He doesn't understand that I don't feel those strikes the way I should. Hell, I don't think I've felt anything the way I should in a long time. Not like I used to. I try to tell myself that maybe that' a good thing. That numbness is better than pain. But I'm not so convinced anymore, and neither is my family. I try to shrug it off like I'm fine. Except given the way they've been eyeing me, I'm not fooling anyone.

I'm scaring everyone around me. And it sucks. Not only because I don't want them scared, but mostly because I don't know how to stop it.

"The referee has called a stop to this match at two-minutes and forty-nine seconds into the second round," the announcer begins. "The winner by TKO, Finn 'The Fury' O'Brien."

The crowd screams and pumps their fists in the air when my hand is raised. I take the few seconds I need to thank my sponsors, my camp, and my brother, because that's what I'm supposed to do despite the fog clouding my senses. I wish that disconnect had something to do with all the hits I took, but deep down I know that it doesn't.

I'm back in the locker room before I know it getting stitched up, too many people talking at once. God, I barely hear their questions or my responses. But they're there, and somehow I make it through.

"I'm worried about you, Finnie," Kill says when everyone piles out.

"Don't. I'm not drinking tonight. I'm headed home," I assure him.

"That's not what I mean," he says. He's sitting in a fold out chair, his arms resting against his muscular legs. "I think you need to talk to someone."

I stretch out my arms. By now they're so tight, they pull against the bones. "I am. I'm talking to you."

I don't have to see him to know he's shaking his head, or that he's looking sad, disappointed, and maybe something else, too. "I'm not who you should be speaking to," he says. "Not for what's going on in your head."

"You're enough," I say, even though I know it's no longer true.

"Finn," he begins.

I don't wait for him to finish, leaving the changing area and heading toward the showers. "Go find Sofia and Wren," I call over my shoulder as I strip out my shirt. "See if they're up for some dinner."

I don't remember peeling the rest of my clothes off. That numbness I've been feeling too much lately claiming me like a mist until it fully engulfs me. Fuck. It's like I've stopped living even though for the most part I think I'm still alive.

I lean against the tile with my arms spread, allowing the water to beat against my back. It's too hot. I should turn it down, but I don't bother. Eventually, like everything else, the sensation fades.

I'm not sure how long I'm in that position. A few seconds? A few minutes? But then Easton and his trainer Yefim are suddenly there. "You got lucky, O'Brien," Yefim calls out, taunting me with his thick eastern European accent.

Shit. Like all the trash talk before the fight wasn't enough.

"Did you hear me, you pussy?" he fires back when I don't answer. "Did you hear me, you goddamn coward?"

Coward? Fuck you. It's what I think, but not what I say, focusing instead on the streams of water that gather along my feet before they swirl into the drain.

It doesn't help. The rage that's building, the one I only manage to barely keep in? It stirs in my gut like a heavy pot filled with hate, sin, and all the curses my Ma would still beat my ass for saying.

"What're you doing?" Yefim asks.

His voice is closer, he's drawing near. It doesn't matter that I'm standing here naked. He wants to be next to me. I shudder, that feeling I keep buried drilling its way up.

"I know about you," Yefim says, not bothering to keep his voice low. "But everyone knows, don't they? Even if you don't want them to."

My body shakes a little more, but it's not from the cooling water. It's from his words and all that anger they trigger. *Don't do it. Don't go there.*

"You like to keep it a secret. Don't you, pussy?"

Yefim laughs when I keep my trap shut. He thinks I'm backing down, just like Easton did before his face met the mat. "He's crying," he calls out to Easton. "What? Not so tough now?"

That's where he's dead wrong. Every muscle I've conditioned serves a purpose—to take down those who fuck with me. And right now, Yefim is seriously fucking with me.

"You like to pretend that it's girls you like, don't you?" he says. "But that's not true, is it? Oh, no, that's not true at all . . ."

I raise my chin, knowing that someone's not leaving without bleeding, and I've bled enough tonight.

Yefim kicks at my calf. "What? Nothing to say? Can't speak without your boyfriend here?"

"Boyfriend?" Easton asks, laughing. "No fucking way."

"Yes. Way," Yefim insists. "Didn't you know this little pussy takes it up the ass—"

I punch him so hard, I feel his teeth crack against my knuckles. For someone with decades of boxing experience he never saw me coming. But I see Easton flying at me out of the corner of my eye. I toss him over my shoulder, slamming him hard onto the ceramic tile floor. Like in the octagon, I throw myself on top of him, my fists colliding against his skin.

Voices rush forward, telling me to stop. A woman screams, but I don't stop fighting off the bodies trying to grab me, breaking through the arms wrenching me back. I need to hit him—I need to feel my fists meeting his face—I need to feel *something*.

God damn it. I need to feel alive.

I don't want the pain.

I don't want the terror.

But once more, it's all I feel.

Photo by Kate Gledhill of Kate Gledhill Photography

Cecy Robson (also writing as Rosalina San Tiago for the app Hooked) is an author of contemporary romance, young adult adventure, and award-winning urban fantasy. A double RITA® 2016 finalist for Once Pure and Once Kissed, and a published author of more than twenty novels, you can typically find Cecy on her laptop writing her stories or stumbling blindly in search of caffeine.

www.cecyrobson.com

Facebook.com/Cecy.Robson.Author

instagram.com/cecyrobsonauthor

twitter.com/cecyrobson

www.goodreads.com/goodreadscomCecyRobsonAuthor

For exclusive information and more, join my Newsletter!